CRITICAL ACCLAIM FOR
LYNN S. HIGHTOWER AND

EYESHOT

"Rings with gritty authenticity. You won't be able to put it down and you won't want to sleep again."

—Lisa Scottoline

"A gifted, straight-from-the-hip writer, [Hightower] builds the story in this thriller deftly, luring readers from page to page with fascinating peeks into blood-and-guts crime-solving, with enough humorous dialogue and tongue-in-cheek philosophy to lighten the load. . . . Hightower knows the human condition—especially the Southern one. . . . Pour yourself a cup of java and let Lynn Hightower provide a great escape."

—*The Lexington Herald Leader*

"What gives [*Eyeshot*] its depth and resonance is the way Hightower counterpoints the murder plot with the details of daily life in homicide. . . . This wry, easygoing narrative overlay gives Sonora and her latest adventure an appeal that should draw readers."

—*Publishers Weekly*

"Nail-biting cat and mouse thriller that is reminiscent of Patricia Cornwell at her very best."

—*Bookcase* magazine

FLASHPOINT

"There are some good frissons of psychological terror, interspersed with convincing violence; and the unconfident but courageous Sonora is a lively and sympathetic addition to the ranks of fictional female coppery."

—*The Times* (London)

"Diabolically intriguing from start to finish."

—*Publishers Weekly*

"A powerfully original book . . . Like all the best thrillers, *Flashpoint* leaves you uneasily aware of shadows, especially those that start at your own two feet."

—Reginald Hill

"The pace is swift, the murders gruesome, and the conclusion welcome. Hightower, whose character makes a great addition to fiction's army of female detectives, handles the bizarre elements of her tale with a fresh and lively touch. She is a talent to watch."

—*Sunday Express*

"[Hightower] shows [a] gritty mastery of the police procedural. . . . By reimagining psycho and cop as three-dimensional women, [she] produces something miraculously fresh and harrowing."

—*Kirkus Reviews*

"One to watch."

—*Daily Telegraph*

SATAN'S LAMBS

"Never a dull moment . . . a plot that moves."
—Tony Hillerman

"Crisply written . . . a nice twisting plot . . . memorable characterization . . . a devilishly good book."
—Ross Thomas

"A truly original plot . . . Lena Padget is a very welcome addition to the ranks of fictional private eyes. She is witty, tough, and always a woman."
—Stuart Kaminsky

"Hightower's prose is a quick read—fast-paced and suspenseful."
—*Lexington Herald-Leader*

"Her prose is clear and pacing breakneck."
—*Publishers Weekly*

"Hightower is a writer of tremendous quality."
—*Library Journal*

Books by Lynn S. Hightower

Satan's Lambs
Flashpoint
Eyeshot

EYESHOT

LYNN S. HIGHTOWER

HarperPaperbacks
A Division of HarperCollinsPublishers

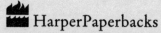 HarperPaperbacks

A Division of HarperCollins*Publishers*
10 East 53rd Street, New York, N.Y. 10022-5299

This is a work of fiction. The characters, incidents, and dialogues are
products of the author's imagination and are not to be construed as real.
Any resemblance to persons, living or dead,
is entirely coincidental.

A hardcover edition of this book was published
in 1996 by HarperCollins*Publishers*.

ISBN 0-06-109609-1

HarperCollins®, ®, and HarperPaperbacks™
are trademarks of HarperCollins*Publishers*, Inc.

Cover design by Richard Hasselberger
Cover illustration by Jean Paul Iris/FPG International

First printing: November 1997

Printed in the United States of America

Visit HarperPaperbacks on the World Wide Web at
http://www.harpercollins.com

❖ 10 9 8 7 6 5 4 3 2 1

For my buddy, Jim Lyon
Couldn't ask for a better friend

ACKNOWLEDGMENTS

My thanks to Robert Youdelman, P.C., Attorney at Law, who graciously took time out of his demanding schedule to keep me out of trouble.

To Detective Maria Neal, Criminal Investigation Section, who was available for questions and to talk plot, and who counted up body parts and told me what I was missing.

I count myself lucky to work closely with three talented and brilliant people—my agent, Matt Bialer; my HarperCollins editor, Carolyn Marino; and my Hodder & Stoughton editor, George Lucas. It is a rare privilege to tap the instincts of three people whose opinions and creativity I trust.

To artist Steve Sawyer, and entrepreneur Cindy Sawyer, who made themselves available on a moment's notice to discuss plot and artistic vision.

To the Tennessee state trooper who kindly did not arrest me while I was parked beside I-75 scouting locations for body parts.

To the students and staff at the University of Cincinnati, who were kind enough to provide maps, directions, and insights.

To Doug Collins, who was good enough to act as my videographer.

To the usual gang of helpers and readers: my kids, Alan, Laurel, and Rachel, who screen to the best of their ability during deadline days, up to and including facing down law enforcement; to Bill Swinford, one of my favorite attorneys, for being a friend.

My thanks to Lindsey Hunter and all my buddies at Silverstone Farm who help me work and train and play with my horses. See you in the next book.

To Sharon Hilborn and Tamra Gormley of the Commonwealth Attorney's Office for questions answered.

EYESHOT

eye-shot: the distance that a person can see; range of vision.

1

Peter Peter, Pumpkin Eater
Had a wife and couldn't keep her
Put her in a pumpkin shell
And there he kept her very well

—*Children's nursery rhyme*

It was one of those moments when Sonora hated police work.

Butch Winchell sat across from her in the interview room, laying the family snapshots out on the table. There was brown-eyed Terry, three years old, Power Rangers sweatshirt barely covering a pouchy tummy. And baby sister Chrissie, struggling sideways in her lap, fine hair a wisp at the top of her head, sister's hand clutched in a tight and tiny grip.

Their mommy was missing.

Sonora liked it that the Winchell kids had normal names. None of the soap opera specials—Jasmine, Ridge, Taylor, or Noelle. She ran a finger along the edge of the table. Outside it was ninety degrees and sunny, but it was cold in the interview room. Everywhere in the city people were going boating, swimming, out to movies.

Homicide detectives never had any fun.

Sonora looked across the table at her partner, Sam Delarosa. If the baby pictures were bothering her, he'd be worse off. Softer hearted.

He smiled at her, gave her his "come hither" look. He was a big guy, big shoulders, dark brown hair side-parted and falling in his eyes. He looked young for his age, boyish—though Sonora, who knew him well, noted the careworn signs of worry around his mouth, and at the corners of his eyes. He had the kind of small-town, country-boy, Southern charm that made women want to confide in him, and men automatically include him as one of the boys. There was no doubt that he was the kind of guy who opened doors for women, watched football, and didn't like to shop. His normality was one of the things that attracted Sonora. They'd worked homicide together for five years.

And it was the second come hither look Sonora had gotten out of him this week. She was sure they had put all that stuff way behind them. He must be messing with her mind.

She smiled back, heavy on the eye contact, and he gave her a second glance before his eyes went back to Winchell.

"Her name is Julia, Detective Blair." Winchell laid one more photo beside the rest. He looked up at Sonora.

Just like her kids, Sonora thought. Quick to pick up on a moment of inattention. She pushed hair out of her eyes. Too long, too curly. She wondered if cutting it would tame it down or pouf it up.

She picked the picture up off the desk.

It was a quickie Polaroid with the sticky glaze of constant handling. She gave it a long look, passed it across the table to Sam.

There was something breathtaking about Julia Winchell.

The hair was magnificent—red-lit brunette, thick and curly, rising from a widow's peak, pulled back from a heart-shaped face. She had a high forehead, a touch of severity about the mouth. The lips were lush, heavy at the bottom, the eyes almond-shaped, deep brown, with well-defined eyebrows. She had narrow shoulders, long slim fingers, delicate porcelain wrists.

She was the kind of woman you would expect to find vacationing in Paris, or exploring the countryside of southern Italy. She would order clothes from J. Peterman, shop at Abercrombie & Fitch.

Hard to believe the woman in the picture could be the wife of this ordinary man who looked petulant, uncertain, and afraid.

Married young, Sonora thought.

Winchell picked up the Styrofoam cup of coffee Sam had brought him and raised it to his lips, but didn't drink.

Bad coffee? Sonora wondered. Nerves?

"Mr. Winchell, would you like a soda or something?" she asked.

He shook his head. He'd be a medium to small, if attractiveness was measured like T-shirts, black hair wet with gel, heavy black rims on the glasses, a round sort of face. Sloping shoulders, paunchy stomach. The kind of extra weight nobody noticed on a man. The kind of extra weight that sent women screaming to the salad bar.

Somebody's brother, somebody's cousin, somebody's killer.

Sonora figured on a high probability that the man sitting across from her had killed his wife, provided she turned up dead. She might just have run away from home. Back when Sonora had been a wife, she'd wanted to run away from home.

But not enough to leave two little children behind, both babies still.

Winchell hunched forward in his chair, shoulders tense. He had hollows of darkness beneath his eyes. "You can't see it in the picture, but she's also got a tattoo on her ankle." He pushed the glasses back on his nose. "It's not cheap-looking, okay? She did it graduation night when she was a senior in high school, and her mama like to kill her. It was just kids cutting up. She and her friends had been out to a Chinese restaurant to eat, and decided that they should get their birth year symbol tattooed on them somewhere. Hers is the year of the dragon—she was born in '64. None of the others went through with it. Can't blame them, if they were born in the year of the rat or the monkey or the pig or something. It's really kind of neat-looking, blue and green with red eyes and a long red tongue."

Sonora leaned forward, memory stirring, cop instinct on edge. "Did you say left ankle?"

He hadn't said. Sam looked at her.

"I think . . . yeah, it was her left ankle, definitely."

Both men looked at her expectantly.

Sonora didn't care to elaborate, not with Butch Winchell and those baby pictures staring her in the face. It wasn't the kind of theory you shared early—not if it involved a severed leg found alongside the interstate highway. It was a long shot anyway. The leg had turned up a whole state away. Julia Winchell had disappeared in Cincinnati, Ohio, not where-some-ever Kentucky. What gave Sonora pause was the way the leg had been taken off.

It was sweaty work, cutting up bodies. Most killers took the hard road, sawing the leg straight off at the thigh, with the usual combination of brute force and ignorance. Working from the joint was a lot easier, same as boning chicken. In the instance Sonora was thinking about, the top of the leg had been severed at the ever so practical hip, but the foot had been taken off over the ankle, well above the joint. Inconsistent, she had thought, when she'd heard the story. It had bothered her at the time.

A dragon tattooed over the anklebone might explain it. A killer intelligent and cool-headed enough to consider the practicalities of dismemberment was not likely to leave a tattoo for easy identification.

Sonora sat back in her chair. "I'm confused, Mr. Winchell. Do you and your wife live in Cincinnati?" From his accent, they'd have to be Southern transplants. Unhappy in Ohio, like other Southern transplants. It would be interesting if they were from Kentucky, home of bourbon, racehorses, her partner Sam, and various and sundry body parts.

"We run a diner in Clinton."

"Clinton is where?" Sonora asked.

Sam scratched his head. "Tennessee, isn't it?" His area of the country.

"Yes sir, right outside of Knoxville. That's where I grew up, Knoxville. I . . . we bought the diner four years ago. It's just a little place in downtown Clinton. But it's a beginning, and for us . . . for me, anyway, it's a dream come true."

Sonora noticed that Winchell was clenching his fists. She figured the diner was a point of contention in the marriage. Dream fading in the day-to-day grind of reality.

"Julie up and decided a while back she wanted to go to this conference here. In Cincinnati."

Sonora knew where here was.

"A restaurant conference?" Sam asked.

Winchell looked at his feet. "Nope. This was one on running a small business—tax advice and everything geared for people whose business is small-scale." He shrugged. "Pretty much a waste of time if you ask me."

"Did she?" Sonora said.

"Did she what?"

"Ask you."

He grimaced. "Julie is a independent female, which I admire, usually."

Lip service, Sonora thought.

"I didn't really think we could afford it. Especially not the airfare. Julie said she'd drive and keep expenses down and we could take this off on our income tax."

Sonora nodded. "So it was already a sore subject when she left."

He opened his hands wide. "It was settled. But then the transmission went out on the Mazda. My opinion was, she ought to call it off. Car repair bill coming in . . ." He took a breath. "Her point was we'd already made the deposit to the people running the conference and we weren't going to get that back. The airfare on short notice was ridiculous. So she did a car rental—got a weekly deal. That way she wouldn't leave me without a car, and she'd have wheels while she was up there. Here, I mean."

"Pretty determined to get away," Sam said mildly.

Winchell's hands hung heavily between his knees. "She said she needed some time to herself."

"How far is it?" Sonora asked. "You say the conference was here, in town. How far from Clinton?"

"It's about a four-hour drive, give or take."

"Okay," Sonora said. "So then what happened?"

"She, umm, she didn't come home."

Sonora nodded, kept her voice gentle. "That much we figured. It would help if you could go into a little more detail. When was the last time you talked to her?"

"Well see, what happened was kind of odd. I was supposed to pick her up at the car rental place, she was going to be driving down late that Sunday afternoon, after the conference. But she didn't call and she didn't call. I couldn't get her at the hotel. We'd sort of fixed the time around six, that I would pick her up at the car rental place around six o'clock. And since I didn't hear from her, I just went on out there, see if she'd show up. And she didn't."

"How long did you wait?" Sam asked.

"About forty-five minutes. I had both the kids with me. All excited because Mommy was coming home. But Mommy didn't come home." His voice broke and he rubbed his chin hard. He was getting a five o'clock shadow and the stubble of beard rasped against his fingers. "Nobody at the rental place had heard anything from her. If it had been just me, I'd have waited longer, but the baby was getting tired and Terry was fussy. So I went on home." He took a breath. "The minute I get the car in the garage I hear the phone ringing. So I run for it, leave the kids strapped in their car seats. But whoever it is hangs up. Fifteen minutes, and it rings again and it's her. Julie."

Sam nodded. Winchell bit his lip.

"She was upset, I tell you that from the get-go. I could tell she'd been crying." He closed his eyes and ran his hands through his hair.

Sonora wondered if the gel made his fingers sticky. It had dried, so maybe not.

Winchell opened his eyes. "She told me that something had happened. She said she couldn't come home for a while, she had to take care of it."

"What was it?" Sonora asked.

Sam gave her a look. He thought she interrupted too much.

"I don't know," Winchell said.

Sonora frowned. "How come you don't know?"

Winchell leaned forward, close to Sonora. "See, used

to be, her first question would have been the kids. Are they okay, you know, the whole worried Mommy bit." His shook his head. "She didn't even ask. Not at first."

"Did you ask what the problem was?" Sonora said.

Sam rolled his eyes.

Winchell looked at his hands. "I don't . . . we didn't get to that."

"You mean you had a fight," Sonora said.

"It wasn't a fight."

"What was it then?"

"I just . . . here she is going on about how she can't come home, and not word one about how I'm making out with the kids, who I've had on my own all this time, with precious little help."

Sonora exchanged looks with Sam. Shocking—married people having a fight. Next on Oprah. She wondered how often Julia Winchell had handled the kids on her own with precious little help. Knew better than to ask.

"She got mad and hung up."

"And you haven't heard from her since? Nothing at all?" Sam asked.

Winchell shook his head. "No, and it's not like Julie. She's no grudge-holder. She'd 've called me if she could. Now if it was her sister, that'd be something else. But Julie, she gets mad fast, then it blows over. And even if she was mad at me, she'd call just to see about the kids and talk to them. Only thing that's kept me going is I know she's got to be alive, I just don't know where or what's going on."

Sonora cocked her head to one side. "How do you know that?"

Butch Winchell smiled at Sonora—a social smile from a man who looked like he needed last rites of the heart. Sonora had seen other men look that way, killers some of them. She studied his sad eyes, the large white hands (the better to strangle you with, my dear). The fingers were artistic and delicate compared to the chunky heaviness of the rest of him.

He scratched his cheek. "Somebody's using our credit cards. The limits are all run up."

2

Winchell was not a stupid man. He should not have missed the endless possibilities—none good—of his credit cards maxing out. He just wasn't ready.

Sonora stacked the Polaroids, smiled at Winchell in a noncommittal way. Pity would scare him, right about now. It would be better all around if he was thinking straight.

"Just a few more questions, Mr. Winchell. Details to clear. You said Julia had—has a sister. If you could give us a number, I'd like to give her a call. Also, what about her hotel? Did she check out, have you been over there?"

Winchell's lips went tight. "She's staying at that Orchard Suites place down by the river. According to them she hasn't checked out, but she won't answer any calls and the guy as much as told me nobody'd seen her. But he wouldn't let me into her room. She's using a credit card that's just got her name on it, or they might've let me in. They don't seem to care that I'll be footing that bill."

"Speaking of which, we'll need your credit card numbers, the last statements." Sonora cleared her throat. "Also, was your wife hospitalized any time recently? Her latest medical records might help us out."

Winchell pushed his glasses up on his nose. "With the babies, she was. I can get that for you."

Sonora smiled again. "Sooner the better." She checked her watch, waved a hand at Sam. "Detective

Delarosa can get this going for you. Maybe get some of the basics faxed. Sam?"

He nodded, gave her a watchful look, turned a gentle smile on Winchell. "There's a phone we can use out here."

Not going back to his desk, which butted right up to hers. Good Sam, Sonora thought. He, at least, had picked up on the significance of the hospital records. He always hated asking that question, because sometimes people cried.

Sonora took the picture of Julia Winchell and her two babies and headed for her desk.

She settled into her chair, checked her watch. Two o'clock. Two hours till shift change. The peculiar Friday feel of restless energy and ennui was thick. Sunlight streamed through the windows like a beacon.

Sonora dialed a number she was beginning to know by heart. Listened to it ring. Conversations with Small-wood were getting more and more frequent.

She'd met him months ago, on his day off, when he'd left Caleb County, Kentucky, to tell her about a local murder that dovetailed with one of her own. She'd been going through a bad time then, and his voice on the other end of the line had gotten more and more welcome.

He fed her the interesting pieces of the bad and the ugly he came across in day-to-day work and gossip—a sort of cop-to-cop come-on.

"That you, Smallwood?" Sonora pictured him in his deputy uniform, one foot on the desk.

"Girl." The voice was country Southern, and deep.

"Answer me a question."

"Yes, I do accept your kind invitation to dinner. Or is that supper, in Cincinnati-speak?"

"Pay attention, Smallwood. You remember that severed leg you were telling me about?"

"Always business with you, isn't it? Yeah, I remember."

"Where exactly was that found?"

"Down I-75 south, between London and Corbin." His voice got sharper, more focused. "You got something?"

"I don't know. Hope not, actually." She spread the pictures of Julia Winchell's little girls across the desk. "You ever hear any details on the victim?"

"Nope, but it's not like I would. I know somebody down there, though, she's going with my cousin."

"Nice to know you fit the typical Southern stereotypes."

"Let me put you on hold real quick, and I can find something out."

"Is this a Cincinnati quick, or a long Southern minute?"

"Knit something, why don't you?"

The line clicked, and Sonora balanced the phone on her shoulder, turned in her chair, saw Gruber doing the same.

"We've got to stop meeting like this," Gruber said.

On hold and stirring up trouble, Sonora thought. He was from New Jersey, dark and swarthy—sad brown eyes. An air of challenge women found interesting. He'd picked up weight, all of a sudden, but he still looked good.

"Is this the secretary? Can I speak to a real cop?" Smallwood, back in her ear. "You there, Sonora?"

"Where else would I be?"

"I could think of a couple places. Anyhow. Results aren't back from the state lab, but unofficially the victim is female, between the age of twenty-five and thirty-eight, leg severed over the ankle, but taken off at the hip joint."

"Blood type?"

"A-positive."

"Any scars, tattoos?"

"Not that I know of."

Sonora made a note.

"You going to tell me what you got?" Smallwood asked.

"Missing person, woman from Clinton, Tennessee, disappeared up here at some kind of seminar."

"I must be missing something. Why would her leg be showing up in Kentucky? This be because she's from Clinton? Think maybe this leg just kind of migrated on home?"

"Pay attention, Smallwood, and listen to how a real cop thinks. This woman has a tattoo, a dragon, right over the left anklebone. I just thought it was funny. Killer took off the leg at the hip joint, which makes perfect sense, though none of them ever do it, do they? Then he goes and sweats the foot off over the ankle, which makes no sense at all unless there's a tattoo he's trying to hide."

"You say this vic is from Clinton?"

"Yeah."

"Cause London's on the way there."

"Is it?" Her next stop was going to be a map.

"South down I-75. Maybe not such a long shot after all. You getting cop twitches on this, Sonora?"

"We call it instinct, Smallwood."

"Maybe you want to come on down then."

"Maybe." Sonora looked up, saw Sam and Winchell headed her way. "I'll get back to you, Smallwood, and thanks for the help." Sonora hung up. Smiled at Winchell, who trailed Sam like a baby duck following his mama. Cop imprinting.

She picked up a high school transfer paper she needed to fill out for her son, and waved it in the air.

"Just for the record, Mr. Winchell, can you tell me your wife's blood type?"

His eyes went flat. "A-positive."

Sonora turned the pictures on her desk face down, so she didn't have to look at Julia Winchell's babies.

3

The Orchard Suites Hotel was on the Ohio River in Covington, right across the bridge from Cincinnati. Sam eased the Taurus up and down the parking lot.

"No sign of the rental on this end," he said.

"What color was it again?"

Sam looked at her. "You mean you've been looking up and down your side and you don't—"

"1995 Ford Escort, red. Just double-checking."

"Tell me about that leg again. You say it had a tattoo?"

"No, Sam, I said the foot was cut off well above the ankle—"

"That would be the shin."

"Thank you, *doctor*. Think about it, Sam. Hip taken off at the joint, which makes the most sense."

"Except nobody ever does it that way."

"But this guy *did*. So why's he take the foot off *over* the ankle joint?"

"Cut there first, saw how much trouble it was, got smarter on the next cut and did it at the joint."

Sonora frowned. Sometimes she didn't like it when Sam made perfect sense. "Maybe. Or maybe he was cutting it off over a tattoo. This victim was a female between the ages of twenty-five and thirty-eight and the blood type matches Julia Winchell's."

"Face it, Sonora, most victims of that kind of crime

are young females. And half of America has A-positive blood." Sam pulled the car into the circle drive in front of the lobby. "I wonder what Julia Winchell was upset about."

"Probably going home."

"She was pretty damn set on getting up here. You think she was fooling around on him?"

"You saw the picture."

"You got to feel for this guy, Winchell," Sam said.

Sonora slammed the car door. "Not if he did it, I don't."

It was cool in the hotel—not quite chilly, and a relief from the heat and humidity rising in gasoline-tainted waves from the asphalt parking lot. The lobby was wide and noisy, full of fountains and people in sports shirts and sandals. A tired-looking woman in lime green shorts herded a knot of preteen girls out the front door. Two of the girls turned and looked at Sam. There were giggles.

"I think I'm the butt of a joke," Sam said.

"A familiar sensation I'm sure."

"You always get bitchy in the heat."

The desk clerk was tall and had bushy eyebrows, and a nervous habit of clearing his throat. He handed Sam a card key.

"There was a man here, earlier, asking about her. He said he was her husband."

"Black hair, glasses, name of Butch?" Sam asked.

The clerk nodded.

"That's the husband."

"We have to be very careful about who we—"

Sonora waved a hand. "No problem, I'm glad you brought it up. You definitely didn't let him in?"

"Definitely."

A good thing, Sonora thought. Winchell was never

officially in the room. If they got forensic proof he was, that would nail him. "She got any messages?" Sonora asked.

"I could look," the man said.

Sonora looked at the man's name tag. Van Hoose. "So look already."

He ducked to the other side of the counter, and Sam gave Sonora his rudeness disapproval frown.

"Seven." Van Hoose handed Sonora a computer printout. "This is a list of the calls she made. And here are the messages, never picked up."

Sonora looked it over, followed Sam as he said thanks and moved away from the desk. One of the numbers seemed familiar.

Sonora looked up at Sam. "We got your public library. A bunch from Winchell. Return a call to what looks to be another room in the hotel." Sonora went back to the desk clerk. "That what this is? One of the other rooms?"

He nodded.

"Look that up, why don't you, and let me know who was staying in that room at the time the call was made."

Van Hoose hesitated. But they were the police after all. He went to his computer.

Sam drummed his fingers on the counter. Sonora laid her hand over his to make him stop.

"The call came from a Mr. Jeffrey Barber in room three-twenty-seven."

"Checked out when?"

"July sixteenth, on a Sunday." He handed Sonora a slip of paper. "This is the name, address, phone number, and plate number he filled out for registration."

Sonora smiled. "We may have to hire you, Van Hoose."

"What's your procedure when a guest disappears?" Sam asked.

Van Hoose shifted his weight to his left foot. A bone popped in his hip. "We check the credit, and if the card's good, we keep the room a while."

"How long?" Sonora asked.

"Honestly? It's a management call. Depends on the guest's credit and how bad we need the room."

Sam patted the desk. "Okay, thanks."

Sonora followed him through the lobby, to the elevators. Punched four.

"They got free breakfast with the room here," Sam said.

"Very important," Sonora agreed, closing her eyes. She leaned against the back wall of the elevator, which stopped at the second floor to let in two couples, freshly bathed, perfumed, pantyhose and heels.

Sonora wondered what Smallwood was doing tonight. Probably not working.

The elevator stopped. Sonora got the rat-in-a-maze feeling brought on by hotel corridors.

She gave Sam a look out of the corner of one eye. "You seem to know your way around this place."

"This is where I bring my women. They like that river view and I like the breakfast."

Julia Winchell's suite had that hotel air of maid service around clutter. It opened onto a sitting room: TV, desk, table and chairs. Hunter green couch. There was a bar with a coffeepot and small refrigerator. The room was freshly dusted and vacuumed, pillows plumped. Stacks of paper, books, and a small, open briefcase crowded the top of the desk.

Sonora gave the couch a second, wistful look. Her dog Clampett had chewed up the cushion on the one in her living room, and it left a trail of stuffing every time someone sat down.

She peeped into the bedroom. The bed was made, and a teddy had been neatly folded on the ridge of pillows that stretched across the king-size mattress.

Sonora picked it up. Smelled the wave of sweet flowery scent, fingered the soft black silk, admired the spaghetti straps that crisscrossed along the back.

She heard Sam whistle as he opened and closed the tiny refrigerator behind the bar.

"Old pizza," he shouted.

"Save me a piece."

"What?"

"Look in the bathroom, Sam. Count the toothbrushes."

His steps were heavy in the hallway. Sonora knew he could walk lightly if he wanted to. She'd heard him do it once or twice.

He put his head in the bedroom doorway. "Two. Both dry as a bone."

Sonora waved the teddy. "I guess she wasn't just here for the riverfront view."

"Poor son of a bitch."

"I assume you mean the husband. Who now has a very good motive."

"Keeps us in business."

Sonora headed for the dresser drawers, wondering if Julia Winchell was the kind of hotel guest who unpacked.

She was.

Sonora found a silk nightie, slate blue, Victoria's Secret price tag hanging from the side seam. She had one like it at home in her closet, hooked over her lingerie bag. Julia had paid full price for hers; Sonora had waited for a sale.

Which might mean a special occasion, as far as Julia Winchell was concerned.

She had a tendency toward white or black, tailored shirts and khaki pants, longish skirts, straight cut, size eight. She shopped at The Limited, spent a lot of money on shoes that were well worn, and size seven and a half.

A full cadre of makeup clotted the bathroom counter—neat but not obsessive. Julia Winchell had brought her own makeup mirror. Bubble bath from home.

Sonora took a quick mental tally. Mascara, eyeliner, blush, two shades of lipstick. All partially used, nothing new except one of the lipsticks. Sonora opened the older tube, rolled it out. Rum Raisin Bronzer.

There were theories that you could read a woman's character by the shape of her favorite lipstick. Sonora had seen an article on it once in the *Inquirer*.

She looked back into the bedroom at the black silk teddy, the crisply ironed white shirt hanging on the back of the bedroom door. There was a quietness in the room, already a layer of dust on the worn floral suitcase. Julia Winchell wasn't coming back.

"Sonora?"

It was the way Sam said her name that got her attention—a particular tone of voice.

She put the tube of lipstick back on the bathroom counter. "What, Sam?"

He had his back to her, a sheaf of paper in his left hand.

The phone rang.

Sonora raised an eyebrow at Sam. He nodded, and she picked up the desk extension. There were several phone numbers jotted down on an Orchard Suites scratch pad, one with a 606 area code. Julia Winchell was from

Tennessee, which was 423, Sonora knew from calling Smallwood. She was pretty sure that 606 was Kentucky. The leg had shown up in Kentucky.

"Hello?" Sonora pitched her voice low. At a guess, she'd say Julia Winchell was an alto.

Silence.

"Hello?" Sonora said again. She heard a click, looked at Sam. "Hung up."

"Sit down, Sonora. You should look at this."

"What is it?"

"I think I know why Julia Winchell decided not to go home. It isn't what you think."

"What is it?"

Sam had Julia Winchell's open briefcase on the couch. He moved it to the floor, picked up a sheaf of papers that looked like handwritten notes and a newpaper clipping with ragged edges.

Sonora settled on the couch. Sam handed her the newspaper clipping. "Let's start with this. Recognize the picture?" He sat on the arm of the couch, knee touching hers. Tapped the newspaper. "Look at the date."

Sonora got her mind off the knee and looked at the paper. It was neatly cut from the Saturday edition of the *Cincinnati Post*, the Metro section, dated July fifteenth, the day before Julia Winchell had been supposed to drive home to Clinton. She raised an eyebrow. Read the caption. "District Attorney Gage Caplan put closing arguments before the jury today in the trial of ex-Bengal football pro, Jim Drury, accused of running down Xavier University co-ed Vicky Mardigan. Drury, a popular hometown boy made good and local celebrity, attended Moelier Catholic High School, a school well known for nurturing football players. He has done spot coverage for local television stations during the football season for the last nine years. Mr. Drury played for the Bengals from 1979 to 1986."

Sonora looked up at Sam. "Caplan's going for vehicular homicide."

Sam grimaced. Vicky Mardigan had been dragged thirty-eight feet down Montgomery Avenue, and left to die in front of the White Castle in Norwood. She was breathing when the 911 team got to her, but hadn't survived the night.

"You think Caplan has a prayer of nailing him?"

Sam shrugged. "Drury says she walked out in front of him. How's Caplan going to prove otherwise? His word against a dead girl's."

"Sam, he dragged her half a mile down the road."

"He says his foot slipped when he tried to hit the brake. And there were no alcohol or drugs in the guy's blood—that'll work against Caplan."

"You've heard the rumors."

Sam nodded. Every cop had. Drury was a known maniac on the road. Short-fused, he took his anger out behind the wheel. He'd been pulled over time and again by uniforms, but he was Drury for heaven's sake. He usually signed an autograph and went on his way.

"Yeah, Sonora, but you can't take rumors to court. I've worked with Caplan a couple of times, no question he's good. Most of 'em, you hand them the case file, they look it over fifteen minutes before they go into the courtroom, if you're lucky. Caplan does his advance work, and he charms the shit out of the jury."

"Gee, Sam, thanks for the visual." Sonora's foot itched. She rubbed her shoe against the carpet, wondering if she should take it off and go for total ecstasy.

Sam turned sideways, so he could look at her. "Julia

Winchell left a lot of little notes behind in that briefcase, Sonora. She saw a murder. Or thinks she did."

Sonora gave Sam a lopsided smile. "By chance she mention the killer's name?"

Sam grimaced and Sonora thought he looked sad. He tapped the news clipping in Sonora's hand. The one with Gage Caplan, ace District Attorney. "As a matter of fact, she did."

Sonora tilted her head to one side. "Somebody he's putting away?"

"No, Sonora. Him."

4

Sonora looked at Sam. Looked back at the picture in the clipping. "Did I understand you? You're telling me Julia Winchell saw a murder—"

"I'm saying she thinks she did."

"And the killer was Gage Caplan? *This* Gage Caplan?" Sonora waved the clipping. "Champion of the underdog, defender of law and order, friend to cops, kids, yada yada yada?"

"How many times do I have to say yes?"

"Until I get you to say no. *Who's* he supposed to have killed?"

"His wife."

"His wife? That establishes a motive, I guess."

"Seriously, Sonora—"

"Seriously, Sam, his wife is alive and well. They had a picture in last week. Caplan the family man. Wife and little kiddy."

"*First* wife, Sonora. This all happened eight years ago."

"So why didn't she bring it up eight years ago?"

"She did. Nobody believed her. And she only saw the guy, she didn't know his name. Till she picked up the newspaper two weeks ago, and there he is."

"Give me details, Sam."

"I don't have details." He stood up, pointed to the sheaf of papers on the desk. "This is all I got. Notes. Stuff she jotted down."

"It's thin. Except . . ."

"Except what?"

"This list of calls she made. I thought one of those numbers was familiar. She was calling the DA's office."

"Look, Sonora, I'm not saying it's true. Calling the DA's office proves not a thing, except she may have had a screw loose."

"Her husband doesn't describe her that way."

"He maybe is the one who killed her."

"If she's dead."

"There is that."

Sonora smoothed the clipping out on her knee. Frowned at the headline. CAPLAN CLOSES IN. The picture had been taken in the courtroom, from the side, Caplan talking to the jury. He was a big man in a nice suit—not too nice, you'd never picture this guy in a pinkie ring. He was attractive—carrying a lot of extra weight, the way ex-athletes often do, but it sat well on him. His hair was thick and full, razor cut.

A district attorney with definite jury appeal. And popular in the ranks.

Sonora skimmed the article.

The defense attorney was Judith Kelso, another hometown girl, which was a smart move on Drury's part. She was a short, squat blond, and she was moving hard and heavy. Much had been made of Drury's squeaky clean blood test, his all-American hard-jawed good looks, his community service with the Shriners, his struggle to be a good father to his kids, despite the divorce. This was a golden boy, who deserved the benefit of the doubt.

Vicky Mardigan, a nineteen year old from Union, was not pretty. In her pictures she looked chunky and small and she had a bad complexion. The photos from the accident scene were hard to take. The jury had needed a recess.

Women's rights groups had picked up the case, for reasons that were not clear to anyone. They were holding vigils downtown, trying to take back the night. Sonora wasn't sure they'd ever had it.

In the bullpen, Drury was getting three-to-one odds in a new twist on the usual football betting pool. Caplan was the only reason Drury's odds weren't better.

Business as usual.

Sonora laid the newspaper clipping gently on the coffee table. "Make a prediction, Sam. Is Caplan going to convict?"

"If anybody could, he'd be it."

"See, that's the problem, Sam. I agree with you. Almost every cop in the city agrees with you, including, I might add, our chief of police."

Sam looked at her. "We could let it go."

"Maybe she'll come back," Sonora said flatly. She looked up, caught both her own and Sam's reflection in a mirror that hung over the desk.

Two unhappy cops.

"She ain't coming back," Sam said.

5

The shift had changed over and everyone had gone off duty except Molliter, who was on nights. Molliter was a tall, rangy redhead with a sour look. Known to be religious. He was at his desk, eating pineapple rings from a square Tupperware container.

Sonora shuddered. Settled at her desk. "My phone light's not blinking."

"No messages? Where are your kids?" Sam asked.

"Heather's at some skating thing. Tim's at the mall hanging out and annoying the security guards."

"How'd they get to these places?"

"A combination of their grandmother, one parent with a van, and a friend's big brother who drives. Wait till your Annie gets older." Sonora watched him out of the corner of her eye. Last year, it would not have been a safe comment. "How's she doing?"

"Two Bs, the rest Cs on the last report card. She's behind but she's catching up."

Sonora opened her bottle of tea. It was nice to ask after Annie and get something other than a medical report. This time last year she'd been in the hospital, enduring blood work and testing in an ongoing battle against leukemia.

Sonora peeled the yellow and white tissue paper from her sub sandwich. "Okay, Sam, you take this Barber guy and I'll take Julia's sister."

"I'll take the sister."

"No, I will." Sonora saw no telltale smear of tomato sauce on the paper. She opened the bread of her sandwich. "Gross, what is this?"

"Crab and seafood salad. You got mine."

They switched sandwiches.

"You got a nice phone voice, Sonora. Barber will talk to you."

"You just want the sister because you hope she looks like Julia."

"What is this?" Sam asked.

"It's Snapple, Sam. Mango Madness. I thought you'd like it."

"Real cops don't drink Snapple."

"Give it here then."

He pulled the bottle out of her reach.

Sonora dialed the number Butch Winchell had given her, got a busy signal, and put the phone on redial. She chewed meatball and jalapeño pepper and was halfway into the sub when the phone rang once, and was answered immediately.

Sonora swallowed a mouthful of bread. "My name is Blair, Detective Blair, and I'm trying to reach a Liza Hardin?" She grabbed a pen with greasy fingers, heard Sam snicker.

The voice was wary. "I'm Liza Hardin. I'm sorry, who did you say you were?"

"Detective Blair, with the Cincinnati Police Department. A Mr. Butch Winchell has reported his wife, Julia, missing, and he gave us your number and said—"

"Oh, yeah, I'm her sister."

Sonora flipped open a notepad. "Do you have a few moments to talk with me, Ms. Hardin?"

"Of course."

"Have you seen or talked to your sister any time recently?"

"I talked to her . . . um, a few days ago. Sunday morning, the seventeenth."

"Sixteenth," Sonora said.

"Whatever. I talked to her that Saturday night, too."

"When she was in Cincinnati?"

"Yeah. Really, I talked to her every night she was there."

Phone lines humming, sister to sister. "Do the two of you usually talk every day?"

"Um, no, only when . . ."

"Yes?"

Hardin cleared her throat. "Just when there's stuff going on. When we have things to talk about."

"What was going on?" Sonora asked.

Hardin did not answer.

"Ms. Hardin, have you heard from your sister at all since Sunday morning of the sixteenth?"

Harden's voice softened. "No. I haven't."

"Don't you think that's odd?"

"Yes. I didn't know what was going on. Butch called me and he said he was headed your way. He didn't find her?"

"No ma'am, he didn't. And you're sure she hasn't been in touch?"

"Absolutely."

The woman sounded definite. Truthful.

"Ms. Hardin, I know you don't want to betray any confidences here, but we're concerned about the where-abouts of your sister. Do you think it's possible she might have left her family, um, willingly?"

Hardin's voice went flat. "No, I don't."

"No doubt?"

"You know about the affair, don't you?"

Sonora thought about it. "Can you confirm that there was an affair, and give me the man's name?"

"Yes, there was an affair, and no, I don't know his name. But she didn't run off with him, Detective. The affair was not going well and he was the last thing on her mind."

"What was on her mind, do you know?"

Hardin took a breath. "It sounds . . . dramatic. But my sister saw a picture in the paper. A picture of a man she thinks killed somebody eight years ago. She was upset about it, and she was going to the police."

"I can double-check, but we have no record of her filing—"

"I talked her out of it. Of going to the police. I thought she would just make an ass out of herself. She decided she'd look into things herself, don't ask me how. I was hoping she'd give up on it and come home. It seemed . . . pointless."

"She didn't give you any idea what she intended to do to check things out?"

"No, but we got interrupted." Hardin's voice took on a rough edge. "That whoever it was she was seeing was at her door, upset about something, God knows what. He was very high maintenance, that's one thing she did tell me, and driving her up the wall. She said she'd call me later, but she never did."

"You must have been worried."

"Very. But I wasn't quite sure who to tell."

"What do you know about this murder she thinks she saw?"

"No thinks about it, Detective, Julia isn't a nut. She told me about it, but it's been years." Hardin paused. "I know it happened when she was on campus. She went to the University of Cincinnati, did you know that?"

"No," Sonora said.

"Look, I've got a date and he should be here any time, and I've got ten minutes to put on makeup and get these electric rollers out of my hair. Can I think about this and call you back?"

Sonora gave her the number and hung up. Ten minutes was going to be a hell of a rush. She looked over at Sam. "How'd you do with Barber?"

"He's a photographer. He's not home. It's Friday night and nobody's available."

"Let's get out of here."

6

Sonora was dawdling in the parking lot, not sure she was ready to leave Sam, not sure she was ready to launch into the mom-thing. She got into the Blazer, put the key in the ignition so she could roll the window down and talk.

"I want this Chevy," Sam said.

"Tim wants me to keep the Nissan so he can drive it when he gets his license. You don't want to buy that one, do you? I'll give you a deal."

"I know it too well." He slapped the top of the Blazer. "You ever want to sell this one, you let me know."

They looked at each other. The sun had gone down but it was still hot. Sam had sweat on his upper lip.

"What you going to do tonight?" he asked.

"Go home. Clean house. Pay bills." For some reason, she had been going to say call her brother. Maybe because it was his car she was driving. He had left her everything in his will.

"What?" Sam said.

"Don't ask me why, but I was going to say call Stuart."

Sam squeezed her shoulder. "I wish I could tell you these things go away, Sonora. I think you just learn to live with it."

She was. Learning to live with it. One brother, murdered in hot flame and agony, because he was related to a homicide cop after a serial killer.

Someone honked a horn, and Sam looked over his shoulder and waved. A regulation blue Taurus unmarked cop car pulled close alongside the Chevy, loose gravel crunching beneath the tires.

Gruber and Sanders. Sonora gave Sam a look. If there was ever a mismatched pair of cops.

Gruber was a hard-ass guy from New Jersey, with an attitude to match his experience. Sanders was the little girl next door who wanted to grow up to be a mommy and a schoolteacher.

"You guys forget the way home?" Sonora asked.

Gruber rubbed a hand across his face. "Home? Where's that?"

Sanders stuck her head out the window. She had straight brown hair that hung to her shoulders. "Another clown down today."

Sam nodded. "We heard. Lion's Club Fair, same thing?"

Gruber shifted the car into park. "Yeah. Bobo's in the dunking booth throwing out insults to the crowd, waiting for somebody to bean him with a ball. Instead, some guy cuts him in half with a thirty-ought-six, bolt-action rifle."

Sonora rested an arm on the open window of her Chevy. "Doesn't anybody see this guy coming?"

Gruber snorted. "Hell, yeah, lots of people. You going to argue with a guy with a deer rifle and an attitude?"

Sanders shook her head. "Those poor clowns, sitting on that perch in the booth. There's nowhere they can go."

"Except under," Gruber said. "They got Bobo clowns quitting in droves." He held up a bag of doughnuts, stuck them through the window over Sanders's head. "Help yourselves, guys, courtesy of my partner here." He saluted Sanders, who grimaced at the doughnuts.

"We're trying to set up a stakeout," she said. "Catch this guy coming."

Sonora was looking into the bag, deciding between caramel iced and chocolate sprinkles. Sam took cinnamon cake.

"I'm going to wear a clown suit and sit in the booth and Gruber's going to collar this sucker, you see if we don't."

Gruber turned and looked at Sanders. White powdered sugar flaked the beard stubble on his chin. "Who says *you're* doing the decoy? You got dimples. Cops with dimples can't be decoys."

"It's a regulation, I think." Sam licked cinnamon off his fingers.

Sanders folded her arms. "I already talked to Crick. He said whosoever shall fit into the clown suit with vest underneath, shall therefore be the clown decoy." Sanders smiled at Gruber. "We already got the suit, I've tried it on, and you'll never fit."

"Wha— Is that the reason behind all the sub sandwiches and pizzas and candy bars you been bringing me?"

Sanders smiled gently.

"I bet I've put on fifteen pounds in the last three weeks."

"Maybe more," Sanders said.

Gruber stuck a finger in his waistband. "God bless. Now what am I going to do?"

Sonora took the bag of doughnuts off his hands. "Do what women do."

"Which is?"

"Induce vomiting."

7

Sonora drove with the windows down. Stuart had loved country music all his life, and for some reason, lately, she found herself listening to his tapes. She stopped at a red light, turned the volume down.

She had been a die-hard rock fan all her life and did not want to be caught listening to country.

It was a long drive home, all the way into Blue Ash. She got to the house after dark, which at least meant she didn't have to notice how much the lawn needed mowing.

She headed up the stairs from the garage, saw, with no surprise, that her kids were on the floor in front of the television set. Clampett leaped off the couch, trailing clumps of yellow foam stuffing, tail wagging and thumping the wall. He stepped on Sonora's foot and jumped for the bag of doughnuts.

"Hi kids."

Tim looked up. He was on his back, one leg bent, head pillowed by the only couch cushion free of dog bites. His hair was black, close-cropped, which gave him a tough look he cultivated. His jeans were oversized and bagging. Sonora always wanted to tell him to pull them up.

"What's in the bag, Mom?"

Heather got up. "Doughnuts, stupid." She pushed her glasses back on her nose. Her hair, dark and fine, streamed loose from a braid. "Can we have some?"

"If you can get to them before Clampett does."

"Mom," Tim said, "can you wait a while before you go into the kitchen? Me and Heather are going to clean that up later on."

Sonora overslept the next morning. She drove fast, dropped Tim off at a friend's, and Heather at her grand-mother's. Homicide had no respect for weekends.

She headed for the city, wondering how she could justify being so late. Decided to stop and talk to Caplan on the way in, go through the motions, meet Sam and regroup. No one would know how long she had talked to him, or waited around until he could talk. She could go to the office like a worker bee, instead of slinking in, hang-ing her head.

It was a plan.

She didn't know where Caplan lived, but it would be a good bet to try his office. There was a chance he'd be working. Even if he'd given his final arguments, he had to prepare for the sentencing segment, in case he won. The Drury thing was probably muscling in on his weekends.

There were cars in the parking lot, which Sonora found encouraging.

She went through a door into a hallway, heard laugh-ter, a young male shouting, "Yeah, right," then a female voice, also young, that said, "You sure you don't want me to stay?"

Sonora got the feeling, as she rounded the corner, that the woman would have liked to stay. A male voice, rich with the medium depth of a good baritone, said, "Hell no, you kids get home and enjoy what's left of your weekend. I'll see you first thing Monday morning. Early, the both of you."

The kids, Sonora saw, were a man and woman

anywhere from twenty-two to twenty-five, wearing jeans and khakis, Saturday casuals. They had the sheen of up-and-coming youngsters who had sufficient pocket money and fun on what weekends they took from the office, and the pale complexion of kids who worked long hours.

Sonora immediately recognized the man at the door who was waving them off. He wore his shirtsleeves rolled up and his strong forearms were crisscrossed with glints of gold-brown hair. His body type might have been called fat in a man more unattractive, but not this one. His clothes fit him well, and he wore them with the air of comfort a man gets when he is happy with who he is and where he is going. His hair was dark tobacco brown, the waves well cut and under control, and he had the big shoulders and muscular build of a man who is good at physical things.

He smiled at Sonora, a one-sided smile, and she noticed that his eyes were very blue. He folded his arms, cocked his head to one side.

"You have the world-weary air of a cop."

The "kids" in the hallway gave Sonora a long look.

"You're Caplan?" she said. Just making sure.

"We haven't met."

His handshake was firm, and he covered her one hand with both of his and gave her a speculative look, the kind a man gives a woman. Sonora had not expected him to be quite so taking in person. Like all the best DAs, he had a certain presence that would be a plus in the courtroom, or anywhere else, and she liked the steady way he returned her look, and the intelligence she read in his eyes.

She was glad she had worn the silky white shirt. "Specialist Sonora Blair. Homicide."

He grinned. "*Really*. Surprised we haven't run across

each other till now. You brought down that nutcase last year, Yorke, wasn't it? Serial killer? Liked to play with matches?"

"Selma Yorke," Sonora said. Liked to play with matches was one way to describe a woman who hand-cuffed men to the steering wheels of their cars, doused them with gasoline, and set them ablaze.

He looked over Sonora's shoulder at the two in the hallway. Made shooing motions. "Get along and get rested up. I'll be working your butts on Monday."

They obeyed immediately, footsteps echoing.

Caplan waved an arm, cop-friendly. "Come on in, and excuse the mess. Trying to nail myself a vehicular homicide, so we're working late nights and weekends."

"I appreciate your time. Your name is legend, you know." Sonora caught the smile, boyish and on the edge of shy, as she followed him through the doorway.

It was a busy room, too many desks in too small a space, and it had the familiar tired smell of old coffee and cold pizza that Sonora recognized from long nights in the bullpen. The trash cans were full, some of them over-flowing. One desk still had a light on and a typewriter uncovered and was snugged in an alcove right outside of the open office Caplan led her into.

His desk was as close to immaculate as a desk could be after weeks of intense work. A brass lamp cast a pool of light over the flat black surface, set in heavy, well-polished mahogany. An open briefcase housed an Apple PowerBook, taking up the slick and dusted right corner. His computer was set to the left on an arm of mahogany, and the screen was up, color monitor.

Not government issue, Sonora thought, looking at the bookshelves, the credenza, the flowered love seat, and oriental carpet. Looked like something you would find in a well-heeled law office, where they handled things like bankruptcies and corporate taxes.

Brought a few goodies from home.

A double-frame holder sat on a bookshelf, off the desk, nontraditional. Caplan couldn't see it but everyone else could. On one side was the picture of a little girl, six or seven, maybe a bit younger than Heather. The child was Amerasian, hair jet black and shoulder length, eyes slanted and cornflower blue. Her skin had a fragile porcelain look and she wore a red velvet dress with a sash so big that either end of the bow peeked out from both sides of her tiny waist.

Her smile was wide but unconvincing, and she looked tense. Her eyes were sad.

The companion picture was a contrast of informality. The woman wore wide khaki shorts that stopped at her knees, chunky waist cinched with a drawstring belt. Her sleeveless blue denim shirt looked worn but comfortable. She had chin length, thin, dark blond hair, an odd sort of clown nose, and a figure that an unkind person might dismiss as dumpy.

She looked shy, as if she knew that she was unphotogenic, and that the camera would not be kind.

"My family," Caplan said.

Sonora nodded, muttered "lovely" under her breath. The woman could not be the biological mother of the little girl, but those big blue eyes looked like Caplan-issue.

Sonora took the newspaper clipping from her briefcase. Handed it across the desk. "Good picture."

Caplan did a double-take when he recognized himself, then leaned back in his chair. "My wife went out and bought a dozen newspapers when this came out. Sent them to all her relatives. She grew up on a farm, so I guess she figures that when the barn cats don't scare the mice, these will."

Sonora gave him a sideways smile. "Don't add that one to your collection, it may be evidence."

Caplan scooted his chair in close to the desk, smile fading. "What do you mean, evidence?"

The relaxed feel of the room went away. Caplan had a wary look that put Sonora on guard.

"I've got a woman who's come up missing. Julia Winchell. She had this clipping in her hotel room."

He shook his head, a look of polite perplexity wrinkling the brow. Sonora was watching and he knew it. It made them both nervous.

"Julia Winchell? Sorry, I don't know her."

Sonora nodded. He said the name as if it meant nothing. She studied him, thinking that probably it did.

Caplan rocked from side to side in his chair. "It's odd, though. I mean, whoever she is, she clearly cut this out with a purpose. You think she has some connection to the case?"

Sonora waved a hand. "Anything's possible, we're just in the initial stages. She's not from around here."

Caplan leaned back and waited. He wasn't going to ask.

"She's from Tennessee," Sonora said. "In town for some sort of small business convention."

"Married?" Caplan asked, voice dry.

"Married. Two little kids."

He was nodding. "You know, it's possible—"

Sonora waited. Let him say it.

He waved a hand. "Sometimes the family thing is overwhelming. Wife gets away from the diapers and the house a couple days, gets swept off her feet. She'll probably call in a week or two when the novelty wears off." Caplan scratched his chin. "I know I sound a little hard.

It's not something I'd say, except to someone like you who knows the business."

"We think it's possible she witnessed a murder." Sonora smiled. Bland.

"No kidding? She file a police report?"

Sonora shook her head. "It was something that happened a long time ago."

Caplan pulled his ear. "That's kind of weird. You think maybe she called our office or something?"

"No stone unturned. That's why I'm here."

"Which makes you good at what you do." His voice stayed friendly, but he had an air of preoccupation. He tugged the middle desk drawer. It stuck, and he yanked it hard. "Messages," he muttered, dislodging a fist full of pink telephone slips with jagged edges. A pencil spilled onto the floor and Sonora could see the edges of an unruly stack of papers and old envelopes. Caplan shoved the drawer shut and flipped through the messages, humming. "Revolution." The Beatles.

He looked up and caught Sonora's eye, brows raised. "Nobody here by that name, but my secretary may have screened it, or someone else could have taken the call. It's been a mess around here lately."

Sonora looked at the immaculate desk.

"Bea should be gone by now. We're in pretty good shape, so I told everybody to leave at noon. I've got to get home myself. My wife's expecting her first child, and she's been feeling bad the last couple of days. Probably the heat. Anyway, I'll ask Bea on Monday if she took a call like that, have her check with the staff. I'll get back to you on it."

Sonora nodded. "Appreciate your trouble."

He shook his head. "Not at all. Two little kids, huh? What ages?"

"Three and fourteen months."

"Um." He looked truly regretful. He was a family man. He had kids of his own. "Anything at all I can do to find their mama, don't hesitate to ask."

Sonora shook his hand again. "Thank you."

He stood up. "Is that blouse silk?"

It wasn't, but Sonora wasn't about to say rayon. She wasn't about to say anything. He was hitting on her. Damn.

"Stay in touch, Detective. We could do the lunch thing, when my schedule clears."

"Let me know what your secretary says."

"About my schedule?"

"About those phone calls. And thanks for your time." Sonora turned away, wondered why the secretary had left her lamp on and her typewriter uncovered, if she had gone home. She looked over her shoulder at Caplan, caught him watching her butt. She inclined her head. "This your secretary's desk?"

Caplan moved across the room behind her, looked out. "Yep."

Sonora waved a hand toward the lamp, the typewriter. "Maybe she's still here."

Caplan put both hands on Sonora's shoulders and scooted her gently out of the way. He turned the lamp off. "I don't—"

Something landed hard very close by, and a woman's soft voice could be heard, muttering.

Caplan pursed his lips. "Maybe she *is* here. I sent her home a little while ago, but Bea's a real hard worker." He headed toward an open door behind the desk. Sonora saw metal file cabinets, a copy machine, stacks of paper, forms, envelopes. "Bea? You in there?"

Sonora trailed him through the door.

Caplan opened his arms wide. Grinned. "I thought you went home."

"First I heard of it." She was black, thin, close to retirement age or beyond, and though there were lines of fatigue from her nose to her lips, and bags of exhaustion under her eyes, her smile was sweet, and she greeted Sonora with genuine warmth.

"Bea, this is Detective Blair. She's a homicide investigator from downtown." He waved a hand. "Bea Wallace. Runs the office and everybody in it."

"So long as I've got you fooled." She leaned against the open filing cabinet, then rocked back on her feet, looking from Caplan to Sonora. "How can I help you out?"

The accent wasn't local, but from farther south. Maybe Kentucky, but to Sonora's ear, she'd guess Tennessee.

"I'm trying to track a woman who went missing a couple weeks ago. Julia Winchell. According to our phone records, she called your office here, several times."

Bea Wallace folded her arms, closing the file cabinet with her back and resting up against the dull gray metal. "Say that name again?"

Sonora turned sideways, facing her. "Julia Winchell. She probably asked for Mr. Caplan. She clipped his picture out of the newspaper."

"Julia Winchell. The name doesn't ring any bells. But we've been getting all kinds of calls since we started the Drury prosecution."

"I bet you have," Sonora said.

Bea Wallace tapped her cheek. "We did get one strange one though, come to think of it. Little girl wanted to know what the statute of limitations was on a homicide."

"There isn't one," Caplan said.

"What I told her. And she wanted to know if I could give her any details about . . ." she glanced at Caplan, "about a particular homicide."

"Which particular homicide?" Sonora noticed Caplan going solid and tense.

"She'd caught that article about you in the paper, Gage. The one that gave that background stuff on your first wife. Sorry. She wanted to know how long Mr. Caplan's been a district attorney. That kind of thing."

Caplan nodded, thin-lipped and grim.

Sonora gave Caplan a sideways look. No doubt, then, that the call was from Julia Winchell. She had the usual cop's aversion to coincidence.

"What'd you tell her?" Caplan asked.

Bea Wallace shrugged. "She didn't sound like the typical nutcase, but how can you tell? We've had a lot of calls since the Drury thing started. This kind of case brings out the bad ones."

"In droves," Caplan said. Grimaced.

"I don't like it when they get personal about Mr. Caplan. So I didn't tell her anything."

"She call back?" Sonora said.

Bea looked down. "Just once."

"What about?" Sonora asked.

"Wanted to know what Mr. Caplan's wife's full name was. His first wife."

"And she was killed?" Sonora said.

"Murdered," Caplan said. "Brutally."

"She wanted to know if they'd ever caught the killer."

Caplan shifted his weight. Stared at a spot on the wall, somewhere between Sonora and Bea Wallace.

Sonora pushed hair out of her eyes. These people did not give ground easily. "And you said?"

Bea Wallace stood still, both feet planted side by side. She would not meet Sonora's eyes. "I said no. They did not catch the killer."

8

The parking situation tipped Sonora off—after-hours, no special events, and all the slots in front of the Board of Elections Building filled, both sides. These were not cop cars. Cops tended to drive two types of cars. The older guys, the guys with families, favored the beige Taurus or Camry, cars that didn't stand out to the highway patrol, cars that were the equivalent of stealth bombers on the interstate. One could tote the kids in comfort, and indulge in an excess of speed without the embarrassment of glad-handing a brother officer into forgiveness. The younger cops drove Chevy Malibus and Camaros, with souped-up 454 engines for speed, and modified turbo 400 transmissions that gave torque and muscle.

The underpaid press tended toward Chevettes, Vegas, and Escorts.

Sonora looked at the mix—a Lincoln, an LTD, a van, Chevy Blazer, one small blue Mazda. Looked like John Q. Public.

She headed into the building, took the elevator to the fifth floor. She heard the buzz of voices as soon as the doors opened. The noise reminded her of high school hallways between classes. She passed the empty glass booth of reception and went through the swing door into homicide.

She veered sideways immediately, reflexes sharp, to get out of the way of a woman who walked past with the air of the person in charge. Sonora did not recognize her. She was tall and big-boned, wings of gray in the swept-back, coarse brown hair. Her dress was that deep shade of purple that seemed to appeal to British royalty and women past menopause. The dress was belted in the middle, setting off a well-toned, nicely proportioned figure, though the shoulders were large, and the hands and facial features oddly mannish.

The woman caught Sonora's look, lifted her chin, and breezed past, finding herself face to face with the swing door. She turned and frowned, and Sonora leaned up against the wall, arms folded, thinking that this was a woman people were probably at pains not to cross.

"Where *is* this mythical coffeemaker, or can I persuade someone to actually get me a cup?" She looked at Sonora expectantly, and held a mug out, as if in supplication.

Sonora noticed that the mug was her turquoise Joseph-Beth Booksellers cup. "You don't want *that* one."

The woman braced her legs. "What?"

"That mug. You don't want to drink out of that one, it's got lipstick stains on the side."

The woman turned the mug on one side and squinted, then pursed her lips. "You're right." She curled her lip, handed the mug back to Sonora. "Thanks."

"Anytime."

Sonora continued down the hallway, stopping at the coffeemaker that steamed on a table by the left-hand side of the wall. She wondered how the woman in purple had missed it. She put coffee and cream into the mug, rocked it gently to disperse the white powder, smiled when the mix turned the right shade of mocha brown, and headed for her desk, noting, as she went by, that both interview rooms were full.

"Sonora?" Sam leaned out of Interview One, right behind her.

He loped down the hallway, brown hair sliding into his eyes. His tie was loose, shirt ballooning from the waistband of his pants. He looked boyish and tired, as if he hadn't slept.

"How'd you get all these people here so early?" Sonora said.

"I guess they get out of bed before you. You up all night cleaning and paying bills and doing the mom-thing?"

Actually, she had let it all go to hell and curled up with a book. She gave Sam a noble look, tinged with sadness. "I chose to be a single mother. I'm not complaining." She yawned and covered her mouth. "Stopped at Caplan's office on my way in."

"Yeah? How'd it go?"

Sonora frowned. "A little weird."

"Weird how?"

"Just a feeling I got. Everything he *said* was right, anything I can do to help, all that. But he told me his secretary had gone home, and she hadn't."

"Arrest that man."

"I got the feeling he didn't want me talking to her."

"Maybe he wanted you to go away so he could get his work done and go home."

"Maybe. But she did call. Julia Winchell. The secretary talked to her."

He rocked backward on his heels. "Aha. What did she want?"

"She wanted to know about Caplan's first wife. And how she got killed."

"Nancy Drew at work."

"Which is what I need to be. It's wall-to-wall cars outside, how many people you got up here?"

"Five or six," Sam said. "Hundred. Locals. Called and invited to drop by."

Sonora hid a smile. "Who's the sweetheart in purple?"

"Valerie Gibson, the conference coordinator."

"Scary."

"I'll take her," Sam said. "You cover the couple in Interview Two. Molliter's working the lady in one."

"I thought he was on nights."

"He wants the overtime and we need the help."

Sonora gave Sam a hard look. "What's wrong with the couple in two?"

Sam smiled sweetly, and scooted down the hallway, fast enough to let her know she'd been stuck. She stopped for a minute outside the hallway to peep in at them, saw the woman, sixtyish, rummaging in an expensive-looking tapestry purse, waving one hand in the air. The man sitting next to her was frowning and watching intently, as if his life depended upon what might or might not come out of the purse.

Sonora took a sip of coffee and ducked inside. The woman was unwrapping sticks of Wrigley's Doublemint gum. She gave one stick to her husband and unwrapped another, looked up and caught sight of Sonora.

"Are you the secretary, miss?"

The woman would be short when she stood up, Sonora thought. Five two at the most. Still taller than Sonora herself, but a good deal heavier. She wore a lavender blouse that looked more like real silk than rayon, and looped in a big bow across the collar that had been buttoned tightly around her neck. The ends of the bow fluttered across what she would undoubtedly call her bosom, and dipped below the high waistband of the navy skirt that flared and folded, the hemline midcalf. Her shoes, under the table, looked sensible and new, the toes squared, the heels chunky. The oval lenses of her glasses magnified her eyes.

"I'm Police Specialist Blair. I'm a detective."

"Gum?" the man said, chewing discreetly.

Detectives merited gum, Sonora noted. "No thanks." She shook both of their hands and sat down. The woman set her purse on her lap.

Sonora gave them a smile that was likely more preoccupied than friendly, threaded a reel of tape into the old warhorse of a tape recorder, and asked them both to state their names.

"Barbara Henderson Miller," the woman said, eyes big and alert behind the thick lenses of her glasses. "And this is my husband—"

"Alford C. Miller," he said, leaning toward the recorder.

"What's the *C* stand for," Sonora asked, thinking maybe *Crabby*.

"Carl," he said. And blinked.

Sonora rubbed the back of her neck. "As I understand, one of you, both of you—"

"Both," Mrs. Miller said. Alford nodded.

Sonora was not surprised that they had not needed to hear the question. These people would know the answer before you decided what to ask.

"Both of you attended this small business conference at the Orchard Suites?"

Mrs. Miller's purse slid sideways and a checkbook, flowered glasses case, and roll of butterscotch Lifesavers spilled out. The Lifesavers hit the floor and rolled under Alford's chair. Mrs. Miller caught the checkbook and glasses case, pressing them into the folds of her thick polyester skirt.

"You didn't close it, Barbie." Alford leaned sideways to pick up the butterscotch Lifesavers.

"I *did* close it, I heard it snap. Didn't you hear the snap?" She looked at Sonora.

"I wasn't paying attention. Are the two of you local? You live in Cincinnati?"

"We live in Union," Alford said.

"So you didn't stay at the hotel?"

Mrs. Miller took a tight grip on her purse. "Oh yes we did. We like staying in hotels. You get breakfast."

"It comes with the room," Alford explained.

Sonora took a breath, let it out slowly. "Mr. and Mrs. Miller. Did either of you see or talk to Julia Winchell during this conference?"

"Well, how could we not, it wasn't that big a conference," Mrs. Miller said.

Alford thumbed his ear. "You mean that black-headed girl Detective Sam showed us? In the picture?"

"Yes."

"He play football in school?"

"He was on the badminton team," Sonora said. She did not want to get into Sam's glorious football history.

Alford was still working the thumb. "That can't be right. UC doesn't have a badminton team. Do they?"

"He went to school in Kentucky," Sonora said.

"We certainly *did* notice *Mrs.* Winchell," Mrs. Miller said.

"Pretty little girl," Alford said absently. "She seemed very nice at first." He gave his wife a dark look and both of them nodded.

"At first?" Sonora said. With these two it might be best just to let them talk, provided she could keep them on the subject.

Mrs. Miller leaned forward, mouth going tight. "She

seemed nice at first, maybe a little offish, keeping herself to herself some."

"Shy," Alford said.

"Reserved. With some people, not with everyone. For instance, Mr. Jeff Barber certainly seemed to be a particular friend."

Sonora made a note. Alford leaned forward and cut his eyes sideways. Sonora was tempted to print GO TO HELL on the notepad, but she couldn't pay attention and write upside down at the same time.

"I take it Mr. Barber was enrolled in these courses too?"

Alford shook his head. "Not courses. It was a one-week conference. Lectures, panel discussions, workshops. Really, it should have been a two-week thing. That would have been more effective."

"But double the fee," Mrs. Miller said.

"Maybe, maybe not. With economies of scale—"

She was losing them, Sonora thought. "Can I get either of you a soda, cup of coffee?"

Their heads swiveled as one, their eyes bright, as they allowed that a soda would be a welcome thing.

"Let's clear up this Barber thing before I run out to the machine." Sonora had kids. She knew how to do this. "When you said they were good friends. Did either of you get the feeling they knew each other before?"

"They *said* not," Alford said.

"You asked?" Sonora looked at him.

He nodded.

"They certainly got *very* chummy *very* fast." Mrs. Miller gave Sonora a significant look.

"For instance?"

"Oh, but I don't like to say."

"Mrs. Miller, I'll remind you that Julia Winchell has

been missing for over fifteen days, and she has two young children waiting at home. You need to answer all of my questions to the very best of your ability."

Alford made the kind of clucking noise you would make to a horse. "That just makes it that much worse, when an irresponsible young mother can't behave."

Mrs. Miller leaned forward. "Does her husband know anything about all this?"

Sonora closed her eyes, shutting the two of them out for three precious seconds. "About all what?"

"About the way she was carrying on!" Mrs. Miller let go of the purse and it hit the floor, spilling contents that Sonora was now able to inventory with her eyes closed. Mrs. Miller looked at Alford, heading him off. "I did snap it shut, the catch is broken. And I've only had this purse a few months. I think the store should take it back. Don't you think?" She looked at Sonora.

Alford was on his hands and knees, picking up the butterscotch Lifesavers. "Did you keep the receipt?"

"No, she didn't keep the receipt." Sonora leaned back in her chair, placed both hands flat on the table. "You said that Julia Winchell and Jeff Barber were"—she looked at her notepad—"in your words, 'carrying on.' Tell me exactly what you mean."

"They weren't the only ones." Alford. Off on a tangent.

His wife nodded. "You must mean that MacMillan woman. *Sylvie*."

Alford leaned forward. "First of all, they *sat* together. Every single class."

"Saved each other seats," Mrs. Miller said.

The two of them slid their chairs in closer to the table.

"Anything else?" Sonora asked.

"They laughed. A lot. She had this little way of turning her head sideways when he talked."

"Very cute," Alford said.

"*Coquettish*. And one day, at a workshop, she came in late and *he* wouldn't let us start till she got there."

Sonora wondered how to spell coquettish. She wrote down flirty.

"Don't forget that Friday," Alford said.

Mrs. Miller patted the table. "That's right. We went to Montgomery Inn. We can't have the ribs. We have to order the chicken for our digestive systems, but we like eating down on the river. So we gave ourselves a little treat and went there for dinner."

"Which *he* called supper, I heard him!"

Mrs. Miller nodded. "And they were already there. *Just* the two of them, in one of those half-circle little booths, sitting very close together."

"And?" Sonora asked.

"They seemed very happy," Mrs. Miller said.

Alford nodded. "They were having the ribs."

9

Sonora left the Millers pining over ribs. She peered into the two-way of Interview One, saw Valerie Gibson waving an arm in the air, and Sam cringing. She went in quietly.

Gibson was holding forth. "One of the best conferences we've ever had. A very congenial group, with a palpable esprit de corps."

Sonora decided that any woman who used *palpable* and *esprit de corps* in one sentence deserved to be interrupted.

"Sam, can I see you just for one minute?"

Gibson swiveled sideways and raised one eyebrow. "*That* is the secretary who took my coffee cup."

"I'm just a temp," Sonora said.

Sam made soothing noises at Gibson and followed her out. He shut the door and leaned against the wall. Gave Sonora a look.

"Get anything out of her?" Sonora asked.

"I think what you mean is did I get anything useful. The answer to which is not much. Anything out of your couple?"

"Unmitigated joy." She leaned her back against the wall, lowered her voice. "It does look like our girl was—" She paused, picturing Julia Winchell's haunted face in the photograph, her two children. Remembered how unhappily she herself had been married way back when.

She had been about to say "doing the nasty," but changed it to "stepping out."

Sam cracked a smile. "As in *stepping* out or stepping *out*?"

"Shut up, Sam. She was getting close to this Jeff Barber guy at the conference, just like we figured."

"Close, Sonora? That Victoria's Secret special looked very close."

"Yeah, have it your way, Sam. She was fucking Jeff Barber. Any luck yet tracking him down?"

"Been trying to catch him since first thing this morning. Want me to give him another call?"

"Now would be good." She followed him into the bullpen. Waved at Sanders, who was at her desk, on the phone.

Sanders had a high wattage glow that made Sonora decide the call was definitely personal.

Young love.

She thought of Keaton, and pushed his image out of her head. When a relationship went bad it was always better to sever the connection, and not do the back-and-forth agony dance. Better, but hard. He would always hold her peculiarly responsible for the death of his estranged wife, even though she'd saved his neck. It was not fair, but it was real life.

Sometimes it seemed the whole world was paired off except her. She was getting tired of lying to people about what she did Friday nights.

"Sonora?" Sam tucked a wad of tobacco into one cheek.

"What you got, Sam?"

"Jeff Barber runs a photography studio in a strip mall out on College. I talked to his wife—"

Sonora raised an eyebrow. "So there is a wife."

"Yeah, *I'm* shocked. Wife said he'll be working in the darkroom all day. Probably be home late tonight, maybe around ten."

"So he didn't run away. I bet he'd rather talk at the studio."

Sam moved his shirt off his wrist, looked at his watch. "Let's wrap this thing up here, and go out together."

Sonora smiled. She was not going back into that room with that couple. "Why don't you hold the fort here, Sam? I think I better jump on this Barber thing while I can. See you later."

She put her coffee mug down, then picked it back up. Better take it along to be safe.

10

The strip mall, out exit seven in Montgomery, was dying the slow tortured death of buckled asphalt, grass sprouting through the cracks, broken concrete headstones for parking spaces. A blue mail-drop box showed four pickup times, the latest at 6 P.M.

Most of the storefronts were dark. Barber's studio was next door to a pet store, Animal House, front door propped open with a brick. A condenser dripped rusty water onto the worn concrete sidewalk. Sonora heard the squawk of a parrot and the shrill sweet chatter of parakeets. According to a hand-lettered sign in the front glass partition, they were running a special on Animal Science Diet. Sonora thought of Clampett, content to eat whatever was on special. He was getting on in years. Would he live longer if she put him on an Animal Science Diet? She wondered what an animal science diet was.

The humidity was making her hair curly. Frizzy, actually. The *F* word. She straightened her tie, and pushed the door open to Barber Studio Internationale, thinking he could call it *Internationale* till the cows came home, but tomorrow this would still be Cincinnati.

There were yellowed wedding pictures in the window— a bride gazing happily into a bouquet of white roses that were too beautiful to be real. Another shot showed a pregnant woman in a white flowing robe holding a pink rose to one cheek in a soft camera focus that said Madonna,

Madonna, Madonna. A heavy silver cross hung around her neck.

Sonora gave the picture a second look, thinking that it would be more realistic to have the woman bending over a toilet tossing her cookies. She wondered how that would look in soft focus.

Little brass bells tinged as she entered the studio, but the man inside was singing along with Roy Orbison in a duet of "Crying," and didn't hear her come in.

Sonora put her hands in her pockets and rocked back and forth on her heels. She had on new Reeboks, white high-topped Freestyle, with REEBOK stitched in shimmery silver on the sides. Sonora liked her tennies new and unscuffed. She admired them for a moment, then looked around the studio.

A lot of vinyl in that state-park shade of brown used for signs and picnic tables. The carpet was indoor-outdoor, thin and reddish, and there was a green couch next to an old silver ashtray—the old, freestanding kind that opened in the middle to make a chasm for cigarette butts and ashes. It was the kind Sonora had liked to play with when she was a child. The kind her mother had told her to leave alone.

The vocals swelled, harmonizing with Roy's, *cry ee eye ee ing*. A man pushed his way through a saloon-style swing door, caught sight of Sonora, and stopped dead.

"You're among friends," Sonora said. "I'm an Orbison fan."

He watched her, like a startled mule deer that is making its mind up whether or not it will spook and run.

Where would he go? she wondered.

He was exactly what she had expected. Handlebar mustache, thick, black, and long enough to chew. Eyes deep-set and brown, shadowed by half-moons of fatigue.

His lips were thick beneath the mustache and he needed a shave. His hair was longish, like he was overdue for a haircut, collar-length in the back, shorter on the sides, and parted to one side.

His shoulders were stooped, like an old man's, though he looked to be no more than thirty-five or six.

"I sing 'Blue Bayou' in the shower, myself," Sonora said. She wanted him off-guard and friendly. For starters.

He gave her a sad smile. In the dog world he would be a basset hound and would howl on the night of the full moon, and at ambulance sirens. He went over to the boom box and shut the CD off. Looked over his shoulder at Sonora. "My guess is you're getting married, am I right? Second time around, and this time it's going to work?"

She held out her ID. "You guess wrong. Police Specialist Blair, Cincinnati PD."

His eyes took on a glaze of shock. He licked his lips. "What exactly is a police specialist?" His voice had gone down an octave.

"A detective. In my case, homicide."

"Homicide," he repeated.

"Forgive me, Mr. Barber, but you look like a man expecting bad news."

"Would you . . . would you like to sit down?"

Sonora looked at the couch. She'd sat on worse. In her own living room. "Thanks."

11

Of course he smoked. Generic brand, white packaging, cigarettes that smelled as bad as they looked. The air conditioner was laboring, and it gave off a sour musty smell.

A small picture of Barber, a woman, and two children was displayed in a frame on the coffee table. If Barber had taken the shot, it would go a long way toward explaining the lack of Saturday afternoon clientele.

"Nice family," Sonora said, picking up the picture. The helpmeet had curly brown hair, chin length, a full face, and glasses. The children were school age, first and second grade from the looks of them. One boy, one girl, standard issue, bowl haircuts.

"They were."

Sonora checked his left hand. Saw the thick gold band. "Were?"

"Died, all three of them. Ran up under a tractor trailer truck on I-75. My wife and daughter went instantly. My son hung on a couple of days. Happened five years ago."

Sonora looked into his face, saw that he was smiling the bland sheepish smile people plaster over a welter of grief. His demeanor was apologetic. He had not meant to bring tragedy into the room, it was just there ahead of them.

She told him how beautiful his children were, and that she was sorry.

"What were their names, your kids?" Sonora asked.

"Christy and Wesley. Christy for my sister. Wesley for Kathy's dad. Kathy was my wife."

The names came awkwardly on his tongue, and Sonora looked at his eyes and decided that he mentioned them almost never, and thought of them every day.

"You've remarried?" Sonora said.

He looked puzzled. "No."

"We called your house. Talked to a Mrs. Barber—"

"Ms. My sister. She goes over and leaves me dinner every day."

"That's nice."

"It would be if she could cook."

Sonora gave him a half-smile in acknowledgment of the hit, but wondered why he didn't let his sister off the hook, if he didn't want the meals. She slid back on the couch. "Mr. Barber, how long have you known Julia Winchell?" She watched his face. "You do know her, don't you?"

"I, uh, I met Julia at a conference on running a small business."

He liked saying her name, she could tell. Red flag number one.

"When was the last time you saw her?" Sonora took out her mini recorder. Checked the tape, turned it on. "Excuse me, let me ask that again. Mr. Barber, when was the last time you saw Julia Winchell?"

He moved sideways, shoulders low even when he sat. "At that last workshop, I guess. The one on dealing with the IRS."

"And that was the last time you saw her?"

He nodded.

"Say yes," Sonora said, tapping the recorder.

"Sorry. Yes."

"When was that, exactly?"

"Saturday, late in the afternoon. The fifteenth of July."

"You call her? Afterwards?"

Pause. "No."

"Has she called you? Written you? Gotten in touch with you in any way?"

"Why would she? You haven't—Has something happened?"

"Mr. Barber, have you called Julia Winchell since that last workshop on the IRS? Her hotel, her home, whatever?"

"No ma'am." Very softly lying.

Sonora sighed, rubbed her forehead, held up a finger. "Number one, you're making this hard. And number two"—another finger—"you're not helping me. I see your point of view, believe me, but I got to tell you you're not helping yourself at all here."

She was playing with him. Julia Winchell had gone somewhere, if only to a shallow grave by the side of the road. And if suspect number one was the husband, the lover was candidate number two.

"Work with me on this," Sonora said.

"I'm not sure what you—"

"Describe your relationship with Mrs. Winchell."

His color drained, left hand making a fist. "Is she . . . you said you were a homicide detective. Is Julia . . . did something happen to her?"

"Were you expecting something to happen to her, Jeff?"

He bit his lip. "No. But—"

"But what?"

"*Please,* just tell me."

"She's missing, Jeff. She hasn't been seen or heard

from for two weeks. She hasn't called about her children for fifteen days. You may be the last person—"

"To see her alive?" he asked.

"Jeff, you keep harping on that. Why do you think something happened to her? You do, don't you?"

"I don't know."

"You know."

"I don't." He gave her the puppy dog look.

It probably worked, with kinder females than she'd ever be. She wondered how long he'd been trading on his tragedy. Glanced at the picture of his family. "If your children were missing their mother—"

"Please don't do that. Don't use my children."

Sonora nodded, pursed her lips. "Mr. Barber, it might be a good idea for you to answer my questions downtown, as they say, and with you the attorney of your choice."

"But *why*? If she's missing—"

"See, you're not working with me on this, Jeff. And I don't understand why you won't help me. I'm not an unreasonable person." She opened her arms wide. "But if you won't work with me, it makes me think you've got something to hide."

"I *will* work with you."

"You're going to have to do better than you have been."

He nodded at her.

"Jeff, let's start at the beginning." She pitched her voice low now, quiet honey. "What was your relationship with Julia Winchell?"

He put both palms on his lap and wet his lips. "We were friends."

"More than friends," Sonora said. A statement.

"She was married," he said flatly. Looked at Sonora.

She stayed quiet and he shifted sideways in his chair. "We hit it off, we were friends. Men and women can be friends."

Sonora waited. She had conversations like this with her son. Waiting for the truth to come. Barber looked around the room the way Tim did when he didn't want to tell her something. Were they looking for a way out? Of a conversation?

Sonora kept her voice soft and matter-of-fact. "I'll make it easy on you, and tell you what I know. You and Julia Winchell were having an affair. It's not like a new concept, okay, Jeff? I'm sorry to intrude into your privacy, but if you care for Julia you'll help me out."

"I cared for her. I loved her."

"Tell me this, Jeff."

He waited, expectant.

"Why are you using the past tense?"

12

Jeff Barber was not happy to be downtown at the Board of Elections building talking to Sam. Barber was having a break and a ham sandwich with catsup.

Sergeant Crick stood in the hallway, arms folded. He glared at Sonora. "Catsup? On a ham sandwich? And you let him?"

Sonora yawned, covered it with her hand. "I'm not his mother."

"If you were, I'd tell you to get him a haircut."

Crick was clearly in his usual good humor, Sonora decided. He wore a shirt that hung loosely across swollen biceps, the collar buttoned tight across the short thick neck. His air of disapproval was a constant and he was broad and massive and intimidating, until you got to know him and were legitimately afraid.

"How long they been boinking?" Crick asked.

"He won't admit to the boinking. He says they just met at the conference."

"He's full of shit," Crick said.

Sonora inclined her head. "True."

Crick shifted his weight from his left leg to his right. One of his bones popped. He had brown eyes, intelligent and wise, and he stood too close.

"So, Sonora, why *don't* you believe him? Just because he looks like a lying shit?"

"For one, the sister says there was somebody. For

another, Julia Winchell brought lingerie with her. One black teddy, and one blue nightie."

"Maybe she always wears them. Call up her husband and ask him."

"I was just thinking there might be a kinder way."

"Like *please* does your wife wear black teddies? Since when were you kind?"

"See," Sonora said. "You caught me. I'm not being kind. I don't know if Butch Winchell knows his wife was fooling around. If he does, we got motive. I'd kind of like to have my stuff straight and hit him with it when I can watch his face."

Crick scratched his nose. "Let's say they been screwing a while, long enough for this little girl to get her lingerie together. Theorize on that. How you going to prove it? The sister ever meet him?"

"No."

"Know him by name?"

"No."

"So then?"

Sonora leaned back against the wall. "See if he's ever been to Clinton, Tennessee. See if they went to school together, way back when. Phone records. Maybe he's been calling her house. He called her hotel room, we got that cold."

Crick shook his head back and forth, clearly unimpressed. "He'd brush that off in no time. Say it was conference stuff. What's this guy do for a living?"

"Photographer."

Crick frowned at her. "Hell, there you go."

"Pictures?"

"If they just got together, maybe no, maybe yes. But if the sister and the nightie hunch prove right, they've known each other a while. What photographer could resist taking pictures of his lady love?"

"Think so?"

"I was in love once. I think so."

Sonora waited outside the door of Interview One while Jeff Barber ate the second half of his sandwich. Sam sat across from him, watching him chew and swallow. Sonora considered inviting Sam out for a conference, decided no. He could follow her lead. Anything else would look too contrived.

She heard footsteps behind her, heavy and light.

"*Sonora.*" Gruber. Sounding pissed.

She turned sideways, saw that Sanders was with him, thin-lipped, cheeks flushed. She'd never seen Sanders angry, but this might be it.

"This is my personal life and nobody's business but mine. We are not going to have this conversation," Sanders said.

"Oh yeah we are." Gruber had his jaw set hard.

Sonora looked at him. "If Sanders says we're not having this conversation, we're not. I got work to do, and kids at home eating pizza and watching MTV and Mayberry reruns instead of doing their chores. I'd like to get back to the house to make sure they're not conducting satanic rituals at the end of the driveway. You know kids today."

"See? She's too busy, anyway." Sanders folded her arms and puffed air between her lips.

Sanders petulant and angry in the space of a minute. Sonora looked at her, then back through the two-way. Barber was still chewing. He ate a Frito.

One more bite of sandwich, and she was going in.

"Here's what we want to know," Gruber said. "How can you tell if the guy you—" He looked at Sanders.

Lowered his voice. "The guy you're crazy about is married."

Sanders leaned close. "The symptoms are these—"

Sonora held up a hand. "Why are you asking me?"

"We figured you'd know," Gruber said.

Sonora gave him a look. "I don't even want to think about why you said that." She looked back through the two-way. Barber was on his last bite. There was catsup and a large white bread crumb on the left corner of his mouth.

"Look, Sonora, if we're bothering you." Gruber waved a hand.

"You are bothering me, but I'll give you what I got. One. When's he call you, Sanders? Between eight and five? That means he can't call you from home." She glanced at Sanders, saw her go still and watchful. "Two. Did he fall in love and decide you were soulmates in the first forty-eight hours? Married guys are usually in a hurry. Three. Does he watch the clock when you guys are together? Because if he's married, he's usually supposed to be somewhere else. And four." Sonora glanced back through the two-way. No more ham sandwich. She was definitely going in. She looked back over her shoulder. Saw Sanders heading down the hall toward the ladies room.

"She left after three," Gruber said. "What's four?"

"You're a guy, you were married, you probably already know." Sonora headed through the door into Interview One.

Barber was not glad to see her. She handed him a napkin. "Catsup on your mouth."

He took the napkin and wiped his lips, crumpled it into a ball.

Sonora sat on the edge of the table, swinging her

right leg. Barber still had the bread crumb hanging from his mouth. She knew it was going to drive her crazy. "Okay. Let's speak hypothetically here." She looked at Sam, who poured a handful of Fritos in his hand.

Barber crossed his legs, thighs pressed tightly together. He flipped a wave of dark hair out of his eyes and the bread crumb fell off the corner of his mouth. Sonora breathed a sign of relief.

"Now, Jeff, let's say, just for the heck of it, and hypothetically you understand, that while you been here talking to Sam and eating your sandwich, that I got a court order and went to your photography studio there. And let's say I found pictures of Julia Winchell. Pictures taken *before* this conference. I'd have to decide you've been lying to me, and I'd want to know why. I might suspect you of something awful. I might have to talk to your friends and neighbors and also, not incidentally, to my sergeant and a judge about my suspicions of you." She stopped talking for a minute, watchful. Heard Sam crunching Fritos. Sonora leaned in close. "We got witnesses, Jeff. People who know the two of you were together, people who will testify that you and Julia Winchell were having an affair.

"Now, Jeff, Julia's been gone fifteen days—as far as we know, in touch with nobody. Her husband's worried about her. *I'm* worried about her. What I don't understand is why *you're* not worried about her. It makes me think you already know what happened to her."

Barber leaned forward, elbows on his knees, and covered his eyes with his hands. He looked like he was going to be sick.

Could have been the sandwich, Sonora thought.

She noticed that his palms were large and square. She pictured them around Julia Winchell's neck. Cop imagination.

Sonora gentled her voice. "We need to find her, Jeff.
We need you to talk to us, tell us everything you know. I
think—I get the feeling that you know something that
could help me find her. You need to talk to me, Jeff. Talk
to me for Julia's sake. You care too much about her not to
help us. Don't you, Jeff?" Sonora took a breath. "Jeff?
You with me here?"

He raised his eyes, hands still covering his mouth.
"Of course I care." The words were muffled behind the
thick fingers.

"If you care you'll talk to me."

He looked from Sonora to Sam. "I think . . . I think
something did happen to her."

Sam quit crunching Fritos.

Sonora nodded at Barber. "Been worried about her,
haven't you?"

He nodded.

"It's got to have been hard for you. Nobody you can
ask, nobody you can talk to. How long you been worrying,
Jeff?"

"Since she didn't call." He swallowed so hard it made
Sonora's throat hurt. "She was supposed to call. We were
going to . . . to meet together. But she didn't, and so I
knew something had to be wrong."

The male ego, Sonora thought, glancing back at Sam.
Something had to have happened to her, or she would
have called.

"How long have you two been . . . together? Jeff?"

Barber let his hands drop between his knees. "I was
down in Knoxville picking up a lens a buddy of mine
was selling. He was retiring, getting rid of a lot of his
equipment, and I went down to buy stuff off him.
They're doing a lot of construction on I-75 down near
Knoxville, so this guy tells me my best bet getting home

is to take Maybryhood Road and go through Clinton. That way I bypass all the mess and the traffic tie-up. Said there was a good place to have lunch there—the Blue Moon Diner. Near some place where some twins used to have a restaurant, I don't know. But that's where I met Julia."

He said her name with a gentle hunger.

"So you met her in the diner," Sonora said.

Barber brought up a bright red flush. "A woman like that, running a diner in Clinton, Tennessee? Have you seen pictures of Julia?

"She had beautiful cheekbones, a kind of round, Slavic bone structure. I asked if I could take her picture. I did, and went home. Could *not* forget her. So we—we talked on the phone, a lot of that. I told her about this conference, the small business thing."

"Whose idea was it for her to come up?"

"Mine. But she wanted to come. I think she did." He frowned. "She wasn't happy at home. I mean, she wasn't *un*happy, but she wasn't happy either. To be honest, she was fine either way without me. But I wasn't fine without her. It's like . . ." He looked at the wall. "It's like she woke me up. I've been on autopilot since . . . for a while now. First it had to be that way, then it just got to be the way it was. I mean stupid stuff. Like I didn't notice how ratty and dusty my office was, till I got Julia in my life. I don't know what I'll do without her."

You could clean your office, Sonora thought.

Sam leaned sideways. "When was the last time you saw her?"

"We had dinner at the Montgomery Inn, the one on the river." His voice had gone low and gravelly. "We were supposed to go out again the next night. But there wasn't a next night."

Maybe she had indigestion, Sonora thought. "What happened?"

"I went back to my room late. We were supposed to meet for breakfast—they have a breakfast buffet. It comes with the room."

Sam nodded, man to man. The importance of a breakfast buffet was not lost.

"She called my room early that morning. Said for me to go on without her. She seemed distracted and, I don't know, kind of angry. I thought she might be mad at me, so I tried to talk to her, but she said she'd call me later."

"Did she?"

"I didn't wait. I thought something was wrong. Like between us. So I went to her room."

Might be true love, Sonora thought. Passing up that breakfast buffet.

"What was up?" Sam said.

"She had a newspaper. One of those ones they leave outside the door. I wish they hadn't."

"Why's that?" Sam said.

"She had it folded back to a picture of that prosecutor who's going after that Bengals player. Drury."

Sonora nodded. "Keep talking."

"She's using nail scissors to cut this article out of the paper. Says she saw this guy Caplan kill somebody eight years ago."

Sonora looked at Sam, then back to Barber. "Tell me exactly what she said."

He swallowed. "It happened while she was in school."

"She say what school?" Sam asked.

"University of Cincinnati. I mean, people get killed around there every year. I thought she must have meant some kind of thing in the streets. But she said this happened inside. And she saw it."

"Did she report it?" Sonora asked.

"She told the security guard, but when she took him back inside, there wasn't anybody there—no body, no murderer. Guard thought she was a crank. But she was really positive about it. She got a good look at this guy, and she's sure it was Caplan."

"Who got killed? Did she know the victim?" Sam asked.

"It was a girl, that's all she told me. And she was pregnant."

"Anything else?"

"That's all. She was trying to decide what to do about it. She felt funny about going to the police, since it had been so long ago. Eight years. She was going to look into it, that's what she said."

"Look into it how?" Sam asked.

Barber shrugged. "I know she went to the library, because she asked me for directions on the best way to get there. Said things had changed so much in the last eight years she couldn't find her way around. I wanted to go along with her, but she said no. That's the last time we talked."

"Did you call her again?"

"Yeah. But it was like I was on the back burner all of a sudden. She got real busy, and I could never catch her in her room. Since then, no calls, no letters."

Sonora tilted her head to one side. "You wrote letters?"

He nodded.

"Where'd you send them? Not to the house, is my guess."

Barber shifted in his chair. "She had a post office box," he said. Matter-of-factly.

"Let me get that address off you," Sonora said. Matter-of-factly.

13

Sonora was working from home, which was not always a good idea, because it meant she could watch the kids while working, a possible oxymoron. It did allow her to wear sweatpants and not comb her hair.

From the kitchen came the clink of Heather's spoon against a cereal bowl. The rustle of cellophane. Clampett, asleep on the couch behind Sonora, was suddenly awake.

"Let her eat," Sonora said to the dog.

Clampett yawned. Stretched and stepped down from the couch on top of the map she had opened out onto the floor. He was a big dog, in excess of a hundred pounds, thick coat, blond, three-legged. He'd shown up on their back porch years ago, hair thick with mats, burrs, and ticks spread liberally about his person, stomach running on empty. The kids liked to make up stories about his shady past.

The current fiction involved Cuba and political asylum, mainly because of Clampett's interest in a fake plastic cigar the kids had stashed in the dress-up box in the laundry room.

Clampett licked Sonora's wrist, and tasted her pen. A stream of saliva dripped from the dog's mouth and landed somewhere in southeast Ohio. Sonora shoved him sideways, and he padded into the kitchen.

Sonora squinted at the map, looking for where she'd traced I-75 with the pen. Red, she decided, was not the color to have used. The map was already full of red lines, and hers was lost in the shuffle. She frowned and wondered what color she should use. The map was a rainbow, no color noticeably missing.

"Clampett, *no*." Heather's voice, from the kitchen.

She found the line she'd traced just under a hole from one of Clampett's toenails, followed it to where the map left off in northern Kentucky.

"Dammit."

She snatched up the map, turned it over. Ohio, Indiana, northern Kentucky. Everything but Tennessee, which was what she needed. She folded the map, wondering if she had a map of Tennessee in the glove compartment of her car. The map did not want to go back into the original accordion folds. Sonora unfurled it and tried again.

"Clampett, *stop*."

A bowl clattered against the kitchen floor. The map bunched when it should have folded and Sonora wadded it into a large ball, and threw it across the room.

The doorbell rang.

Sonora looked at her watch: 11 A.M. Sunday morning. Seventh Day Adventists?

She got to her feet slowly, the small of her back stiff and achy. Boy were these guys in for it. She ran down the stairs, opened the front door. The heat and humidity hit her like a glove in the face. She could almost feel the air-conditioning being sucked away, and it wasn't even noon yet.

Sam stood on the front porch, glancing over his shoulder at a pickup truck pulling a maroon fishing boat.

"That hurts," he said, grimacing, turned to Sonora and screamed.

"Oh shut up. I don't look that bad."

"If you say so."

Sonora noticed that *he* looked good. Freshly showered. Khaki pants and a denim shirt.

"You're going to burn up in that shirt," she told him.

"I'll roll up the sleeves and show my biceps." Sam followed her in through the door. "You got anything I can eat while you get a shower?"

"We going somewhere?"

"To work, girl. Talked to the Clinton, Tennessee sheriff's department." He checked his watch. "Something like an hour ago. Julia Winchell's turned up."

Sonora paused on the steps. Sheriff's department. So Julia Winchell was dead. She hadn't realized she'd been hoping. "Where'd they find her?"

"Some of her. Head, hands, and feet, bound up in a plastic trash bag. Snagged on somebody's trotline in the Clinch River. Guy went out and checked it early this morning."

"Positive ID?"

"Not confirmed, but the sheriff there seemed pretty sure. Gar had gotten into the bag, but there was the long hair and the widow's peak."

"She had a widow's peak?"

"Yeah. Didn't you notice, in the pictures?"

"I guess."

"Anyway, we've been invited to go down for a look, and I said we'd be on our way."

"Why didn't you call me?"

"Line's busy."

"Use the business one."

"That one's busy, too."

Sonora headed into the kitchen. "You dialed it wrong, Sam, nobody's been on the phone all day. Heather just got up, and the boy never stirs till late afternoon."

She glanced at the kitchen extension, saw two blinking red lights. "Well hell."

"Hi, Heather," Sam said.

Sonora glanced at her daughter, absently pulled the long dark hair off her shoulders and out of the cereal bowl. "Heather, give Sam some Lucky Charms while I go kill your brother."

Tim was still in bed. The room was thick with dust and an electric guitar was parked on the floor next to a practice amp. Sonora stepped over a pile of clothes that emitted an odor that would do a locker room proud.

"Mom, do you mind not just barging into my room?"

Tim's hair, short and spiky, stuck up from where he'd been sleeping on it. His face had broken out along the chin. The sheets of his bed were wadded along the side and he had clearly been sleeping on bare mattress.

"Off the phone," Sonora said.

"But, Mom—"

"And then you explain why you're on my business line."

His eyes widened. "I thought it would be okay, because it's Sunday."

"It's never okay. I'm a cop, Tim. People get murdered on the weekends, too. Consider yourself a prime candidate."

He glared. Mothers rarely amused fourteen year olds. "You don't have to yell."

"This, I promise you, is not yelling. Why are you talking to two people at once?"

"I'm doing a conference call."

Sonora looked at her son and wondered if teenagers went through phases so you wouldn't miss them when they moved out.

"You have one minute to get off. Sam's here. I have to go to work. They found—"

"Something horrible, I don't want to hear it. Mom, everybody's going to Kenneth's to swim. Can you drop me on your way?"

"What about Heather?"

"I have to *baby-sit*?"

Sonora backed out of the bedroom. Shut the door hard.

Sam wandered into the hallway, cramming a handful of dry cereal into his mouth. "What's with the phone?"

"He's fourteen years old and he's having a conference call."

"If that boy's got a girl on each line, I'm going in there to shake his hand."

Sonora rubbed the back of her neck. "What was it that led me to procreate in the first place?"

"Probably too much to drink." Sam picked up the map, tossing it up and catching it. "Have a moment with maps, did you, Sonora?"

14

The sheriff's office was in a cinderblock building next to the Farmer's Co-op. Sonora opened the door of the Blazer and let Heather and Clampett out. Too hot to leave them in the car.

She looked at Sam. "You know, if you die and go to hell, you could wind up here."

"Speak up, Sonora. Make sure we get off on the right foot with the locals." He opened the door.

"Hang on to Clampett's leash," Sonora said, glancing at her daughter. She could use some cleaning up. Her pale blue shorts were loose around her thin, tan legs, and her white tank top was smeared with grape from a cup of Hawaiian shaved ice they'd stopped for on the way down. She wore plastic sandals with silk daisies on the front. Her toenails needed trimming. Her shoulders were pink with sunburn, arms broken out in goose bumps from the chill inside the police station.

Clampett's toenails clicked against the worn yellow linoleum, and he zigged and zagged through the small lobby, sniffing. Heather held tight to the leash, along for the ride.

"That dog taking you for a walk?" The woman behind the desk was tiny and thin, hair cut short, dyed white blond. Her eyes were thickly circled with eyeliner, expertly applied. She had a deep tan that gave her young skin the patina of alligator hide, cigarette husk in her voice.

Sonora put her ID on the woman's desk. "Detectives Blair and Delarosa, Cincinnati. Homicide. I think Sheriff Sizemore is expecting us."

The girl looked at Sonora curiously, then glanced at Sam. The nameplate on her desk said SYLVIA LOVELY.

Good name for a porn star, Sonora thought.

"It's that Julia Winchell thing," Sam said. "You didn't happen to know her?"

The girl shook her head. Her neck was long and pretty. Her earrings dropped all the way to her shoulders. She glanced at Sam's left hand, noticing the wedding ring.

"No, I didn't know her." She leaned over her desk, picked up the phone, punched a button. "Monte? You got those folks from Cincinnati here waiting." She looked up. "Said to tell you he's real sorry for the wait, and he'll be off the phone in just a minute." She nodded her head toward the couch. "Y'all can take a seat if you like, shouldn't be but a minute. Can I get anybody a pop? We got coffee made up, too."

Old coffee, Sonora thought, judging from the smell.

Clampett was licking the bottom of a blue can of Cherry Coke when a door opened and Sheriff Monte Sizemore walked into the room.

He was taller than Sonora, which wasn't saying much. His hair was brown, cut short in the way of state troopers and marines, gray-flecked at the temples and across the top. His uniform was well pressed and had likely been spotless when he'd put it on that morning. The bottoms of his shoes were mud-crusted, and the cuffs of his pants had been drenched, then dried into mud-stained wrinkles. There was a large round stain over his left knee and his shoes squeaked.

He shook hands with Sam and Sonora, bent down to say hello to Heather and Clampett.

"How long you been on the case?" he asked Heather.

She smiled and dipped her head, pushed her glasses back up on her nose and leaned against Clampett, who drooled down her leg.

"I think your puppy wants his own Coke," Sizemore said.

Heather tilted her chin. "I already gave him a drink of mine."

Sonora grimaced, wondering if Clampett had gotten his drink before or after she'd gotten hers.

Sizemore patted Heather's shoulder. "I got a granddaughter about your size. She loves to draw horses. How about if Sylvia gives you a pad of paper and a pen and you draw me a horse while I talk to your Mama?"

Heather frowned. "I don't know how to draw horses."

"Then draw something else," Sonora said.

15

Sizemore led them to the break room, shut the door. He limped, just barely. The door creaked as he closed it.

"Need to oil that," he muttered, heading across the floor.

Sonora stood close to Sam, spoke under her breath. "Tell me he's not heading for that old refrigerator."

"Probably next to his lunch."

The refrigerator was harvest yellow, one of the double-wide models, and it hummed. An erratic trail of water snaked out the left side, staining the shiny linoleum. Grill shelves were stacked against the wall. Sonora remembered when harvest yellow had been all the rage for kitchen appliances. Now everything was black and white. The new black and white. The old black and white wouldn't cut it.

Smallwood took a fork off the top of the refrigerator, wedged it into the latch, and opened the door.

Sonora, standing close, felt a cold breath of air, smelled the dark ominous odor. She took a step closer.

Bottles of 7-Up and Orange Crush lined the inside door, held in place by a bowed and scratched band of aluminum that was working loose near the door hinge. Sonora looked over her shoulder and caught Sizemore's eye.

"I needed some place quick, Detective. We got your little girl's drink out of the machine."

She nodded.

The shelves had been removed to make room for a Coleman cooler that sat on the bottom over the crisper bins. The cooler was faded red, scratched across the front, as if someone had gotten malicious with a key.

Sizemore bent forward to pick up the cooler, and Sam stepped forward and took one end, guiding the cooler to the floor.

The smell gathered strength.

Sizemore straightened up, groaned and touched the small of his back. He wiped sweat from his forehead with a neatly folded handkerchief.

"Y'all want a look, I guess."

Sonora leaned down and opened the lid, tilting it back on its hinges.

She was immediately engulfed in a whangy miasma that hit with the force of a ripe garbage dump—a fetid mix of fish, rotting meat, and blood.

The bag was a Hefty cinch-top, drawn tight and double secured at the neck with a worm-like strand of fishing line. It was shiny black and damp, sweating beads of condensed water.

"Is this the original bag?" Sonora said. It looked to be in too good a shape.

Sizemore spoke through his handkerchief. "No, that bag was ripped open, and fish had been into it. The original's in there, though. What's left of it. I double-bagged it just to keep . . . anything from falling out."

Like when you buy canned goods at the grocery, Sonora thought. She reached for her purse, and a pair of latex gloves.

Sam fished a tiny pocketknife out of his blazer and cut the fishing line.

"Let me put some newspapers down," Sizemore said,

moving quickly. He slid a thick wide padding of newspapers on the floor, and Sonora removed the bag from the cooler.

A thick splat of water stained the front page of the *Clinton Register* right over the article about trouble at the Main Street McDonald's. Sonora held her breath, taking air in nasty shallow snorts. Water streamed down one side of the bag as she rolled the top away.

Plastic garbage bags had long been a boon to criminals and homeowners alike, storage being a problem in many lines of work.

A small foot bulged through a ragged tear heel first, meat sagging, bone exposed along the top of the foot. Long black hair was twisted through the toes. The interior bag was battered brown plastic, stained and smeared with things uncomfortable to imagine. It was open at the top, revealing more black hair. Sonora pushed the shredded plastic to one side, and began to unpack.

The tally included one severed head, face hidden by heavy black strands of hair. In her mind's eye, Sonora saw the picture of Julia Winchell with her two little girls gathered into her lap. She held the image, trying to match it to the head that dripped onto the pad of plastic and newsprint.

She reached back into the bag, removed two hands and two feet, the right one taken off at the ankle, the left severed well over the joint. Sonora gently peeled and unwound the long black hair that stuck to Julia's face like cellophane against an iced cupcake.

The face was swollen pale and unrecognizable. The mouth was open and Sonora took the flashlight Sam handed her and pointed it inside. The meat of the tongue was gone, eaten back to the nub. The woman had small white teeth and no cavities, a tiny delicate mouth, turning black with rot.

The right eye was a gnawed, empty socket, thick with unhatched fly larvae.

"She's been outside some," Sonora said.

Sizemore was nodding. "Boy who found her left her out in his minnow bucket while he decided what to do. Brought all this up on his trotline, first thing this morning."

"His minnow bucket," Sonora said softly, with a sigh. The left eye was still intact, small blood vessels swollen and burst. She looked up at Sam.

"Strangled?" he asked.

"Looks like. Petechial hemorrhaging, so strangled or hung."

Sam grunted as he stretched the latex gloves over his thick hands. One size fit all—which meant they hung over the edges of Sonora's fingers, and went with difficulty over Sam's.

"Go slow," Sonora said. "These have been in the water awhile."

"Slippage?" Sam asked.

"Looks like."

He picked the right hand up carefully. Bits of flesh had been nipped away, and what was left was pale white around the midnight blue mottling of rot. The flesh was swollen, giving it a thick, glove-like look, and it had been in the water long enough that the pelt of skin was pulling loose from the structure of bone.

She had small hands, even swollen with gas and bloated with water, and they looked tiny and fragile in Sam's thick long fingers. The index finger was gone on the right hand, just above the knuckle joint, and Sonora thought of torture and hungry fish, and wondered which it was.

"Any defense wounds?" she asked.

Sam turned the hand palm up and shoved it in her direction. "I don't see anything. What do you think about the chop?" He turned the edge up, for better viewing.

Sonora turned her head to one side, squinted.

Clean severing, leaving the fine-tooth grain of a serrated cutting edge.

"Some kind of saw," Sonora said.

"Chain saw?" Sizemore asked.

Sonora shook her head. "Too fine for that."

"Hacksaw," Sam said, glancing over his shoulder at Sizemore. "Don't you think?"

The sheriff swallowed but stepped forward. Took a hard look.

Sonora knew he wanted to leave them to it, and wished that he would, but he was too polite to go, and she was too polite to ask.

"I've used a hacksaw a time or two," the sheriff said, voice deep and tight. "I'd say could well have been, though tell you the truth, I don't have my reading glasses on, and I'm not much used to this end of the job." He looked at the stub of index finger. "I'd say a gar got hold of that right there."

"Excuse me," Sonora said. "What the hell is a gar?"

Sizemore looked at her kindly. "Kind of a cross between a fish and an alligator. Little legs and sharp teeth."

"Ick." Sonora tilted her head to one side. "What you think, Sheriff Sizemore. Is this Julia Winchell?"

He looked away from the floor, and studied the outer wall, as if there were a window there. "I can't say for sure, but with that hair and all, and her up and missing. I'd say so."

Sonora reached for the left foot, turning it to one side

to expose the ankle. The skin was coated with moss and snagged leaves. She pushed them away, revealing a mask of blackened decomposition. She wondered if there was a dragon tattooed underneath.

16

Julia Winchell's killer had run into bad luck when the plastic bag containing her severed head, hands, and feet had snagged on a trotline draped across the bottom of the Clinch River.

Sonora looked across the water to a small park. She wished Heather was on one of the swing sets, instead of crammed in the back of the sheriff's car with Clampett, air conditioner straining in the hot humid air. The sun was formidable, and beer consumption was high among the spectators of the softball game across the river. Sonora smelled charcoal and hot dogs, saw the large black grill, the thin drift of smoke. The softball players seemed out for blood, in spite of the afternoon heat. Likely a grudge match, Sonora decided.

Sheriff Sizemore looked over at Sam. "Not to interfere, but your brakes were squealing on that Blazer. They feel mushy when you drive?"

Sam smiled good-naturedly. "Felt fine to me."

Sizemore shrugged, pointed through the trees. "The ole boy who dredged up that garbage bag lives back there. Got a mobile home just behind those trees. Not far."

Sonora looked over her shoulder at the trim fields, green and fragrant against the water. "All this land his?"

Sizemore shook his head. "Belongs to Cleaton Simms, been in his family for years. No, this ole boy used to do some handy work for Cleaton's daddy—he still helps keep the tractors up and the machinery going. Name's George Cheatham. Hell of a mechanic, but he's old now, and slowing down, and his wife is in bed most the time with the diabetes. He looks after her." Sizemore glanced up and down the river. "It's a good spot, out here. George does a lot of fishing."

The mobile home was vintage fifties, aluminum painted sky blue so long ago the color was mostly memories and paint flakes. It was hidden behind the trees, all the windows cranked open with old-fashioned levers and sticks. The front door was propped open, screen door shut. The outside metal looked like it would be hot to the touch.

There was no breeze. Sonora could not imagine the mobile home being anything but unbearably hot inside.

A stack of old tractor tires was a presence on the left. One had been set down and filled with sand. A plastic sand pail and broken off shovel, both a faded yellow, sat to one side of the tire, and a child's Tonka dump truck sat on top. An orange cat sat in the middle of the sandbox, blinked, turned his back, and began digging.

Sizemore noticed Sonora's look. "Their grandkids come sometimes. Cleat fills it up with sand for them every year."

The screen door creaked and the sheriff raised a hand. He looked at Sam and Sonora. "This is George Cheatham. This is the old boy that found her."

Cheatham wore khaki work pants, mud-stained around the bottoms, heavy work shoes, unlaced, tongues flopping, and a worn white T-shirt that hung loose on his thin neck and arms. His skin had the rough and red bronze veneer of years of work in the sun, and his hair was short and fine and steely gray. He walked slowly, like his back hurt, and dragged his feet. The toes of his shoes were scuffed and scarred, so dragging his feet along was more habit than reluctance to make their acquaintance.

"George, these are the detectives from Cincinnati I told you about."

George nodded. His hand shook when he offered it to Sonora and he looked a little white around the lips. Sonora glanced over his shoulder. Saw a curtain move in a window of the mobile home. It was too bright out to see inside. Probably the wife, wondering if they were coming in.

"I'm Specialist Blair, this is Specialist Delarosa."

Cheatham shifted his weight like his feet hurt. "Y'all like to come on in and sit down? Get out of the sun?"

"I appreciate the offer, Mr. Cheatham. But what would really help is for you to tell us what happened and show us where you found the . . . the bag. Let us take a couple of pictures." Sam held up a camera.

Sonora put a fresh tape in her recorder. Sweat trickled down the small of her back. The heat was making her queasy.

Cheatham nodded. His mouth worked in nervous little chewing motions. "My boat's down this way, y'all want to see?"

Sonora glanced over her shoulder—the sheriff's car was out of sight behind the trees. She nodded at Sam. "Head on down. I want to check on Heather, then I'll catch up."

"Want to bring her down?"

Sonora glanced at Cheatham. He wouldn't talk freely about dismembered body parts with a seven year old around. Neither would she.

"Nope." Sonora headed back through the trees.

A man stood next to the sheriff's patrol car, his back

to her, arms resting on the open window. She could see the top of Heather's head, and Clampett sitting in the driver's side. The front dash was fogged with dog drool and snout marks.

The man wore a faded pair of Wranglers, a white cotton T-shirt. Cute butt, which didn't stop Sonora from wondering what he was doing chatting up her seven year old, and why Clampett didn't bark.

Her feet hit gravel and the man turned.

"Girl, you look like you're going to tear my head off. Don't recognize me?"

She didn't right at first. His hair was longer than the last time she'd seen him, thick and brown, and his face was tan. He looked fresh-scrubbed and cool, sunglasses hung from the neck of the T-shirt. His cheeks were pink from a fresh shave, arms more muscular than she remembered, coated with coarse tan hair.

"Smallwood."

He gave her a sideways look, fluttered his lashes provocatively. "You can call me Deputy, if you want."

"I'm still trying to figure out why my dog doesn't bark at you."

"I have a way with animals. Usually sheep."

She was going to shake his hand, but he gave her a hug instead. She caught the faintest whiff of scent. He smelled good. She liked it when men smelled good. She wished she wasn't so hot and sweaty.

He nodded at Heather. "These rookies get younger every year."

"It's take your daughter to work day."

"Mom's going to take me to the morgue when I'm older," Heather said.

"Much older," Sonora muttered.

"*And* teach me to shoot." Heather gave him a cheerful

grin. "Mommy, I'm hot. Can Clampett and me get out of the car?" A film of sweat coated her forehead, and her cheeks were flushed.

"Yeah, hop on out."

"What's going on?" Smallwood asked.

Heather was fumbling with the door handle, and he opened the door, gave her a hand out.

Sonora stepped away from the car, voice low. "Got a find here that may match up to what you got in London."

"Head, hands, and feet," Heather said. She looked at Sonora. "That lady in the office told me."

"Good of her to bring you up to date. What brings you out here, Smallwood?"

He smiled. "This is Southern law enforcement. We all know what goes on in each other's backyards. Plus, we did kind of find the leg on our watch, if it turns out to be a match."

"Did you know Julia Winchell?"

He shook his head.

"You want to walk down with me, talk to the guy who found her, take a look around?"

Smallwood glanced at Heather. "What you going to do with little bit here?"

"Take her along. It's too hot to sit in the car."

Smallwood glanced across the water to the little park full of swing sets, softball players, lush green grass, and noisy children.

"Why don't I take her over there till you get done with your business?"

Sonora hesitated.

Smallwood smiled patiently while she turned the pros and cons over in her mind.

"You sure you don't need to go down there with me?" she asked.

"I've seen a trotline before."

"Not like this one, I bet. And how you getting over there to the park?" She glanced at the sheriff's patrol car.

"I've got my Jeep just over there. You didn't think I walked down from London, did you, Sonora? Brought my dog, too. We'll take yours along, and they can keep each other company."

Sonora frowned. "Clampett's kind of big. He can be a little aggressive."

Smallwood grinned. "I figure Tubby can handle the shock."

"Don't let Clampett hurt him."

Smallwood laughed and Sonora gave him an uneasy look.

"Heather, you want to go to the park with Deputy Smallwood, and swing on the swings?"

"Clampett's coming with me?"

Sonora nodded.

Smallwood put his sunglasses on. "Everything's under control, Mama. You go ahead and do the nasty down there, and I'll take the dogs and the kid to the park."

Sonora hugged Heather, told her again to be good, and headed back the way she had come. She turned back once, as she hit the tree line, and looked over her shoulder. Heather was skipping along beside Smallwood, asking him about Tubby, Clampett at her heels, tail wagging.

Sonora frowned. She was very cautious about allowing men into her children's lives. She barely knew this man and she'd broken relationship rules already. Not that she was planning to have a relationship.

She brushed the hair out of her eyes and headed back through the trees to the water that had hidden Julia Winchell for the last couple of weeks.

17

When Sonora came through the trees to the muddy edge of the river she heard the hum of insects, and the low, easy laugh of men just beginning to feel comfortable with one another. Sizemore and Cheatham had known each other for years, and Sam could always be counted on to work that good ole boy magic that is the special province of Southern men.

They were sitting on an old yellow rowboat that had been turned over to expose flaking paint and a hull that had been scraped raw.

Sam was eyeing a white plastic bucket with a John Deere symbol on the side, flies thick at the edges. "How long'd you keep it in there?" He got up and peered inside. Grimaced.

"Keep what in there?" Sonora asked.

George Cheatham looked up. "The, um—"

"The plastic bag," Sheriff Sizemore said, at the same time Sam said, "Make a guess, girl."

Sonora looked inside the bucket, which held about three inches of dirty brown river water, two tiny silver fish with meaty white bellies, and something that seemed to have the teeth and tail of a fish, and the hands and feet of a 'gator. Dead flies skimmed the top of the water.

"What *is* that?" Sonora asked, pointing to the 'gator thing.

"Water dog," George said.

"Gar," Sizemore told her.

Sam looked at Sonora. "You really never saw one before? They bark when they're onshore."

"They do not," Sonora said, frowning at him, but Sizemore was nodding his head. "Was it, that gar thing, was it in the bag with the . . . was it in the bag?"

Cheatham nodded. "Smell of blood attracted it, then it tore on in there. I kilt it with a baseball bat I keep in the bottom of the boat."

Sonora looked at the boat, mud banked against the edges where it had dripped water. She looked back in the bucket. A sliver of brown plastic floated next to the gar, whose damaged head swelled and bloated in the heat. More flies arrived, circling the top of the bucket. Sonora felt the sun on her head, the sweat running down her back. Her shoes were caked with mud.

They could take that gar back, and analyze the stomach contents.

Sam clicked his recorder on. "Mr. Cheatham was just getting started on his story."

Sonora settled next to Sam on the overturned boat. Cheatham turned another five gallon bucket—this one said PAPA JOHN'S MILD GOLDEN PEPPERONCINI on the side—and sat on the edge. He scratched his chin.

"I run the trotline out last night around dusk."

Sonora looked at Sam and he whispered in her ear. "Fishing line. Baited all the way across, goes across the river, sits on the bottom, maybe, and snags fish." He looked up at Cheatham. "What'd you bait it with, Mr. Cheatham?"

"Cookie dough and night crawlers."

Sam looked interested. Nodded his head.

"Went down real early this morning, 'bout six-thirty when the sun come up, and brought up the line. Found this bag hanging off the middle. So I pull it up and dump it on the bottom of the boat there." He rubbed rough palms together, making raspy noises, like cricket legs at dusk. His left shoulder twitched at regular intervals.

"Never seen nuthin' like it before and never hope to again. That water dog up and crawls across my foot and I bash it good with my bat there." He nodded toward the stained aluminum bat. "And I head on home, shaking like nobody's business, I don't mind telling you."

"Did you check the rest of the line?" Sonora asked.

Cheatham nodded. The shoulder twitched.

"Anything on any of the other hooks?"

Cheatham shook his head. "Nuthin' of a unusual nature. Turtles. Got a good-sized wide mouth bass. Good eating for tonight, anyhow."

Sonora watched for the shoulder twitch. "Then what happened?"

"I come close to heaving the whole mess on back in the water, then I start to wondering where's the rest of her? So I poke around a little where the line was, but didn't find much. I didn't look too hard, it was giving me a funny feeling, sitting out on that boat with . . . you know, in the bottom."

Sonora glanced out across the river. "Right about where were you, Mr. Cheatham?"

He rubbed the back of his neck. Pointed to the right, away from the ballpark. "Right down there just a piece— see where that tree's laying sideways like? Had one end of the trot line tied around it, but I hid it on the other side. Didn't want nobody messing with it."

Sam nodded.

Sonora looked out over the water, picturing the old yellow boat bobbing in the ripples, the park quiet, sun just up, accordions of reflected light skimming the water's surface. Fish jumping, making ripples. Cheatham emptied his last cigarette out of a crumpled pack of Camel Lights, struck a wooden match on his black-rimmed thumbnail. The acrid smell of burning tobacco drifted around their heads. Cheatham inhaled deeply, dragging a good way into his last cigarette like a man starved.

Sam took pictures. Jack Cheatham sat on the upturned bucket, cigarette loose on the left side of his mouth, a hesitant smile on his face, like a man who's been trained to smile for the camera, no matter what.

18

Sonora watched them from a distance—Heather going up and down in the big swing, Smallwood pushing her higher and higher.

There was no parking this far back in the park, so Sam edged the Blazer off the road into the grass. He put the car in park, tapped the steering wheel. Looked at Sonora and grinned.

"So that's the famous Smallwood. He still calling you every couple of weeks?"

Sonora nodded. Watched Clampett, on his feet, circling the swing set, growling at any child or adult who came within fifteen feet of Heather.

He seemed to tolerate a smaller dog, who sat and watched Smallwood and panted in the heat. The dog was packed tight as a sausage casing, with short blue-gray fur and black ears. He watched the playground with a look of intelligence that was unnerving.

"Where'd the little dog come from?" Sam asked.

"Smallwood's. Weird-looking mix."

Sam shook his head at her. "That's a blue heeler. Cattle dog. I haven't seen one since I was a kid."

"I'm glad Clampett didn't hurt it."

Sam laughed. "You been worrying about the wrong dog, Sonora."

She shrugged and got out of the car. Heather was

smiling, swinging higher and higher, hair blowing, and Sonora felt sad.

It was the daddy thing. Zack was an absentee father when he was alive, and Sonora knew that if he had lived, their marriage would have ended around the time she had buried him. But Heather and Tim were missing out on the strong male influence thing.

On the bright side, there had been insurance money.

19

Sonora let out a sigh when she saw the McDonald's across the street from the Winchells' small blue house.

"What?" Sam asked.

"McDonald's," Sonora told him.

"You hungry?"

She looked pointedly at her daughter. Sam nodded, and pulled into the parking lot. Sonora turned around and looked at Heather.

"Can Clampett have a cheeseburger?" she asked.

They left Heather locked in the Blazer with the windows down, Clampett gulping a cheeseburger, Heather working on a chocolate sundae. The first chocolate smear was already drying on the passenger's side headrest, and the windshield was fogging with Clampett's warm breath. Sonora had left the radio playing, and shown Heather the house, catty-corner to the McDonald's and across the street, which Heather was under no circumstances to cross.

Sam and Sonora headed down the sloping asphalt parking lot toward Main Street, which was torn up and clogged with trucks, men in hard hats, a steam roller, and a huge lighted arrow mounted on a trailer that kept traffic herded into one slow-moving lane.

Mounds of dirt were piled on the side of the road.

Broken concrete and asphalt were liberally mixed in the reddish brown soil like raisins in a muffin.

Sonora glanced down at her Reeboks. These were her oldest pair. Probably be easier to throw them away than clean them up. It was 6 P.M., but the sun was still high. It felt like the middle of the afternoon.

The Winchells' house was fifty, sixty years old, red brick that had been whitewashed, the paint peeling. Mounds of dirt were humped at the end of a gravel drive. The yard was sparse, weedy, but trimmed. There were flower boxes in the front window, thick with pink and white begonias.

A rusty red wagon sat by the edge of the driveway. It had been packed with stuffed animals. A tiny bicycle, no more than two feet tall, lay across the front porch.

Sam picked the bicycle up, set it gently on the sidewalk beside the front steps. He looked at Sonora.

"I should have stayed with football."

Sonora knew what he meant. Times like this she wished she was a secretary. "Football gave *you* up, remember?"

"If I forget I have you to remind me."

Sonora took a breath. Tried to relax. Her back felt rigid and achy. She rang the doorbell, heard thumps—small feet on hardwood—an angry screech. The door stuck, then opened. Winchell held the baby in the crook of his left arm. His sleeves were rolled up and the front of his shirt and top of his pants were wet. Sonora recognized the child from the pictures that still sat on her desk in Cincinnati.

Butch Winchell pushed his glasses back on his nose. "Hi."

The baby was wrapped in a yellow terry-cloth towel that was draped and hooded over the top of her damp, drippy head. She grinned at Sam and Sonora, showing a spread of tiny milk teeth.

"*Move*," she said.

Winchell glanced down at the little girl. "This is Chrissie. Her first word was *move*, the second was *mine*."

Possible future in police work, Sonora thought.

"Mr. Winchell," Sam said.

Winchell held up a hand. "Come in, and we'll talk."

He was oddly relaxed and matter-of-fact. He led them into a living room with polished hardwood floors. A cheap but colorful oriental rug, rose and black, warmed the room. There were wood shutters on the window, and the walls had recently been painted a soft yellow. The furniture was old, salvation army era, but there were mahogany bookshelves built into the walls, a stone fireplace, and a television tucked into an antique oak pie safe.

With the ease of experienced parents, Sonora and Sam negotiated the coloring books, crayons, and Duplos that littered the floor. Sonora settled on the edge of an old green couch. She avoided the armrest, which had a mysterious yellow stain. Sam took a recliner, maroon vinyl, that looked as if it had survived—barely—the kittenhood of a series of bad cats. Foam spilled from a tear in the cushion. Sam tucked it back in absently, realized what he was doing, and quit.

"Let me put Chrissie in her sleeper," Winchell said. "Be right back."

Sonora waited till she heard his footsteps on the staircase. "You called him, right?"

Sam looked at her. "You were standing right there when I did it."

"I mean, you told him why we were coming out here, right?"

Sam nodded. "Told him it would be a good idea to have someone with him. Maybe to look after the kids."

Something was pressing into her back. Sonora fished behind her and pulled out a worn blue book with a cracked spine and tooth marks on the corner.

Dr. Seuss. *Green Eggs and Ham*. She handed it to Sam, looked at her watch. They had a four-hour drive back.

Sonora drummed her fingers on the armrest, away from the yellow stain. Noticed a little girl, the three-year-old, staring at them from the hallway. She stood in the shadows and her features were hard to make out. She was small, tummy swelling over her shorts and pouching out from under a chocolate-smeared T-shirt that was getting too small.

"Come on in," Sam said.

She took three steps forward. She wore pink flip-flops and held a half-eaten cookie high up over her head. She had tucked a purple weed into her hair, snug behind her ear.

"Why you got that cookie over top your head?" Sam said.

"Got it at the Mortons' next door. Didn't want Bernie to get it."

"Bernie that hungry?" Sam asked.

"Bernie's always hungry. He's a dog."

She took a bite of cookie. "My name is Terry. Are you here about Mama? Daddy says we're having a bad year."

Footsteps again, on the staircase. Slow. Winchell came down the stairs with the baby in one arm and a folded playpen in the other. Sam was on his feet in an instant, reaching for the playpen.

"My little girl had one just like this," Sam said,

unfolding the yellow-meshed square and setting it in the center of the room.

The baby screamed, leaned toward Terry and the cookie. Terry shoved the cookie toward her sister.

The baby's mouth popped open, soft lips pursed. She nipped off the end of the cookie, chewing hugely, exposing pink gums. Chocolate-tinged drool spilled down her chin into the folds of her neck, and soaked the collar of the rose-pink sleeper.

"Terry, I just got her cleaned up."

The little girl put the cookie behind her back. "I'm sorry, Daddy. Want me to get a wash rag?"

"Please."

Terry looked at Sam. "Will you help me turn on the water?"

Another conquest, Sonora thought. He even got to the young ones.

"You bet I will. Go on and put that little one into the pen, Mr. Winchell. I'll keep an eye on your babies." Sam looked at Sonora and she nodded.

"Mr. Winchell, while Sam's doing that, let's go into the kitchen for a minute and talk." Sonora smiled at him and pushed through floor-length wood saloon doors.

It was a small kitchen, dark, imitation red brick linoleum peeling away from the edges of the wall. A metal highchair, butter yellow, was scooted up to the edge of the table. The metal food tray was clumped with baby oatmeal which, Sonora knew from experience, would now have the consistency of concrete. A baby spoon, the end shaped like Mickey Mouse, was on the floor under the table. Two laundry baskets sat next to the back door.

There were dishes on the counter, an open loaf of bread near the sink. The table was old brown Formica, stainless steel legs, and cluttered with a two day supply of milk-filled bowls clotted with dead soggy cereal. An open box of Frosted Flakes sat next to a box of Froot Loops. A plastic mug shaped like a parrot had slipped on its side, a trail of dried orange juice snaking to the edge of the table. A bottle of Flintstones vitamins, three left, one purple Fred and two green Dinos, was open next to a sticky looking salt shaker. There was no pepper in sight.

Pictures ripped from coloring books were taped to an almost new double-wide refrigerator. You could get ice cubes and ice water out of the door. Sonora wanted one like that.

She thought of Julia Winchell, facing this dark cramped kitchen every morning. Working long hours only to come home to laundry, bills, kids.

Much like her life.

The room at the Orchard Suites would have been an oasis—a two-room suite with maid service and a complimentary breakfast buffet right off the lobby. Black silk teddy on the pillow at the head of the bed.

Was Julia Winchell having an affair because there was trouble in her marriage, or because she needed a vacation?

"Excuse all this mess," Winchell said. He pressed his back to the counter in front of the sink. Licked his lips.

Sonora nodded. "Mr. Winchell, Detective Delarosa talked to you on the phone about why we're here."

"I got Kool-Aid in the refrigerator. Or I could make you some iced tea."

"No thanks."

"It's grape." There was sweat on his forehead.

"No thanks."

"Want to sit down?" Winchell pulled two chairs away from the cluttered table, chair legs scraping the linoleum, making black scuff marks that barely showed against the red.

Sonora noticed that Winchell's pants hung loose, his eyes dark shadowed. Not sleeping or eating. His cheeks were pink and smooth. Probably shaved for the first time in a long time right after Sam's call.

"Mr. Winchell, is there anyone you want to have with you tonight? Maybe help you out with the kids?"

Winchell was smiling at her, shaking his head. He picked a spoon up off the table, fingering the bowl. Sonora saw that his hand was perfectly steady.

"Mr. Winchell, I think it's possible we may have found your wife."

He kept smiling. Sonora watched him, wondering if she was getting through.

"If we have found her, Mr. Winchell, the news isn't good. It's bad."

"I know what you're saying." The smile had gone shy, but it was still there, and the look in his eyes was sober, the voice deeper and more gravelly.

She was getting through.

"We've found . . . remains . . . that we think are Julia's remains. You can go to the sheriff's office and make a formal identification, but we thought it might be easier, at first, if you took a look at a couple of pictures."

Sheer torture for him now. Sonora took the pictures from her blazer pocket quickly and handed them over. He made no move to take them. Sonora brushed crumbs and clutter to one side of the table, and laid the pictures out, avoiding milk rings and sticky spots.

They'd done what they could in the sheriff's office, laying the head back against the steel table as if Julia Winchell was resting, pulling a white sheet up to her chin to cover the raw, fish-eaten wound of the severed neck, unwrapping the hair from the face. The sheriff had cut a piece of black construction paper and placed it over the empty eye socket.

Still, by no means pretty.

The skin had that pearly gray-white translucence of death, black-tinged with putrescence. And the hands, laid on the table, severed wrists hidden by the sheet, were still missing fingers, one gnawed to the bone.

"*God*." Winchell shuddered and looked away, closing his eyes. "It's not her."

Sonora frowned. "Mr. Winchell, I'm sorry, would you take another look so we can make sure?"

He looked again, eyes narrow, head tilted sideways as if he couldn't face the pictures head on. He shook his head. "No. I'm sure, I'm definite. This isn't Julie."

Sonora took the pictures and put them away. "Mr. Winchell—"

"It's *not* her. How about some Kool-Aid? Be glad to pour you a glass."

He was bringing out the heavy Southern artillery. Blunt courtesy to the right palate for TKO.

"All right, Mr. Winchell. I don't have any more information for you right now, but I'll stay in close touch."

"Of course. Thank you. I'll do the same."

"There's one other thing."

He waited, hands still in his lap.

"Detective Delarosa mentioned this to you on the phone, I think. We need blood samples from your children, so we can run a match with this victim, check the DNA. That way we can make a positive ID—in this situation, or in anything else that might crop up."

He licked his lips. "Could you maybe get the DNA stuff from Julie's sister?"

"We've been in touch. She'll be meeting us at the

clinic in about an hour, give or take, but we still need samples from the children. The Sevier Boulevard Clinic is staying open, we've made arrangements already. Unless you prefer your own doctor?"

"Is there any charge for this?" he asked in a soft voice.

"No sir, no charge."

He nodded. "I need . . . a little time. Clean Chrissie and Terry up, and do some stuff here in the kitchen. Can I meet you there, say half an hour?"

She would never get home. She thought of Heather, waiting, waiting. "That would be fine."

Sonora turned away, taking a breath as she escaped the kitchen. Sam was in the living room, reading *Green Eggs and Ham* to the girls, who were both cuddled in his lap.

"Sam?"

He held up a hand. "Almost done."

Terry glanced up at Sonora, but her absorbed gaze was immediately drawn when Sam turned the page and showed a new picture. Chrissie bent forward, mouthing the corner of the book.

She had to get out of the house. "Be right out front," Sonora said. She headed out the door, screen whanging shut behind her.

She was across the street, no more than a couple of feet from the Blazer, when she heard Winchell call her name. He was standing in the side yard, waving his arms. Sonora figured he'd come out that back kitchen door, bypassing Sam and his little girls. He was pitched forward, body tense.

Sonora looked back at the Blazer. Clampett's head was thrust out the window. She could hear him bark and snarl because someone had dared open the passenger's side door of the car parked next to theirs. Laid back and easy at home, he was a hellacious watchdog on the road. Heather was pulling on his neck, trying to get him to hush.

Sonora headed back across the road. A pickup truck, loaded with gravel, went by slinging small rocks at her feet. She waited for traffic to slow, then break, but cars kept coming in an endless stream, giving her an occasional glimpse of Winchell, pitched forward on his toes, wiping sweat from the back of his neck.

There was a dump truck coming, right behind a white Lexus, ponderously gathering speed. Sonora dashed through the gap, climbed over the gravel and dirt piles, headed down the weedy unpaved driveway back up to the Winchell house.

Butch Winchell had deflated somehow, face sagging. He did not meet Sonora's eyes. He took his glasses off, cleaned them on his shirt. Ran his hands through his hair.

"Mr. Winchell?" Sonora said gently.

He was out of breath, as if he'd been the one darting through traffic. They both were breathing hard.

"Yes, ma'am. I think . . ." He rubbed his forehead with the heel of his hand, put the glasses back on. "I changed my mind, Detective Blair. It's my wife you found. It's Julie."

"I know."

20

The waiting room was cold enough to make Sonora shiver—a good thirty-degree drop from the heat and humidity outside. Sam paced in front of Sonora, Heather up on his shoulders, sleepy but game.

A woman in pink sweats and a white polyester jacket leaned out into the waiting area from one of those equipment-laden rooms where medical people always made you wait.

"We're ready now, Detective."

Sam looked at Sonora. "I'll go. I'm more used to it."

Something in his tone of voice gave Sonora a twinge of guilt. He'd logged more than his fair share of hospital time with Annie. Sam put Heather gently on the floor and walked into the examining room with Butch Winchell and his two little girls.

Heather sat cross-legged on the floor in front of Sonora. Her T-shirt and shorts had seen a lot of action for one day. She needed a bath.

"Where's Sam going?"

"They have to take blood samples from Mr. Winchell and his little girls."

"How come Sam has to watch?"

"Maintain continuity in the chain of evidence."

A wail came through the closed door. Heather put her head against Sonora's leg, and Sonora reached down and lifted her off the floor, settling her sideways into her lap.

They sat quietly, listening to the babies cry. Sonora heard a car door slam, saw headlights, noted quick light footsteps. The glass door opened, bringing in a wave of humid heat and the sound of crickets, and a woman who, at a distance, resembled Julia Winchell.

She had the same hair, brown-black and sleek, with the lush richness Sonora had only seen in Vidal Sassoon commercials. She wore blue jeans, lace up hiking boots, an orange T-shirt that said JAZZERCIZE. She was tallish, five six or seven, with high cheekbones. Her hair was cut chin-length, straight and swingy. Her brows were dark, eyes almond brown. She walked very precisely, careful where she put her feet.

Sonora wondered how alike she was to her sister. Families, in her experience, shared mannerisms and quirks of speech even more than physical similarities. Tribal trademarks, she thought. Had Julia Winchell kept her nails so long and meticulously polished, did she turn her head sideways like that, chew her hair when deep in thought?

Sonora had the familiar urge to know the victim. She had an image, fueled by one Kodak snapshot, and the remains that had been snagged and dragged by the trotline.

Sonora shifted Heather off her lap, stood up. Flipped the ID. Knew Heather was watching. For some reason the kids always liked to see her show the badge.

"Detective Blair, Cincinnati Police Department. You're Liza, aren't you? Julia's sister?"

The woman swung her head sideways and tilted it up. "Liza Hardin. Yes, I'm Julia's sister." They shook hands. "I've talked to you on the phone a couple of times, haven't I?"

There was no Southern in this woman's voice. Sonora

wondered where she was from, and how she'd wound up in Knoxville.

"Thanks for coming," Sonora said.

Liza Hardin looked away. "Did Butch . . ." She took a breath. "Did Butch think it was her?"

"If you don't mind, Ms. Hardin, it would be best if you took a look yourself, and formed your own opinion."

"Sure."

She was going all stony-faced. Sonora decided they'd better get the blood samples first.

21

Sam and Sonora packed the blood samples carefully into the back of the Blazer. It would have been nice to rent a room for the night, but they decided it would be best to get the physical specimens back to Cincinnati and into the hands of the CSU guys. Neither of them wanted to sit in front of a jury and explain how the blood had sat overnight in the parking lot of the local Budget-Tel.

Sonora sat in a booth at the Shoney's Inn Restaurant, nonsmoking, next to the salad bar, and ordered a Coke.

Liza Hardin went for coffee, in spite of the heat.

"Where's your little one?" Hardin asked. Her eyes were red-rimmed and glazed. She seemed to want to talk.

Grief took people that way, sometimes, stunned them into an honest purge of thought and emotion. Sometimes they said things they were sorry for later. Sonora had always thought it was a good time to talk to people, if you had the stomach for it.

Hardin put three packs of Equal into her coffee cup, caught Sonora's look. "If you think this is bad, you should have seen Jules. She put—no kidding—eleven of these in every cup of coffee. Fifteen in her iced tea." Hardin smiled, eyes misty. "Last Christmas I went to Sam's and bought one of those *huge*, econo boxes of Equal—must have been ten thousand packs in that thing. I wrapped it in red foil and put it under her Christmas tree as a joke.

That thing weighed a ton. She kept picking it up and fooling with it. She thought I got her, like, hand weights or something."

Sonora took a long sip of Coke, savored the jolt of sugar and caffeine. "Your sister have a good sense of humor?"

"Oh *God*, she was funny. We always did the joke thing at Christmas. One year she gave me these horrible disco earring balls—I mean, purple sequins, the height of tacky. And I was thanking her, you know, and thinking, what in the *hell*. She got to laughing and told me my real present was in the trunk of her car. That's what started it, it was her. So the next year I got her a goldfish—Jules hated fish, she could not stand to be around aquariums, said they were tedious beyond belief. She got me an M&M dispenser. I'm not going to be able to stand it this year. Christmas and no Jules."

She covered her face with her hands. Sonora waited.

Hardin wiped her eyes with a napkin, blew her nose. "*Sorry*." She looked up, eyes bright. "Where's your little girl?"

"She and Detective Delarosa went to Wal-Mart to pick up . . . a cooler."

Hardin did not seem to find any particular significance in the need for a cooler. Sonora did not explain.

"You have any other kids, Detective?"

"My son is fourteen. Heather is seven."

"Where is he?" Hardin asked.

It was a sore point. "I don't know. No one answers where he swore up and down he would be." Sonora brought out her recorder. A tape was inside, ready to go.

Hardin gave her a wary look.

"I take it that you and your sister were close?" In this instance, a rhetorical question, but Sonora always made a point of starting with the easy stuff. She could listen to Liza Hardin talk about Julia for thirty seconds, and know they were close.

She wondered what it was like to have a sister.

Liza Hardin nodded.

"How was her marriage?"

"I *knew* you were going to ask me that. It was fine, I guess."

"How fine could it be? We both know she was having an affair. You never met this guy?"

Liza Hardin's eyes went narrow for a moment. She leaned back against the turquoise pad of the booth. "No, I didn't want to. I like Butch, and I felt funny about it. I told her if this guy lasted more than six months, I'd meet him then."

"How'd Julia take that?"

"Told me to go fuck myself."

"Had she done anything like this before?"

Hardin looked at Sonora, reached for her coffee cup. Put it back down. "No."

Sonora raised one eyebrow. "You sure?"

"Yeah, I know, I hesitated. Far as I know this was Julia's first walk on the wild side. She didn't know how these things work. But I do. I've done it before."

"Okay. Julia know about that?"

"Some of them. I didn't tell her at first. I thought she'd, you know, be all shocked and disapproving. But I fell in love and got upset and called her once."

"What'd she do?"

Hardin shook her head. "It was the first one I told her about, and she *laughed*. Then I was the one who was shocked. She said she had no idea I'd been having all the fun, wanted to know all about it. That's what got me wondering if her marriage was all it was cracked up to be. She even asked me . . . never mind *what* she asked me, but let's just say it was pointed."

Hardin refilled her coffee from the brown plastic pot, ripped open a blue packet of Equal. "Believe me, we weren't raised like this."

"How long did your sister have a private post office box?"

Hardin frowned. "You know about that? She got it about two, three months ago. Right after she met this guy."

"She open it just for him?"

Hardin shrugged. "Let's say he was the catalyst. But I'm the one who talked her into it. Went with her, paid the first six months rent on the thing. See, I didn't know if her marriage was in trouble. My experience is people say, no, we're fine, fine, oops, guess what, we're getting divorced. That's the way it was for me, some of my friends. The reasons may take years but the actual divorce seems to hit all of a sudden. A post office box is a good thing to have."

Sonora nodded.

"She had a safe deposit box at a bank, too, and a checking account in her name only, different bank from the one she and Butch used. One hundred dollars in the bank account, three hundred in the box. We put it in together. For emergencies. I've been divorced before. I know how this stuff works." She dipped her spoon in and out of the coffee cup, scattering brown drops of liquid on the imitation wood-grain table.

"Sounds like serious trouble," Sonora said.

Hardin's look was intent, as if she had tales to tell. "It's a good idea to be prepared. Remember, I've been there, seen friends go through it. Seen how the person you said forever with, had children with, turns into a

weird nasty stranger. I can't decide whether divorce just
turns people mean, or if you're just seeing them the way
they really are for the first time."

"What was going on with them? Julia and Butch?
From a sister's eye view."

Hardin set the spoon down. "I think, in all honesty,
her marriage was no better or worse than any other.
They've been running the diner for four years—putting in
unbelievable hours. And they started their family about
the same time. Two little girls—beautiful as they are—
and the diner. They've actually been doing pretty well
with it the last couple of years, but it's an impossible
load."

"Butch do his fair share?"

Hardin grimaced. "What man does? And anyway, the
diner is his big dream. Jules was fine with it, but she was
getting restless. She felt like she'd spent four years busting her ass, getting the diner off the ground, making
babies like a hill woman, and she was wanting just a little
time to herself. To get centered, is how she put it. Butch
didn't get that, and the more she tried to pull away, the
harder he kicked. If he'd have let her breathe a little, they
probably would have been okay. That's why that affair of
hers was going nowhere."

Sonora raised an eyebrow, waiting.

Hardin laid her palms down on top of the table.
"Because the guy needed a keeper. His wife and kids died
in a car accident a few years ago, and he grabbed my sister like a lifeline. He was . . . demanding, and difficult.
She used to joke that now she had four kids on her hands,
the girls, Butch, and . . . this guy. The last time we talked,
she said she thought she'd made a mistake. That she was
feeling . . . I don't know, claustrophobic and out of breath
when she was near him. I think she was trying to figure

out how to get rid of him without hurting his feelings." Liza Hardin rolled her eyes. "Ain't no way, of course. And then this big exciting plan to meet in Cincinnati gets made, and she goes up on wings of love, and finds after a few days this guy is driving her nuts.

"*Then* she sees that guy's picture in the paper, and she's off on that like you would not believe. It's been a lot of years since it happened. I was surprised by how upset she was over it."

"She say who this alleged killer was?"

"Some DA—got his picture in the paper, trying some old jock for running down a girl from Xavier."

"She give you a name?"

She frowned, pursed her lips. "She mentioned it. I'd know it if I heard it."

"Helphenstine? Reynolds? Caplan?"

"Yeah, that was it."

"Which?" Sonora glanced at the tape. Made sure it was running.

"Caplan."

Sonora kept her expression matter-of-fact. "How sure was she?"

Hardin waved a hand. "We talked about that, you know? 'Cause it's been eight years. And she only saw him maybe a few seconds. It's been eight years, and people change. Plus he was crying, when she saw him."

"Crying?"

Hardin nodded. "Isn't that weird? I can't remember exactly what she said, but I think he was holding some poor girl under water, she's gagging and thrashing around. And the whole time he's holding her under, tears are running down his face."

"Sweat," Sonora said.

"Jules said crying. It weirded her out." Hardin folded

her arms and leaned back into the booth. "Julia told me she was going to go to this guy's office and meet him. Maybe on some pretense. She didn't think he would remember what she looked like. I told her not to confront him. If it is him, she tips her hand. If it's not, she looks like three kinds of idiot, right?"

"Why didn't she go to the police?"

"Well, you know, Detective, the whole thing is pretty thin. She sees a picture in the paper of a guy she thinks committed a murder nobody believed happened eight years ago. She wanted to check things out a little. Look at it on her own. And forgive me for being blunt. I don't know what it's like with you guys, as in police officers. But your average citizen's usual contact with prosecutors isn't likely to be pleasant. Ever been a witness to a crime? Better to be a criminal. Jules saw a car accident once, and foolishly tried to be a good citizen. Never a good idea."

"I wish I could say I didn't agree with you." Sonora glanced at the recorder. What the hell, Hardin was right. "About this murder your sister thinks she saw. What was your gut feel on it?"

"I don't know. I admit, when Jules called me, I thought it might be some kind of an escape thing. Play detective. Beats going home to a man who's driving you nutso, or dumping a lover who's doing the same. But now, after what happened to her, it kind of makes you wonder."

"You have a key to the post office box?" Sonora asked.

Hardin nodded.

"Where is it?"

"On my key ring."

"I meant the box."

"In Knoxville. Couldn't have one here and the whole town not know about it."

"How far a drive?"

"About thirty-five, forty minutes."

"Is your name on the paperwork?"

"Had to be. Otherwise they'd send the bill and stuff to her house, and Butch would have found out."

"Good. My partner should be here—"

"Hell, no, I'll take you right now. I want to see what's in the box."

22

The post office branch where Julia Winchell had her secret post office box was in a small strip mall on Kingston Parkway, Knoxville's main thoroughfare. They passed through an endless string of offices, malls, movies, restaurants, Blockbuster Videos, liquor stores.

Liza Hardin braked for the parking lot speed bump a split second before she hit it. She drove a dingy white Toyota Corolla with navy interior. The air conditioner worked, barely, flooding the cab with an odor reminiscent of dirty gym socks. The car squeaked, shocks on overload, and Sonora decided that if her son drove this badly when he turned sixteen he would not get his license.

"Forgive the smell," Hardin was saying. "I don't know *why* it does that. It's either the smell or no air-conditioning." She glanced sideways at Sonora. "You got a preference?"

Southerners, Sonora thought. So gracious.

There were plenty of parking spaces. Liza Hardin stopped the car just before it hit the curb. Her front tires grazed concrete. She turned off the engine, pulled the emergency brake into place, and looked at Sonora.

"The afternoon Jules and I came here was her first real day off—no kids, no restaurant—in months. If that tells you anything."

Welcome to real life, Sonora thought, wondering what Hardin did for a living. She got out of the car.

Hardin walked ahead into the post office—small

glass doors partitioned the outer lobby from the service counters that were locked up tight. Hardin bypassed the first inlet of boxes, leading Sonora into the middle alcove.

"Thirteen seventy-five," Hardin muttered. She considered and rejected the various keys on her ring. "Ah. Here, this. It looks good."

She inserted the key into the lock while Sonora said a small prayer.

It was one of the smaller boxes, letter-size and long. The key turned and the door swung open with a squeak. Sonora moved sideways, edging Hardin aside as politely as possible.

Inside she saw a brown envelope, rolled to fit, along with three standard-size letters and a box of Cocoa Puffs, advertisement size. Hardin held a hand out expectantly.

Sonora handed her the cereal.

"What about the mail?"

"I've got it."

Wariness dropped like a blanket between them.

"I have a form and a receipt you need to sign, when we get to Clinton. Paperwork's in my car." Sonora glanced at Hardin. No clue to what she was thinking. "It will be better if these get opened up in the lab, with the crime scene guys. Get what evidence we can from them."

Hardin folded her arms. "Feel free to make me that speech about how you're going to catch my sister's killer. That was always my favorite scene on *Crime Story*."

23

Sonora tucked her daughter into the backseat of the Blazer, folding her jacket into a pillow, using a worn but clean beach towel that had been left behind on the last lake trip as a makeshift blanket. She used the middle seat belt because it was adjustable, and Heather could lie down. She snugged it up till it looked comfortable, wondering how safe it would be.

"When's Sam coming?" Heather asked. Her eyes were closed.

"Just in a minute." Sonora heard the door of the sheriff's office scrape the concrete stoop. The men's voices and footsteps had the quick measured pace that meant they were carrying something either awkward or heavy or both.

The back hatch of the Blazer opened. The air outside was cooler now, but not by much. They'd turn the air conditioner up high when they hit the road, and Heather would need the beach towel to keep the chill off while she slept.

Sonora hoped she would sleep.

"Move it back this way." The sheriff's voice, instructing Sam, who slid an oversized metal cooler into the back of the car.

Heather's eyes opened to slits.

Sonora patted her head. "Go on to sleep, kidlet. We got a long drive ahead."

Heather nodded slightly, and turned on her side. Sonora listened for heavy, regular breathing. Little seven-year-old girls did not need to know that the cooler in the back section of the Blazer held a severed head, two hands, and two feet.

She shut the car door gently, and went to the back of the Blazer. Sam latched the back hatch gently. The cooler, heavily packed with ice, did not move.

Sonora shook Sheriff Sizemore's hand, signed his clipboard of papers.

"I'm sure you people are the ones ought to have this stuff. You got the facilities. And like you say, you got reason to believe she was killed up in Cincinnati, which makes it your baby."

Sonora was not sure who he was reassuring.

Sam shook Sizemore's hand and clapped his shoulder. Their reasons for thinking the crime originated in Cincinnati were thin. But Sizemore wasn't arguing.

"You've been a whole lot of help, Sheriff. Run a good outfit, for a country boy."

Sonora would never have gotten away with it, but Sizemore grinned.

"You folks just find the fella did this, and put a tag in his ear for me. I don't want to see this one ground under the heel of that Aldridge boy over at the state police. Ain't money or pussy in it, he ain't interested." He looked at Sonora, turned pink around the ears. "Excuse me."

She really hated it when they remembered she wasn't one of the boys. "Money doesn't offend me," she said, deadpan. "And you can't fault a guy who likes cats."

"We won't trouble the state boys any," Sam promised. "And you got my number. Give us a call, if you hear anything."

"You bet."

Sonora looked back over her shoulder in time to see the sheriff actually tip his hat. She waved and headed toward the driver's seat, bumped into Sam.

"It's after dark, girl, I'll drive."

"I'll drive."

"You remember last time when I asked if you wanted to pull over and let me drive for a while, and you said you would if you could find the side of the road?"

Sonora glanced at Heather in the backseat. "Okay, you drive." She got into the passenger's side, put on her seat belt.

Sam adjusted the rearview mirror. Looked at her. "Can't fault a man for liking *cats*?"

Gravel spun under the car tires as Sam backed the Blazer out of the lot. He glanced up in the rearview mirror. Slammed on the brakes.

"What now?" he muttered.

Sonora heard knuckles against her window, rolled it down. The sheriff again, red-faced and out of breath.

Please God he doesn't want those body parts back, Sonora thought. They'd signed for them, completed all the paperwork. Invested in a cooler.

"That back right tire looks low," Sizemore said.

"We'll get it checked when we fill up on gas," Sam said.

Sonora smiled. Waved. The sheriff nodded and headed off.

"You notice the tire looking low, Sam?"

"No."

"I guess we can check it like you said. When we get gas."

"Hell no, the tires are fine."

"You didn't even look. What if it is low?"

"I ain't checking it."

24

They hit fog going over the mountains that bordered the Tennessee state line. Sam squinted, following the tail-lights of the truck ahead.

"So then what happened? Anything in the post office box?"

"Two letters and a brown envelope."

He glanced at her, then looked back at the road. Swirls of clammy white drifted across the lights. The road was almost invisible.

"Don't slow down too much—we'll get rear-ended," Sonora said.

"Open that mail."

"It'll make me carsick."

"Then you drive and I'll read it."

Sonora glanced back at Heather, breathing deeply and evenly, eyes shut tight. Her hand rested on her cheek, vibrating with the movement of the car.

At the next bathroom break, she would call home, and this time, Tim would be there. She did not like driving home late at night, in the fog, wondering if he was okay. She glanced back toward the cooler, bent down to the maroon vinyl case by her feet.

The zipper seemed loud in the cab of the car, road noises muffled by the fog and darkness. She looked at the white envelopes.

"Turn the fog lights on, Sam. Switch on the left. Next to that other one."

"What other . . . oh, here." He clicked a switch. The beams of light changed, penetrating the mist instead of reflecting back. "Girl, you could've brought this up a while ago."

Sonora opened one of the envelopes. "Bill from Victoria's Secret. Julia Winchell ordered a black silk teddy and a Wonderbra."

"What size?"

"Medium."

"I meant the—"

"I know what you meant. She owes forty-two dollars and sixty-eight cents. Guess what the interest rate is on this thing, Sam? It's god-awful. Guess."

"Wages of sin."

"Sam, it's not sin, it's lingerie."

"What else you got?"

Sonora opened the other white envelope. "Stuff from the conference, looks like. Information on panels and stuff. *The Small Business-Person Interfacing with the Local Chamber of Commerce.* My God, no wonder she had an affair. Anything would be better than listening to this crap."

"Typical. Get the information out after everyone's left town." He gave her a sideways look. "What's the balance on your Vicky's Secret account?"

"About the size of the national debt."

"What kind of stuff do you buy?"

"Every flannel nightgown they sell." She held up the big brown envelope.

"Open that," Sam said.

Sonora looked it over. "Cincinnati postmark. Dated, let me count on my fingers here. Twenty days ago? Yeah.

About the time she was calling home saying she wasn't coming back."

Sonora was getting queasy. She took a breath, closed her eyes. Ripped open the envelope. Inside was a cassette tape. PROPERTY OF JULIA WINCHELL had been written on a label in black felt pen. On the other side, PERSONAL, in capital letters.

"Whoa," Sonora said.

"What?"

"It's a cassette tape." She held it up.

"Give it here, let's play it."

"No, don't put it in my player, it eats tapes. I've lost two Bonnie Raitts, one Rod Stewart, and a Beatles in the last six weeks."

"Doesn't anything you own ever work?"

Sonora shrugged.

"I don't blame it for spitting out Rod Stewart."

"Are you trying to start a fight?"

25

Sonora bent the bobby pin, pushed it into the lock on her son's bedroom door. The door jammed, but she shoved harder, and slid through the narrow opening.

Tim was sound asleep in his bed. Dirty clothes, dropped in the doorway, made a pretty good barrier.

They had stopped at a rest stop somewhere near Berea, Kentucky. Tim had been home, cooking a frozen pizza, no clue as to where anyone was, no clue Sonora was looking for him. He had seemed genuinely shocked that his mother might be expecting him to make it home somewhere within a two-hour range of when he'd said he'd be in.

Sonora ventured another three feet into the room to retrieve the cordless phone, placed with precision in the boot of a shiny black Rollerblade skate. She took another look at her son, grimaced at the glass that held what looked like old, furry orange juice, and scooted back through the door.

A relief to see him home safe, asleep in the bed. Tomorrow she would ground him.

"Two days, or three?" she asked Sam, who was heading down the hallway, Heather over one shoulder.

Clampett knocked Sam sideways, leaped at Heather, then turned his attention to Sonora, pinning her to the wall with his front feet.

"Get down," Sonora said.

The dog dropped to three legs immediately, and took the sleeve of Sonora's shirt in his mouth.

"Drop," Sonora said.

Clampett wiggled and wagged.

"*Drop.*"

"Two or three what?" Sam asked.

Sonora twisted sideways, opened Heather's door with her free hand. She followed Sam into the bedroom, walking sideways, dog still attached to her sleeve.

"How long I should ground Tim."

"My mama would have blistered me and grounded me for a month."

"Overkill." Sonora straightened Heather's unmade bed.

"You going to worry about toothbrush and jammies?"

Sonora shook her head. Heather was barefoot. Her little sandals stuck out of Sam's pants pockets. "She hasn't stirred since we dropped the cooler off."

Sam took the sandals and set them on Heather's dresser next to a stuffed penguin. Sonora settled Heather in the bed and covered her up. They left the room, pulling the door almost shut. Clampett tried to nose his way back in. Sonora took his collar.

"Time for you to go out."

Sam shook his head. "Too late. Better check the hall by the kitchen."

"He's just glad to be home."

"The wee of joy. You got a boom box for cassettes?"

"Yeah, if it works."

"If it does, I'll give you five dollars."

26

Sonora sat back on the couch and took the first sip of a Corona. The bottle of beer was icy cold and a small wedge of lime floated at the top. She tasted lime pulp on her tongue, leaned back into the couch, and pulled a quilt over her legs.

Sam looked up from the tape recorder. He sat awkwardly on the floor, too big to be cross-legged comfortably, unlike Sonora.

"You could turn the air-conditioning down."

Sonora closed her eyes—her new response to suggestions she didn't like. Passive resistance. She was learning it from her youngest, the resident expert.

Sam picked up the recorder and tilted it sideways. "When's the last time you cleaned the heads on this?"

"Never."

Clampett padded in, tail wagging. He nudged Sam, bulking him with sheer size. The boom box slipped out of Sam's hand and he dropped Julia Winchell's cassette.

Clampett had it in his mouth before Sam or Sonora could move.

"*No.*" Sonora set the beer on the floor, grabbed the dog by the mouth. "*Drop.*"

Clampett looked at her, brown eyes apologetic. But his jaw muscles were tight, and he clamped down harder.

Sonora smacked his nose.

The dog stared at her. Wagged his tail.

She tried to pry his jaws apart.

Clampett ducked his head, held on harder.

"*Drop*, dammit."

Sam took the dog by the collar, tried his jaws. "At the rate you're going, that dog's going to think his name is dammit."

"Get him a cookie, sometimes he'll trade. Get the chocolate chip ones in the top of the pantry."

Sam went into the kitchen. Sonora tried the dog's jaws. No luck. Clampett gave her a sad look. He was a retriever. He was retrieving. His expression begged for understanding.

"*Drop*," Sonora said. "Sam?"

"No cookies."

"I just—"

He peered around the corner, held up an empty, crumpled Chips Ahoy bag. "This it?"

"I just bought those yesterday. Okay, there are sausage biscuits in the freezer. Get me one of those."

"Frozen?"

"Clampett won't care, he eats firewood."

Sonora heard the freezer door open and close.

"Gone," Sam said.

"Couldn't be. Not already."

"Empty box in the freezer. Want me to throw it away?"

Sonora heard him tapping cardboard against the counter. "No, I want it as a keepsake. Look in the fridge for leftover meatballs. Drop, Clampett."

Drool slid down the side of the dog's muzzle and hung in a line of saliva.

"Sam? Meatballs?"

"Nope."

"What *is* in there?"

"Pickles."

"The one thing he won't eat. Okay. Oh, shit, he's chewing. *Stop* it, Clampett." Sonora held his head.

"Don't you have any dog biscuits or treats, or did the kids eat those, too?"

"Go back in my bedroom, and look in the shoe box on the back left-hand side of the closet."

"Don't give him a shoe. Smack him."

"I already did."

"Let me get a rolled-up newspaper after him."

"No, that just makes him playful. He thinks it's the hit-the-dog-with-the-newspaper game. Go get that shoe box."

Sonora listened for Sam's footsteps in the hallway, heard the squeak of her closet door opening.

"Jeez, Imelda—"

"Get the shoe box, and keep the mouth."

She heard rustling noises. The bedroom door shut.

"I'm not going to even ask, Sonora, why you keep Oreo cookies in a shoe box in your closet."

"For emergencies, obviously. If it isn't nailed down or healthy, the kids inhale it. Clampett's lucky he can run fast."

Sam looked at the three-legged dog. "Looks like they've been snacking on him."

"Cookie please. No, hold it up."

Clampett looked at the Oreo cookie, strained forward. Sonora kept a tight hold on his collar.

"Drop for a treat," she said.

Clampett opened his mouth and the cassette hit the floor. He jumped for the cookie and snapped it out of Sam's hand. Sonora grabbed the tape and wiped it on her shirt. Clampett looked from her to Sam, black cookie crumbs on his muzzle.

"Give him another one," Sam said.

"Chocolate is bad for puppies."

"And firewood isn't?"

Sonora put the cookies back in the shoe box and stuck them in the refrigerator. Clampett curled up like a tiny puppy on three-quarters of the couch. She rescued her beer.

Sam pushed her sideways into the dog and took the end of the couch.

"This is cozy," Sonora said.

Sam held up the tape. "Specialist Blair, please explain to the jury why there are tooth marks on Exhibit A?"

"Shut up and play the tape."

27

The first sound out of the boom box was a squeak, followed by a hiss and a string of noises you don't want to hear when you value the tape inside. Sonora looked at Sam; then, like magic, a woman's voice came through amid the crackle of cheap cassette and dirty heads.

Sam grinned.

Sonora wondered how often she and Sam had wished out loud that a murder victim could talk. This one was going to.

"This is Julia Janet Hardin Winchell, recorded in the Orchard Suites Hotel in Cincinnati, Ohio."

Her accent was hard to describe—a unique blend of midwest Chicago and Southern Tennessee. It hit the lush lower registers. She spoke slowly but without hesitation.

Sonora closed her eyes, picturing the long dark hair, the widow's peak, full cheeks, dark slanted brows. Even dressed in the jeans and torn sweatshirt she'd been wearing in one of Butch Winchell's pictures, she had a Victorian look about her, an air of fragile quality.

No wonder Jeff Barber had pursued her across state lines. Sonora wondered what it was about him that had attracted Julia—fill a room with men and she could have had her pick.

Why did she go for Barber, a needy, difficult male? Was she acting out some doomed karma, forever selecting men who would be dependent and smothering, always going for the wrong guy, like every other woman alive?

Good question. No answer. Sonora sat back, closed her eyes, and shut everything out, except Julia Winchell's voice.

"*An odd and upsetting thing has happened, and I am setting down my thoughts and my memories on tape. I am a believer in fate. I think this had to have happened for a reason.*"

Sonora noted the clear enunciation, the self-confident tone of voice. She wished that she, too, believed in fate. It might make her job a little easier.

"*Today I opened the newspaper and saw the face of my killer.*"

Sonora exchanged looks with Sam. *My killer.* Presumably she meant the guy she'd seen all those years ago. But she was dead now, and she'd said *my* killer.

"*When I opened that newspaper I saw a face I saw eight years ago. His name is Gage Caplan, and he is the Cincinnati District Attorney who is prosecuting that ex-football player who ran down the Xavier University co-ed. It is so strange, to have a name to go with a face I can't get out of my head. And to find him in the DA's office.*

"*Eight years ago I was in school at UC, the University of Cincinnati, living in the dorm. I was having a bad day—I had one of my sinus headaches, plus I'd lost my purse. So I took a Contac and went to bed early.*

"*Just when I was about to fall asleep, I remembered one place I might have left my purse that I hadn't looked. I had met a girlfriend for lunch, and we'd connected up in the media room in the Braunstein Building. I thought maybe I left it in there. I'd looked everywhere else.*

"*It was dark out, by now, and raining hard. Not a good idea to be wandering around campus by myself. But*

I had fifty dollars in my purse, and my driver's license, and my Sears credit card, plus my address book that I've had since my second year of high school. Plus all my keys and a new pair of pearl earrings Liza got me for my birthday.

"I decided that muggers and rapists didn't like the rain any more than anybody else, and that the purse might not still be there the next morning, if it was there at all. So I went.

"It was cold out and I was wearing those dumb sandals everybody wore then. I stepped in a puddle first thing, and got my feet wet. I was wearing a jean skirt and no tights because of the sandals, and because my legs were still tan from the summer. And I got cold.

"So when I finally got in the building it was warm, and I had seen a security guard up at the top of the building, smoking, so I felt safe. That was the funny part. Feeling safe.

"I went up to the media room—it was on the fourth floor, which is important. The media room was open, but there was nobody in there. But there was my purse, right on the table where I left it. First I checked the wallet—my money and everything was there, even the earrings. And my head started feeling better, so some of it must have been stress.

"I remember walking down the corridor, feeling sleepy from the pill—it was just a Contac—and thinking if I could make it back safe across campus to my dorm room, I could curl up in bed with a book and the Snickers bar that was also in the purse, and I remember thinking how great that would be.

"I know I heard a door close somewhere, but I didn't see any people. All the lights were on. I know I was making squeaky noises, and little wet footprints on the linoleum. My feet were slipping and I had to go slow. I turned left to go down the corridor—I was kind of turned around, trying to go out the other exit that would be closer to central campus.

"I remember seeing a little black door that said three. Which I thought meant I was on the third floor. Which I wasn't. More on that later.

"I'm walking along and I hear noises. Funny noises, but kind of awful. I heard, like, a sort of cry, then a groan and gurgle. And a man sort of growling at someone. Then somebody crying.

"I looked around. One of the office doors was open. There was a pink sweater hanging on the back of a chair—I don't know why I remember that, but I do.

"There was nobody in the office. Whoever it was, it looked like they just went away for a minute, you know, leaving the door open like that. And I heard some weird stuff, thumps and cries and water splashing or something, coming from across the hall from the ladies room.

"I went in there slow. I was kind of holding my purse across my chest, don't ask me why. I was kind of embarrassed, but there was nobody around. I was scared. It was all kind of weird and out of place.

"The bathrooms in that building are laid out kind of funny. You go inside in kind of a little hall. Then you turn a corner, you turn right and it opens up into the usual thing—mirrors and sinks and stalls.

"I heard water, and someone gasping, like they were coming up for air, and a woman— her voice was young and soft and she was like, crying. In a panic.

"I remember she said 'please' and 'the baby.'

"So I didn't think at that point, I just ran in."

The voice stopped and the tape ran in silence for a while.

"*This part I remember really well.*" The voice had gone flat. "*He was . . . he had her down on the floor, bent over the toilet, like she was being sick. But he was holding her head in the . . . in the toilet bowl. I saw it in the mirror first, the top of his head. She came up again, she was fighting him, gasping, and he got down on his knees, and pushed all his weight, one hand on the back of her head and one on the back of her neck.*

"*She was a little thing. I couldn't figure how she lasted like she did, because he was a big guy, and he looked strong. She was Oriental. She had black hair. At first I thought she was fat, but then I saw she was very pregnant.*

"*And then he . . . I could see he was crying. So weird. I mean he really was crying. And he pushed down on her so hard, she just didn't have a chance. She hit her mouth on the rim of the toilet. The seat was . . . the seat was up, I guess. And I saw blood spurt from her lip and go down the side of the toilet bowl. And he . . . he slid her head, her mouth off the rim, and shoved her head down in the water. And I think she must have swallowed a lot of water all of a sudden or passed out because you could see her just go limp.*

"*And I yelled or screamed at him to stop. And he saw me. And he looked so, stunned, I guess. Tears running down his cheeks. And he kind of strained towards me. I think he was going to come after me, and she moved. At least I think she did, it happened fast, it was hard to tell. But he decided to keep her under, instead of coming after me. He kept her down, her head in that toilet.*

"*But he watched me. I was going to go and try to make him let her up, but she wasn't moving and I was pretty sure she was dead. And he was such a big guy. So I ran for help. I wanted somebody to try and save the baby, if nothing else.*

"*Just before I could move, or run, or whatever, he said. He said, 'Hang on just a minute, will you?'*

"*I . . . it was such a shock, because he sounded so normal. Hang on, be right with you, I can explain. It was funny, because he had a really nice voice, kind of gentle and calm. And I just stood for a second and we stared at each other. And then I started crying, I think, and I ran away.*

"*I ran down the hall and there was a room with the door open and full of people. I couldn't understand why they didn't come when I screamed, but when I went inside it wasn't people, it was mannequins. That was . . . horrible. And I ran out back in the hallway, wondering if the person with the pink sweater had come back, but then I thought whoever it was wears teeny pink sweaters won't be much help either way. If it had been a big old gray sweatshirt I might have risked it.*

"*I remember seeing an exit sign and thinking—*"

The sound of a telephone ringing came through loud and startling.

"*Oh, shit.*"

There was a sound like bedsprings before the click of the machine shutting off.

Sonora looked at Sam. They listened, for a while, to the hiss of empty cassette tape. Julia Winchell didn't come back.

28

Sam wandered into the kitchen, opened the refrigerator, and came back into the living room with the Oreo cookies, drawing Clampett and Sonora's immediate attention.

"I am eating these only because I need a sugar hit to get the energy to drive home. Why are you frowning at me? I'll share."

"Julia Winchell said the woman drowning in the toilet was Oriental."

"Yeah, so?"

"Caplan's got pictures in his office. His little girl is blue-eyed, Amerasian. Which means her mother—"

"Could have been the woman in the bathroom. Hmm." He crunched a cookie, dribbling black crumbs down his shirt front. "Say it's Caplan. What's he doing on campus?"

"How the hell would I know?"

"You are tired and cranky. We'll figure this out tomorrow." He reached down, rubbed the back of her neck.

She closed her eyes. "You're tired, too. Spend the night, why don't you?"

"Remember what happened the last time I did that?"

They both smiled.

Sonora shrugged. "Kids are here, this time."

"They're sound asleep," Sam said.

"The bedroom or the couch?"

"I couldn't resist you. And it would be a shitty thing to do to Shel."

She was not going to listen to the wife lecture. Plus she liked Shelly, and she wasn't sure, but she thought she might feel guilty. Sonora rolled sideways on the couch, pulled the quilt off of Clampett and over her head.

"You going to roll up like a worm in a cocoon or walk me to the door?" Sam asked.

"I'm not moving."

"If you walk me to the door I can accidentally kiss you good night."

"Lock up on your way out."

29

The air-conditioning in the bullpen was emitting a sour smell that reminded Sonora of Liza Hardin's little Toyota. She had come in early, around six, in spite of the late night, but Sergeant Crick was still in ahead of her.

He sat at Gruber's desk, rolling his chair from side to side. He looked like he had slept.

"Hold up your foot, Sonora."

"What?" Her eyelids ached, and her head was hurting. She also thought she might want to throw up, some time or other. No sleep gave her a queasy feeling in the morning.

"Your foot. Hold it up."

Sonora lifted her left foot, aware that her white high-top Reeboks were getting dingy and worn. Maybe new shoelaces would perk them up. She was not supposed to wear them to work, and she hoped Crick was annoyed. If she had to put up with queasy, he could put up with annoyed.

"Damn, girl, look at those."

Sam, over her shoulder. Sonora looked from Sam to Crick.

"I *like* these socks," she said.

"Hot pink," Crick said. "Reeboks and pink socks? You looked at the dress code lately, or you pushing for a transfer to vice?"

"It's just so we know she's a *girl* cop," Sam said.

Sonora nodded at them. "Soon as Gall's starts selling pink handcuffs, I'm first in line."

"At least we know what to get her for Christmas."

Sonora put her arms on the rests on her chair. "While you're admiring my socks, sir, I was wondering what you could tell me about Gage Caplan."

Crick's look was wary. "The DA Caplan?" He folded his arms. "Who wants to know?"

"I want to know. His name's come up in the Julia Winchell investigation."

Sam settled at the edge of her desk, winked. "Sleep well?"

"Better than you."

"Come up how?" Crick said.

Sonora glanced over her shoulder. Saw Molliter, working at his desk, finishing up the night shift. Pretending not to notice their conversation. Caplan was a popular district attorney. He liked cops. He respected them. He put perps in jail. He had a lot of friends in the police department. One of them was Molliter.

Sonora looked at Crick. "Let's go in your office."

"This chair does not fit my butt." Crick got up.

The coffeemaker was on in Crick's office, baking old coffee into toffeelike sludge at the bottom of the glass pot. Crick flipped the switch, waited for Sonora and Sam to settle. He sat behind his desk and smiled. Sonora did not like that smile.

She was a little bit afraid of Crick—most of them were a lot afraid. He had smarts, he had integrity, and he backed his people up. She'd misstepped badly in the Selma Yorke case last year, and here she was, still working.

But being a cop was like being in the army. Crick was a superior officer, not in the rank and file, and, in

Sonora's experience, as soon as a fellow officer left the rank and file they had motivations and agendas that were not obvious and to be avoided.

"Don't trust me?" Crick asked, showing his teeth.

Sam was looking at her like she'd lost her mind.

"I'm organizing my thoughts."

Crick smiled again, a real one this time. In appreciation of a good side step, Sonora suspected.

"Julia Winchell witnessed a murder eight years ago." Sonora expected questions, but Crick did not interrupt— just stayed quiet and coiled like a cat well versed in the art of looking sleepy and bored before the pounce. "She got a clear and long look at the killer. When she went for help and came back, the killer was gone."

"Big surprise," Sam muttered.

"The body was gone, too. In short, nobody believed her and she had to let it go."

Crick leaned sideways. Still no comment.

"So anyway, Julia Winchell comes to town for a conference. Opens the newspaper. Sees a spread on Caplan, over that ex-football player and the hit and run." She looked at Crick. "She recognized him, sir."

He looked at her and sighed. "Say the name, Sonora. I want to be real clear on this."

"She identified District Attorney Gage Caplan as the man she saw murder a woman in the bathroom on the UC campus." Sam was leaning back in his chair with his feet stuck out, but his chin was up.

Crick looked at Sam, soft but watchful. "This bring back memories, Delarosa?"

Sonora looked from Sam to Crick. Decided, for once, to keep her mouth shut. Sam had run into trouble, of the higher-up political kind, just before they'd become partners. Which was why he'd gotten the rookie female partner award. Which was why promotion was not in his line of vision.

"You want off?" Crick asked.

Sam shook his head, slow and deliberate. "I wouldn't mind seeing Sonora off it, sir. She's got kids."

"We've all got kids," Sonora said.

"Not Sanders. Not Gruber."

"Gruber? He's probably got some somewhere," Crick said. "He and Sanders are busy on the Bobo thing. You sure you want to tangle with the DA's office, Sonora?" Crick was clear-eyed, almost sincere.

She actually hesitated. She'd had enough of being the cop you stare at when she'd tracked Selma Yorke last year. Lost her brother and a large chunk of her reputation in the fallout. Neither she nor the kids needed any more fallout.

"We caught it, sir."

Crick nodded. "Let's look at what we've got here. A prominent district attorney has been accused of murder by a nutcase who has subsequently disappeared, then been found in pieces on the side of the road."

Sonora gritted her teeth. Julia Winchell was *her* baby. She'd decide if the lady was a nutcase. "You saying *she's* a nutcase because she had the bad taste to get herself dismembered?"

Crick sighed. Looked at Sonora. "You look like the dachshund in the yard next door when my collie goes over the fence. I'm calling her a nutcase because she sees murders where the bodies disappear and the perps are sort of local celebrities."

"She was pretty clear about what she saw," Sam said.

Crick was still looking at Sonora. "Exactly what did she see?"

"A man drowning a woman in the ladies' rest room in

the Braunstein Building on the UC campus. The victim was Oriental, and very pregnant."

"Very convincing," Crick said. "I just don't remember a body turning up on the UC campus. I think I would remember a pregnant Oriental female drowned in a toilet."

"Winchell went for help and when she came back the body was gone."

Crick ran a hand over his face, rubbed vigorously. The growth of beard sounded scratchy against the rough-callused palm. "Yeah, you mentioned that before. I was just thinking—didn't I just see this plot on a movie of the week a couple months ago? Brian Dennehy? Suzanne Somers? I bet she had repressed memory, or something."

"Not repressed memory, sir. The body was gone."

"Swam away, no doubt."

Sam got up, left the room. Sonora heard file cabinets open and close. She placed her fingertips together, tapped the back of her nails together.

Crick grimaced. "Don't do that."

"What, sir?"

"That thing, there, with your hands."

Sonora held her hands up like they used to in old M&M commercials. "Julia Winchell was strangled and cut up in pieces and strewn like so much garbage from here to Clinton, Tennessee."

"Yeah, I get you, dragging a woman to Tennessee is heinous. She had a lover, right?"

Sonora hesitated.

Crick put a hand out, cupping his ear. "What's this I hear?"

A file drawer slammed shut. Another one opened.

"Yes sir, she had a lover."

"That Jeff Barber guy. The photographer, if I remember correctly. Do I remember correctly?"

"Yes sir."

"Fooling around on her husband. And you bypass the jealous husband and/or lover and go for this convoluted nonobvious bullshit?"

"Okay, sir. We agree it's usually the husband. But—"

Sam came back in, pushing the hair that slid into his eyes back with an impatient gesture that was as familiar to Sonora as the wistful feeling that came with it. He stood next to her chair. Solidarity. And he had a triumphant air that seemed to put Crick on his guard.

"We've all heard yada yada yada that Caplan became a DA after his wife was murdered and the killer never found," Sam said.

Crick leaned back until his chair creaked. He folded his arms.

"This is the file, and a picture of the first Mrs. Gage Caplan." Sam put an open folder and a spread of pictures on Crick's desk. Sonora saw them upside down.

Black hair. She would have been pretty once—but not in the shot that captured her curled in a fetal position around the mound of belly, hair stuck to her delicate neck.

Sonora picked up one of the pictures. The woman's eyes were wide. She was Asian. Small and petite.

"Where's the autopsy report?" Crick was rummaging. Sam passed it across the desk. Sat back down in his chair.

"Sir?" Sonora said.

Crick held up a hand. Achieved silence. Sonora wondered why Crick holding up a hand brought immediate obedience. When she held up a hand people tended to comment on her nail polish.

She considered the way he held the hand. Nothing special. Maybe it was the size of the hand.

"Delivered of a perfect baby girl, death by asphyxiation, minutes after the mother."

Sam winced.

"Micah Caplan. Cause of death, drowning. Found her body by Sonier Creek. Signs of struggle . . ." Crick frowned, kept reading. Looked up at Sam and Sonora. "Either of you looked at this?"

Sonora shook her head.

"No," Sam said.

Crick got up and shut the door. His walk was slow and deliberate. Sonora knew from the tense and in-check way he moved that somebody was in trouble.

He sat back in his chair, voice oddly subdued. "Two things." He held up thick fingers. "Fragments under her fingernails match skin samples taken from her husband. His answer: she had a habit of scratching his back during lovemaking, and they'd had relations that afternoon."

Sonora looked at Sam.

Crick held up another finger. "Second. Cause of death was by drowning. M.E. made a note here, flagged it. Lungs contained traces of surfactants, phosphorus, hypochlorite bleach—samples were consistent with any number of household cleaners. He wasn't happy. The creek had its share of pollution, and while said elements can certainly be found in trace quantities . . . basically, what he's saying here is that wasn't creek water in her lungs."

"If she drowned in the toilet, that's where she'd get all that crap in her lungs," Sonora said. "The surfactants, the bleach. That's all cleaning fluid."

"I want his car," Sam said. "He scattered her down the side of the road—his car's got to be a gold mine."

Crick's tone of voice was dampening. "If he used his car. This is not some juvenile we're dealing with. He's a DA, he works the system. We move too soon, and take the car, even if he doesn't get us blocked, we could blow the whole case. What's the story on the vic's car? It was a rental, wasn't it?"

"Haven't found it yet," Sam said.

"That's not what I want to hear."

Sonora pulled her hair back and tucked it under the collar of her shirt. "He did it, didn't he?"

30

Sonora had a great deal of curiosity about Gage Caplan's wife, so when the white Nissan Pathfinder pulled up in front of the Caplan household, and she saw a woman behind the wheel with a dark-haired child in the passenger's seat, she forgot her irritation with Caplan for keeping her waiting in front of his house.

His power play was childish and interesting. A gauntlet thrown down—why? Because he was guilty? Too important to be bothered?

She watched his family, wondering why they did not go into the garage. The Pathfinder was stark white and pretty, new-looking. It had the air of a car kept snugly under wraps.

The little girl hopped out quickly, jumping off the side of the Nissan and closing the door. It did not catch. She looked to be ten or eleven—hard to tell because she was petite and likely small for her age. Her hair, blue-black and shiny, hung chin-length. She wore tiny jean shorts fringed à la Dogpatch with white lace on the pockets and hem. Sonora caught a flash of a loose red T-shirt and beige lace-up hiking boots—all the rage—before the little girl disappeared around the front of the Pathfinder.

Colleen Caplan was quite pregnant. The little girl gave her a hand out and Colleen said something that made them both laugh.

She was graceless in her pregnancy, backside broad

and spreading. She wore shorts that hung long and loose just above her knees. Her legs were pale—no sun. She wore thick cotton socks, and high-top white Reeboks just like the ones Sonora had on herself. A red maternity T-shirt hung like a lampshade over the shorts.

Sonora got out of the car, shut the door softly, and headed up the driveway toward Gage Caplan's wife.

It was a face only a mother could love, yet oddly endearing, like a boxer puppy, ugly and cute. She had a thick round nose, a round face, marzipan blond hair that was chin-length and straight, parted to one side, and a thin feathered fringe of bangs.

Her complexion was rough, face flushed, and she seemed to move in a fog of preoccupation. She looked worried. Her brow was wrinkled in the kind of deep grooves few people earned till their sixties or seventies.

Colleen had not noticed Sonora, but the little girl had. The woman hopped sideways in an awkward movement that was as playful as it was gauche. The little girl said something and tilted her head and Colleen Caplan turned and saw Sonora.

Her mouth made an *O*, and her shoulders sagged, and the worried look settled back on her face. Sonora felt like the black cloud that came with every silver lining.

"Hello," Colleen Caplan said with a dutiful but wary politeness. "Can I help you please?"

Sonora smiled, reached for her ID. "Specialist Blair, Cincinnati PD. Are you Mrs. Caplan?"

But she had lost the woman's attention.

"That's so amazing!"

Sonora frowned at her. Surely not the woman cop thing. Please not the do-you-pack-heat-like-the-big-boys question.

"Your purse! You just found your ID like that right in the top of your purse! How do you do that?"

"I dug it out before I got out of the car," Sonora said.

"No, don't tell me that, you'll ruin it!" Colleen Caplan gave her a real smile, big and broad and spreading across her face, making her cheeks puff up and her eyes go small. "Pockets!" She patted voluminous side bulges in her shorts. "I don't carry a purse, I can't find anything in it, so everything is in pockets."

"You can't find stuff in your pockets, either," the little girl said.

"This is Mia." Colleen patted the top of the little girl's head. "She is my pride and my joy and the light of my life."

It was said lightly, with a fond smile, and Sonora got the feeling that Colleen Caplan often introduced Mia that way, and always meant it.

"We lost the garage door opener again." Mia bent over and picked at one of the laces on her hiking boots.

"But I do have my keys!" Colleen Caplan patted her pockets again and frowned. "At least I think I do." She seemed out of breath in the heat. Her neck looked sweaty. She peered into the Nissan. "*There.*" Opened the door. A huge set of keys hung from a cobalt blue fuzzy ball that Colleen Caplan held up and waved at Sonora.

Sonora moved around to the other side of the car, opened and closed the passenger door that had not caught earlier.

"Mrs. Caplan, I was supposed to meet your husband here, and—"

"*Come in* then. We have air-conditioning!"

There was no doubt, Sonora thought, looking at the house, that the Caplans had air-conditioning as well as every other household convenience, but Colleen Caplan's words throbbed with such unbridled enthusiasm that Sonora had to smile. And it was very hot.

"Thank you, I will."

31

They went through a side door into the kitchen, which looked clean enough beneath the kind of clutter that accumulates very quickly with a kid in the house. Sonora, looking at Colleen Caplan, almost said two kids in the house.

There were open cans of Chef Boy-Ar-Dee ravioli on the cabinets, a wad of damp paper towels at the foot of a huge white double-door refrigerator. Sonora looked at the fridge. It had an ice-maker and ice water in the door, just like the one in the Winchells' kitchen, except newer. Maybe she would put one on her Sears charge account, and pay it off in six-dollar monthly installments for the rest of her natural life.

The house looked brand new. There was a breakfast nook in the kitchen with an oak table. Everything was white white white. Spotlights showed that there were no cobwebs over the gold-knobbed cabinets.

"Mrs. Caplan—" Sonora said.

"Call me Collie." She opened the refrigerator, which was full of bright red cans of Coke and shiny green cans of Mello Yello. She smiled over her shoulder at Sonora. "Soda? We also have coffee and wine." The last was added awkwardly. A sentence she threw in for sophisticates who liked such things.

"A Coke would be great," Sonora said.

"Let me find the cookies and we'll sit down."

Where to sit proved to be a problem, with Mia peeping into a white-carpeted living room with the air of one in front of a museum exhibit. She looked over her shoulder at Collie. "She's company. We can sit in here if it's company."

Collie Caplan pursed her lips, stopped midstride.

"Oh no we can't." Mia was still talking, sounding regretful. "The no-food rule."

"You know, honey, it's my house, too." Collie smiled but it was a small, tight thing, and it did not light her eyes. She looked worried. She looked tired.

Sonora looked at the white brocade couch. "Please don't ask me to go in there and eat a cookie."

Something like shame passed over Collie Caplan's face. She straightened her shoulders. Winked at the little girl who watched her, hands clasped behind her back.

"Don't be silly, Mia. Spills can be cleaned up, I had the couch Scotchgarded."

Something uncompromising in her voice. Sonora and Mia followed her into the living room.

"Sit down," Collie invited.

Sonora looked around the room, chose a wing-back chair in hunter green leather, set her legs between the edge of the chair and a footstool. Even if she'd been inclined to put her feet up, which she wasn't, there was no doubt in her mind that footstools in this house weren't for feet.

Collie sat on the edge of the couch. Mia settled beside her, thighs touching.

Something about the two of them together, side by side, muscles tense, poised for flight, made Sonora sad.

She told herself to be careful of jumping to conclusions about Gage Caplan, knew when she did that it was a wasted effort. The conclusions were coming fast and furious.

"Collie, want your back pillow?"

"No thanks." Collie's voice had gone quiet. Sonora saw dark circles under the woman's eyes. A lot of sleepless nights. Which might be due to the pregnancy, or might not. Collie patted Mia's leg. "But thanks for asking. Why don't you take the cookies down to our den and watch a video?"

"Can I watch *Pulp Fiction*?"

"No."

Mia grinned suddenly, the smile of a kid who was testing the waters. "It's time for Ricki Lake."

"That will broaden your mind," Collie said darkly, but Mia was already gone.

Sonora waited but did not hear the sound of a television.

"Did my husband say he was going to meet you here?" Collie asked.

Sonora nodded.

"He probably just got held up. I'm surprised he agreed to leave the office. You know the jury's out?"

"He told me they were waiting on a verdict, but he thought it would be a while."

Collie licked her lips. "Maybe the jury came in."

They looked at each other.

"I hope he nails this guy," Sonora said.

"If anybody can do it, it's Gage," Collie said, serious now.

"I hear a lot of good things about him," Sonora said, but Collie picked up on something in her voice, and her eyes went narrow and watchful.

"How long have you and Mr. Caplan been married?"

"Five years." She twisted her khaki shorts in one thick finger.

Sonora smelled vanilla, noticed the dry chips of

potpourri in a crystal bowl by her shoulder. Next to the potpourri was a candy dish, with a clump of hard candy, red-striped pillow shapes, that had stuck together. It was the kind of candy no one ate, no telling how long it had been there. Added a touch of color, at any rate.

"Did you know his first wife?"

Collie shook her head, twisted her finger first one way, then the next. "She was the prettiest thing, just like Mia. Mia's not mine, you know, but she *is* mine, if you know what I mean."

Sonora knew what she meant. Collie and Mia were what she and Heather were, on a good day, what she and Tim had been, before aliens took him away and left her with a teenager.

She knew a good mother when she saw one.

"Mia was only two when Micah died." Collie got up, opened the seat of the piano stool in front of a gleaming black grand piano. Rummaged. Looked over her shoulder at Sonora. "She played. Gage bought this piano for her on her birthday the year before she died. He keeps all her music and her pictures in here. Sometimes Mia likes to look at them."

The photo album was dingy white vinyl, bought in less affluent days. Sticky fingerprints on the front cover. Likely Mia thumbed them quite a bit. Collie handed the album to Sonora, opened it in the middle.

"This is our favorite. Mia and me."

Micah had been small and slight in the way of many Asian women. Her eyes were dark like Mia's, face very round.

"Micah was Korean, Japanese, and American mixed. She got adopted by her dad when he was in the Korean War. They—her parents—they live in Kentucky."

Sonora looked up from the picture. "Where in Kentucky?"

"London."

London, Kentucky was the last place Julia Winchell had bought gas, according to the records from her BP Oil account.

"What's their name?"

"Ainsley. Grey and Dorrie Ainsley. They're Mia's grandparents, so I see them a lot. They've really been good to me." Collie was moving back to the couch, hand tucked into the small of her back. "Dorrie and me—and I, I should say—we have a lot in common." She grinned at Sonora. "Both of us have Amerasian daughters. And neither of us could have kids of our own." She settled back on the couch so carefully, Sonora could almost feel the backache. Collie patted her belly. "This is some miracle baby. I really tried everything before I met Gage. Spent a fortune—time, money, and effort. My first husband and I did. I explained all that to Gage before we got married. But he had Mia and was absolutely positive he didn't want any more."

She stared at the wall over Sonora's left shoulder. "Got one anyway!" She scratched the end of her nose. "*I* was thrilled. For me, it was a dream come true. If somebody would have told me all those years ago I would finally have one of my own . . . I guess it would have saved me a lot of wear and tear and medical bills."

"What happened to your first husband?" Probably shouldn't ask, Sonora thought. But she was curious.

Collie looked at the floor, then back up at Sonora. "Left me. One of those office affair things. They're married. Got kids." She bit her bottom lip. "Both real happy. She seems like a real nice girl."

Sonora cocked her head to one side. "Has everyone

gotten so civilized that the ex-wife has to speak well of the woman her husband was fooling around with?"

Collie's mouth opened, then she laughed. "No, really. I feel sorry for her because she's married to him. Believe me, he's fooling around on her too. I thank God for Gage every day."

Sonora forced a smile. She did not think that Gage Caplan was a husband any sane woman should be thankful for.

She looked down at the picture of Micah. She was wearing one of those fuzzy pink mohair sweaters with white pearl buttons. She held Mia up to the camera, eyes squinting in the sun. Mia was maybe three months old, and her mouth was curled in a toothless baby smile, gums pink and bare, hair a soft black wisp on her head.

"It was terrible how she died," Sonora said mildly, watching Collie.

Collie nodded, and Sonora saw she had the worried look that was beginning to be familiar. "They never caught him," she said softly.

"They suspected Mr. Caplan, didn't they? For a while?"

Collie sat forward, arms wrapped around herself like she was cold, though her face was flushed, and a line of sweat filmed her upper lip. She nodded.

"Did you know him then?" Sonora asked.

"No. I wish I had. It was a terrible time for him, I could have been a comfort. Gage has a very sad side to him, he just doesn't let most people see."

"I'm sure he has a lot of sides to him," Sonora said.

Collie's look was intelligent. "I can't decide if you like him or not. Most women do, you know."

"Do they?" Sonora asked.

Collie nodded. "Oh yes. And they think, why did he

marry *her*. Big nose and overweight." She glanced at her belly. "I look like this even when I'm not pregnant."

"Since we're being blunt," Sonora said. Collie looked at her. "Have you ever had any suspicions that Gage had something to do with Micah's death? I mean, did it never cross your mind?"

"That's blunt all right."

Sonora nodded, kept smiling. In her experience, you could say very outrageous things if you smiled.

"No, of course not. It's never crossed my mind. I know Gage. Do you know exactly how she died?"

"Yes," Sonora said, but Collie kept talking, like she'd never heard.

"Somebody drowned her in a creek. They took her purse. It was weird, because no one could understand what she was doing there. Gage thinks maybe somebody hid in the backseat of her car, or forced her off the road. And of course, what he never tells anyone, is about the overnight case they found in the trunk of the car. An overnight case with a sexy negligee."

"He told you."

"I'm not just anyone. I think it's very . . . very good of him not to bring that up. Not to try and hurt her reputation. When everyone suspected him."

"If another car forced her off the road, there might well be scratches on the paint of her car. There weren't."

Collie scooted back on the couch. "You know the case pretty well."

"I've studied it."

"Then you know she was pregnant."

"Kind of blows the nightie theory."

Collie rubbed the back of her neck. "Not necessarily."

"It's thin, Collie."

"Seven and a half months pregnant. A perfect baby—a little sister for Mia. I used to think about that all the time. It had to be some kind of a monster, to kill her like that when she was pregnant."

It had been Sonora's experience that pregnancy did not give a woman any protection from violence. Sometimes she wondered if it made her a target. She did not share these thoughts.

"Do you think it happens very often?" Sonora asked kindly.

"What do you mean?" Collie was twisting her shorts again.

"That a stranger kills a pregnant woman for no particular reason? Yeah, her purse was missing. But she still had her engagement ring on. Big diamond, it's in the report. She wasn't molested."

Collie's lips turned down in a deep frown that would have been comical on her clown face, if her eyes had not been so sad.

"I just don't get this. I don't get what you're trying to tell me."

Sonora watched her. "I'm not trying to tell you anything. I do know the case pretty well. Is there anything you want to ask me?"

"No," Collie said. Quickly. With force.

Denial was an amazing thing, Sonora thought. But she was on shaky ground.

The phone rang, and Collie jumped. "Sorry. Excuse me." She got up, headed into the kitchen. "Hello? What? No, I do not want a maintenance agreement on a freezer. Well for one thing, we haven't bought one. No. Thanks. No problem."

The phone clicked into place. Collie came back, moving slowly, an anxious look in her eyes. "Are you reopening the case? Micah's death? Do you have new evidence, or something?"

"No, we're not reopening that case, not right now. I'm looking into something else—a missing person. Would you know if your husband has had any calls from a Julia Winchell, anytime in the last few weeks?"

Worry swept across Collie's face like a storm warning. "I . . . we had quite a few hang-ups a couple weeks ago. But no, as far as I know, nobody by that name called here. Our number's unlisted, for obvious reasons. We don't give it out much."

The phone rang again.

Collie laughed, but the smile did not reach her eyes. "Right on cue."

She headed back to the kitchen, hand pressed into the small of her back. Sonora heard her pick up the phone, pitch her voice low. Sonora could not make out the words. She wished Sam was along. He was the best eavesdropper. She'd been to one too many rock concerts.

She heard Collie calling softly to Mia. "Get fixed up, honey. That was Daddy on the phone. The verdict's in."

Sonora heard Mia's gasp. "Did Daddy win?"

"Yes, sweetie, Daddy won."

Sonora bit her lip. At least she knew why she'd been stood up. The good news was Gage Caplan got a conviction. The bad news was Gage Caplan got a conviction.

She was going to bring down the DA who nailed Jim Drury?

Joy.

32

Gage had sent Sonora a message through his wife—which Sonora found high-handed—a request for a favor. He was clearly in the mood to ask.

Would she drive Collie and Mia into town so they could join him and his staff in an impromptu and informal celebration? In return, he would take some time to let Sonora ask those questions she needed to ask.

If he had thought to annoy her, he had guessed wrong. He would be full of himself, in his element. Guard down. She looked forward to watching him.

She would have said she was almost enjoying the chase, but a look at Collie Caplan, strapped uncomfortably into the passenger's seat, and Mia, sitting stiffly in the back in a clean denim jumper and black patent leather shoes, quelled any little thrill of the hunt.

If she got Caplan they were out a dad and a husband. If she didn't, they got to keep a killer.

Sonora glanced at Collie—pregnant, like Micah. What had made Gage Caplan kill a wife who was seven months pregnant with his child? Why could he not wait until the child was born?

Unless the child was the point.

Not his? Could he be that sure?

Collie had made it clear, whether she realized it or not, that Caplan was not happy over her pregnancy.

Plenty of pregnancies began with reluctance, Sonora thought.

She needed to know why the first wife had to go.

33

The office was a mess. Boxes of files, loose rolls of faxes, and a coating of multicolored strings of confetti.

They were drinking champagne out of little plastic champagne glasses. Mia edged close to Collie, who edged close to Sonora. Collie took Mia's hand, and Sonora noticed that the second Mrs. Gage Caplan was trembling.

It could have been a scene from a movie. A young woman, blazer off, in a tight black skirt and tuxedo-style white shirt, perched on the edge of a desk, legs swinging, medium high heels slipping off one slender ankle. She wore a gold ankle bracelet. Sonora noticed Collie studying it.

Collie's ankles were very likely thick and swollen in this heat and at this stage of her pregnancy.

Gage had his sleeves rolled up precisely two turns, exactly right for the sexy man about town. He looked good. He felt good. Physically large, dominating the room with presence and personality, a come-and-get-me-and-I'll-eat-you smile on his face. He had a nice tan.

Sonora wondered how he managed the tan with all the hours he had to have been putting in.

Collie had changed out of the shorts, making the unfortunate choice of a maternity ensemble that was just cause to have the designer shot or sentenced to a pregnancy of his or her own. It was a two-piece affair, in palest pink—tiny puff sleeves and an overblouse draping a pleated skirt with a stretch panel in front.

Sonora had seen better looking lampshades.

The overblouse tied in the back, empire style, with a big bow that would have been appropriate for Mia. It had large pockets, and baby blocks sporting the ABCs had been stitched on each side.

Sonora had always wondered why you could never find maternity clothes in shiny black leather.

"Here they are!" Caplan's voice was a boom of pleasure. Collie blushed. "Come on in, we don't pay rent on the hallway."

A smatter of laughter, cool amusement from the girl in the ankle bracelet.

"Come on, Mia. Give Daddy a hug and tell him you're proud, then I'll get you your first glass of champagne." Caplan poured a tablespoon of liquid into a glass, handed it to his little girl. He squeezed her chin, and she smiled up at him.

"I knew you'd win, Daddy."

There was a wave of approval and Caplan picked Mia up and set her on the desk next to the girl with the ankle bracelet.

The room went tense. Sonora looked up, watchful. For a moment everyone seemed to hold their breath, looking from Collie to Ankle Bracelet. Sonora knew, then, that Caplan and Ankle Bracelet were deep in an affair, one of those office things that everyone knows about except the wife.

And while Collie did not know, she sensed something. She looked like a deer in a headlight, awkward and large in her pink puffed sleeves amidst the leather briefcase set. Her lower lip trembled.

Caplan turned, smiled at her with such tenderness

that Sonora doubted what she had just seen. "My beautiful wife."

Too precious by half, Sonora thought. Rude to ask for a barf bag?

A lesser man could not have carried it off, but Caplan managed. Sonora looked around, decided she was the only one there feeling nauseous.

Formidable, she thought.

"Detective." Caplan handed Sonora a glass. He turned to Collie. "I know, I know, you're pregnant. We have to be careful of the *bay-bee*. Help me celebrate with *just* a taste." He pushed a glass into her hand. She pulled her hand away but he reached for it and made sure she had the glass secure in her fingers before he let her go. She smiled at him.

Quit smiling, Sonora thought.

Collie did not drink.

"It's a major victory, you know." He spoke softly. If Sonora had not been standing so close she'd never have heard him. Someone was telling a joke. "Celebrate with me, Collie girl. It's our big day."

"*Mr.* Caplan." Bea Wallace swooped over to Collie and relieved her of the glass. She smiled at Collie. "Men." Looked over at Caplan. "Sometimes I think you have the brains of a gerbil."

It took him aback. Sonora hoped, for Bea Wallace's sake, that she was a state employee and impossible to fire.

Caplan gave them a smile. "*Don't* drink then. This wife of mine has a mind of her own." He looked at Sonora. "Between the two of them, they'll keep me from getting a swelled head."

"Too late." Sonora said it softly enough that she did not think anyone heard. But Bea Wallace cracked a reluctant smile, and Caplan gave her a look.

"Pardon?"

"I said it's late. Maybe we should talk some other time. After your celebration."

"No, no. Come on in my office a minute." He raised his glass at the room. "Party on without me." No one paid any attention except Mia, watching Daddy-the-Hero. "The detective and I have business. I'll be—"

"Hell, Gage, don't you ever get a break?"

He stiffened. He did not like anyone saying hell in front of his little girl, Sonora guessed. He waved a hand, turned to Collie. "Starting tomorrow, I'm taking some time off." He grinned at Mia. "How'd you like to go down to London and see Gramma?" He looked at Collie. "You and me can take the canoe out. We haven't done that in ages."

Sonora saw Collie's hesitation, the shadow in her eyes.

"It'll be hot," Collie said.

Gage tucked his chin to his chest. "Sorry, hon. I was just wanting a break."

"Oh no, we can go. I can wear shorts, we can swim. It'll be fun."

"You sure?"

"Sure."

He squeezed Collie's shoulder. "There *is* more to life than eating and sleeping, I promise." He waved Sonora into his office.

She noted Collie's crestfallen droop and Bea Wallace's frown. She studied the fold of flesh that lapped over the starched back collar of his shirt.

I *will* get you, she thought.

34

Sonora was disappointed when Caplan closed the door and she had a chance to look around his office. She had expected to dislike him for keeping it neat and orderly, in spite of the pressures and long hours he'd been working to put Drury away.

But the computer was still up and humming. One file cabinet was open.

Caplan moved a stack of files and videotapes off a chair. "Why don't you take the one behind my desk? You might be more comfortable, everything else is in such a mess. Just let me do one thing—"

Caplan scooted behind his desk—box of files under one meaty arm—and touched the keyboard of his computer.

The sounds of a crowd going wild filled the room, with the loud announcement that *Elvis has left the building*.

Caplan grinned. "Better than a beep."

"This chair's fine," Sonora said, taking the one he'd cleared. She rested one foot on the edge of a box of papers. Waited for him to get comfortable in his chair. His intercom buzzed. Bea Wallace sounded harassed.

"WSTR, on line three. You want to take it?"

"Tell Sly I'll be issuing a statement at four-thirty, as planned." Caplan paused. "But tell him I'll beep him and try to talk to him personally first, if I get a chance. Oh, and if the *Inquirer* calls, put 'em through."

Caplan looked up at Sonora, leaned back in his chair. "I'm all yours."

"Congratulations on the verdict. I honestly didn't think you had a prayer."

"Me neither."

"And you still prosecuted? You're either honest, ethical, and not too bright, or a big-time gambler."

He smiled at her, twisting gently from side to side in the well-padded leather chair. His eyes were very blue.

"Enjoying yourself?" Sonora asked.

"A prime moment," Caplan said.

Mistress and wife toasting his success in the next room, television and newspapers at four-thirty to announce the big victory in court. A man riding so high might well believe he could get away with murder twice.

"So. Detective Blair. No blacks or Indians in homicide these days?"

Sonora tilted her head to one side. "Both, I think. So?"

"So what did you do? Who'd you piss off? Must have been that thing last year when you brought in that serial killer—what did you guys call her? Flash?" He stuck his tongue in his right cheek, making it puff out. "Heard you slept with a witness, or some such thing. I guess somebody in this man's army is out to get you, Detective."

"I don't follow you."

"Smart girl like you? Come on. Here you are on my doorstep again. Questions, concerns, problems." He waved a hand. "You suspect me of some kind of involvement in this Julia Winchell thing, God knows what or why. Cards on the table, Madam Detective? I'm a popular guy, I got your clout, I got your pull. I'm the hot potato, so I'm just curious how I managed to land in your lap. You got my sympathy, though, you surely do."

"That's kind of you," Sonora said mildly. "Maybe we're in the same boat. You went up against the football alumni, and I'm going up against a popular district attorney. But hey. Worked for you, didn't it? You're my hero, I guess."

"What is it you want, Detective?"

"Your alibi, Counselor."

"My alibi for what?"

"Tuesday, July eighteenth, from, say, eleven-thirty A.M. till eleven P.M."

"Pretty broad time spread you got there, podna."

Sonora opened her notebook. Looked up innocently. "You have a problem answering the question?"

Caplan shook his head, cheeks drawn, bottom lip pursed. "No. Let me think a minute." He closed his eyes. "Working, I think. Pretty much all I have been doing, these last few weeks. But no, I remember that Tuesday because Collie and Mia went up to Cleveland to go fishing with Ralph. Ralph is her dad." He said the name like it was funny.

"They catch anything?"

"Collie? Doubt it. Dad probably did. I think Mia said she got something. Pretty excited about it, as I recall."

"So you went home about what time?"

"Two-thirty. I'd left my laptop at the house, and I had a file I wanted on it. And I hadn't had lunch. I knew Collie and Mia were in Cleveland with old Ralph, so the house would be quiet. I went home, put on some sweatpants, made myself a sandwich, and worked till late."

"How late?"

"Some time after eleven. I stopped and watched the news, drank a brewski. Claire Pritchard was on with the stock market report, so it was already part-way over. Must have been between eleven and eleven-thirty."

"Anybody come to the door?"

He shook his head. "If they did, I didn't know it. Never heard the doorbell, but sometimes I don't hear it when I'm working at home."

"Anything else?"

He paused. "A confession."

Sonora raised an eyebrow, wary of his tone.

"I made myself *two* sandwiches. And ate a box of glazed Krispy Kreme doughnuts." He slapped his gut. "As you can see, I'll eat anything. Oh, look, she's trying not to laugh. Don't hold it in, Detective, could be harmful to your health." He was smiling, but his eyes looked sad. "This brings back memories, Detective."

"Of what? Micah's murder?"

"I was under suspicion then, too."

"And now?"

He shrugged. "I survived that, I can survive anything."

That Sonora might believe. "Anybody call while you were there, at home?"

"Several people. I didn't pick up. Bea knew where I was, but nobody else did. I was hiding out, trying to get some work done. You don't believe me."

"I think what we've got here pretty much counts as no alibi."

"Pretty much." He picked a pencil up off his desk, balanced it in the groove between his nose and upper lip. "Tell me, you think I ought to grow a mustache?"

"That's of absolutely no interest to me."

"What is of interest, then?"

"What did Julia Winchell look like?"

"Never saw her."

"Want to see a picture?"

"No."

"You kill her?"

"No."

"You cut her up?"

"God, no. Can't even carve meat."

"If you did cut her up, what tool would you use?"

He looked at her. Perturbed, finally.

"You own a hacksaw, Mr. Caplan?"

He hesitated.

"Let me help you on this one. Your wife says you own a hacksaw." She hadn't, but Caplan didn't know that.

"I guess I might have one out in the garage somewhere. So?"

Sonora leaned back in her chair, stretched out her legs. "Most of the men I know have a pretty accurate mental inventory of what tools they have, in the garage or anywhere else."

Caplan grinned. "I'm not most men. I'm pretty secure about my tools, so I don't spend a lot of time taking inventory. You impressed?"

"Believe me when I tell you that I'm not. Are you willing to submit blood and hair samples, Mr. Caplan?"

"For what possible reason?"

"How about a look in your garage? Turn over that hacksaw?"

"Play by the rules, Detective, I have faith in our system of justice. Get a court order and I'll cooperate."

Sonora stood up. "Enjoy your victory, Mr. Caplan. We'll talk again soon."

"I'm sure we will."

Sonora headed for the door.

"Detective. I was wondering—"

She paused, hand on the doorknob.

"What *does* it take to impress you?"

She studied him a minute, caught sight of the file drawer that was hanging open. She indulged herself and crossed the room, snapped it shut. Headed back to the door, looked at him over her shoulder.

"I guess if you got away with murder twice, that would impress me."

35

Sonora walked into the women's bathroom in homicide and headed for the sink. She was hot and sweaty and wanted to wash her face. She should not have made that last comment to Caplan. Never issue a challenge to a stone-cold killer; she had learned that the hard way.

A stall door was just swinging shut, then it opened. Sanders came out.

"They've been here again," she said.

Sonora went and looked into the stall. The toilet seat was up. "You know, they're each and every one of them detectives. You'd think they'd know better than to leave clues."

"Are they never going to get the men's room fixed?"

"Last I heard they're still trying to trace the smell. Some kind of backup in the drain somewhere."

Sanders grimaced. "They can smell it all the way back in Crime Stoppers, and I don't want to be mean, but I am sick of these guys coming in here. They're messy. They're *gross*. I found—"

"Please don't tell me."

"But what can we do about it?"

Sonora pushed hair out of her eyes. Looked in the mirror. Short hair would not suit her face, and if she got it cut, she couldn't pull it back. She looked over her shoulder at Sanders. Still there. "You prepared to fight dirty, Sanders?"

"Like how dirty?"

Sonora took off her shoe, smashed the tampon dispenser. "Never use your gun for this sort of thing, young Sanders. I knew a guy used his gun to hammer in a nail and shot his thumb almost all the way off."

"You're *breaking in* to a tampon dispenser?"

"Un petit larceny. Here." She tossed a cardboard box to Sanders, who actually caught it. "Men are funny creatures, Sanders. Vulgar, crude. But squeamish about the oddest things. Spread these around. It will definitely get rid of the single guys. May work on the married ones, too, some of them anyway."

She glanced at Sanders's feet, looked back again to make sure. High heels again. Sheer black stockings, instead of the usual thick tights. "Lunch with the married guy?"

Sanders blushed, deep dark satisfying red.

Sonora looked away. "Sorry. None of my business."

"I suppose *you've* never done anything like that in your life."

"Sure I have."

Sanders leaned against the stall door. "How'd it turn out?" She teetered back and forth on the balls of her feet, anxious, hopeful. Ready to call 1-900-PSYCHIC to see if all would be well in the name of true love.

Sonora sighed, leaned up against the wall. "I know what you want me to tell you. You want me to say he left his wife and kids, and married me, because we were soulmates and it was meant to be. Please don't let me forget the part where we lived happily ever after."

Sanders's voice was very small. "These things do work out sometimes, you know."

Sonora looked at her kindly. "Yes, they do. I've even known people where it worked out."

"It did?"

"Yes."

"But not for you?"

"For me it was like a virus. I got it once, got over it, and am immune to catching it ever again."

"I wish I knew for sure if he was married."

"Okay, here's a quick check. How long did you know him before he said he loved you?"

Sanders opened her mouth, but Sonora held up a hand.

"You don't have to tell me. Just remember single guys are impossible to pin down, and married guys tell you they're committed in forty-eight hours—they're in a hurry and they got no freedom to lose."

Sanders sat down on a toilet seat and put her head in her hands.

Sonora sighed. "How long?"

"The first night." Sanders's voice had dragged down at least two octaves.

"Look, this isn't like some kind of exact science, Sanders. For all I know, this love of yours is a straight-up soulmate. I've never met him, I can't judge. Come on girl, get up. Decorate."

Sanders dragged little blue boxes out of the dispenser. "It's the married thing that's driving me crazy. I have to *know*. Would you . . . Gruber wants to tail him. See where he goes at night."

"You know, there is a simpler way. You could just ask him, point blank."

"I did."

"*And?*"

"He said he didn't know."

Sonora burst out laughing.

"I don't think it's so very funny," Sanders said.

"I know, Sanders. I wasn't laughing when it happened to me."

"What should I do?"

"Ask him this. Ask him, when he turns over in bed at night, is there a woman there with him. If there is, tell him he might be married."

Sonora took a good long look at Sanders and made up her mind. Hopeless romance wasn't worth a second look. Keaton was hopeless. She decided to have dinner with Smallwood.

36

Sam was at his desk when Sonora went into the bullpen. He looked up as she settled into her chair.

"I already listened to your messages for you."

"Gee thanks, Sam, how come?"

"I didn't have any. And also, because somebody else was listening to them."

Sonora stopped. Looked at him. "Somebody was listening to my messages?"

Sam nodded.

"Who?" Her voice was quiet but hard.

Sam gave her a wary look. "Molliter."

"He say why?"

"Said it was an accident."

"How could that be an accident?"

Sam shrugged. "And by the way, Visa says your payment is overdue."

"Tell me something I don't know." Sonora flipped through the large stack of bills. She'd brought them to the office thinking she'd get to them sooner. Another fantasy gone to hell. Why was Molliter listening to her messages?

"Oh, and your son called. He wants to know if you could take off work early and drop him at some kind of all-age show in what I warn you is a sleazy part of town. And you'd need to pick up three of his buddies."

"Hey, Blair. Your little girl still belching the alphabet?" Gruber. He looked tired and depressed, tie hanging to one side.

"She's got refinement now, Gruber. She's quit with the alphabet and moved on to *Figaro*."

Sam looked up. "Really? The whole score?"

"No, just the first few measures."

"That's still pretty damn amazing." Gruber settled into his chair. Sighed. "This dieting shit is not for me. You ever heard of this fat burning diet?"

Sonora shuddered. "There are about a million of them. How's the clown thing going?"

"Guy uses deer slugs. So even if we get a weapon, which so far no luck, not like he leaves it behind, but even if we get the weapon, they won't have rifling to ID it with. He could wrap the damn thing and send it Fed Ex with roses, we couldn't nail him with it."

"The guys getting hit have any connection?"

"Well, gee, Sonora, you mean besides being clowns in dunking booths who insult one guy too many?"

Sonora looked at the sludge in her coffee cup. Thought of going to the bathroom to rinse it out. Sanders was probably still in there, crying or decorating. "So what are you saying, Gruber? These guys are getting killed because they're obnoxious?"

"You got any better ideas?"

"They *are* obnoxious," Sam said.

"Best lead we got is stuff from the guy's shoe, just don't ask me yet where it's gotten us."

"What shoe?"

"You didn't hear? Cinderella dropped a tennie. Wal-Mart's own version of a Nike. We been thinking about going door to door with every deer hunter we know and inviting them to try on the golden slipper. We're just awaiting authorization to go out and buy us a velvet cushion to carry it on."

Sonora dumped the sludge into Molliter's coffee mug and filled her cup. Put in a double portion of cream to turn things light brown, instead of tobacco brown. Time to branch out. No sense getting into a rut.

"So what was it?" Sam said.

Gruber scratched his chin. "What?"

Sonora looked up. "The stuff on the bottom of his shoe. Bubble gum? Name, rank, and serial number?"

"Creosote," Gruber said.

Sonora leaned against Sam. "Creosote. Where do you find creosote?"

"Places," Gruber said.

Sam stuck his tongue in his cheek, thinking. "Telephone poles. Maybe this guy's a pole climber for the phone company."

"Ought to be easy to find if he uses a deer rifle to reach out and touch someone," Sonora said.

Sam nodded. "Poor son of a bitch is probably just trying to find his own true voice."

Gruber looked at them. "You guys through? I mean, I don't want to interrupt if you got more of this shit to get out of your system. And don't think just because I already heard all these bad jokes at least twice is any reason not to carry on there."

Sam grabbed Sonora's coffee cup out of her hand, took a sip. "I don't think our humor is appreciated." He picked a scrap of pink paper off his desk. "Before I forget, you also had a message from Money-Wise Rent-a-Car."

Sonora took the scrap of paper Sam was holding. "That's Julia Winchell's rental company, Sam. You're just sitting on this?"

"They said personal."

"I told them to ask for me personally." Sonora frowned. Now Molliter knew they'd found Julia Winchell's car. She didn't feel good about that.

"Think her car's turned up?" Sam said.

"It's got to be somewhere. We could call the psychic hotline, or we can call the guys from Money-Wise. What would you do, Sam?"

"I'd get more sleep so I wouldn't be such a . . ." He looked at her. "Irritable person."

37

It drizzled on the way to the airport. Sam drove, air conditioner on high, windows steaming as cold air mixed with hot humidity and tiny slips of rainwater. The roads were slick in spots, drizzle mixed with baked grime and oil spills.

"Turn the wipers up a notch," Sonora said.

"Who's driving, girl, you or me?"

The windshield wipers were on the low, occasional setting. In between swipes the drizzle piled up into what Sonora considered to be intolerable levels.

"I thought Money-Wise didn't have an office at the airport. Sonora?"

"I'm not telling you a thing till you turn the wipers up."

"Why do you have to see? I'm the one driving." He turned the wipers up a notch.

Sonora glanced in the rearview mirror. It was just on five and traffic was getting slow and thick.

"No, Money-Wise doesn't have offices at airports, ever. But for some reason, this car's in the B lot with all the other rentals."

"How'd they find it?"

"Their guys cruise the airport lots on a regular basis. Most people don't realize Money-Wise doesn't have offices at airports—cars get left there all the time."

"So how come it took two weeks to find it?"

"That's what I asked. Guy I talked to said there were

two possibilities. One, it just got there. Two, it's the busy season. Nobody's had time to cruise for cars. Sam, the rain's stopped and that squeak is driving me nuts."

"You want the wipers off now?"

The representative from Money-Wise Rent-a-Car was young, hair trimmed short, neatly dressed in a suit in spite of the heat. He stood with an air of possessiveness next to a red Ford Escort. The first thing Sonora noticed about the car was the windshield, which was cracked.

"John Curtis."

The kid smiled at Sonora, shook her hand gravely, and called her ma'am. She wondered what the possibility was that her son would turn out this way. She wondered if she wanted him to.

The asphalt parking lot was spotted with damp, from the rain. The air had gone steamy, and Sonora's hair was curling on her shoulders. She lifted it off her neck, thought about cutting it very short.

Sonora give Curtis a second look. His skin was white and sweaty, eyes red-rimmed. Out late drinking, she knew the signs.

Typical All-American boy.

Sonora heard Sam muttering into a radio. "Got a key?" she asked the boy.

"Yes, ma'am. But I'm not supposed to—"

"We're impounding the vehicle, which is now evidence in a murder investigation. You know how long it's been parked here?"

"Not exactly, no ma'am. We found it after lunch, a couple of hours ago. It was on our hot list, so I called Mr. Douglas as soon as we found it."

"And this is normal procedure? Cruising airport lots for your rentals?"

"Oh, yeah. People leave them here all the time. Most rental places have airport offices and they assume we do, too. But we don't have one-way rental. You can't, like, rent a car in Cleveland and leave it in Cincinnati."

"Have to take it back where you picked it up?"

He nodded. "Which means we have to be careful when we do cruise the lots. Sometimes people leave them in the airport lot and want it there when they get back. They're not too happy if it isn't there waiting for them."

Sonora nodded. Curtis had the air of someone who faced the firing squad when a customer got unhappy.

Sonora touched Curtis's arm. "Look, it's hot out, and you'll excuse me for being blunt, but you look like you're going to vomit in my crime scene, so—"

"We were out late, entertaining clients. Is this a crime scene?"

"Yeah, and you look like you entertained real well last night. Why don't you go on inside where it's air-conditioned, find yourself a men's room, and throw up. We'll talk some more when you're done."

He gave her a grateful look, headed for the terminal, moving fast.

"Did I hear you tell that kid to go throw up?" Sam. At her elbow, cheek full of tobacco. He was wearing some kind of shaving lotion that made her want to get closer. She didn't.

"Yeah, so?"

Sam got closer to the car. Sniffed, tentatively. "No body."

Sonora dug in her purse for gloves. "No flies, any-way." She checked her recorder to make sure it held a fresh tape.

"Kid get in the car?" Sam asked.

"Says not. We'll get his prints just in case." She pointed to the crack in the windshield. "What do you think of this?"

Sam circled to the front of the car, squatted in front of the bumper. "No damage, here. Wasn't caused by a fender bender. Makes me wonder how it did get cracked."

Sonora opened the driver's side door. Stuck her head inside. The car had been shut up, sitting in the hot sun for days. Heat hit, surly and sweaty, and Sonora took a deep breath, sweat trickling down the small of her back. Hot air filled her lungs. If she was a dog, she'd flop down in the shade and go to sleep.

Instead, she leaned awkwardly over the driver's seat. "What's this? Sam, we got smears all over the—" She squinted, looked closer. "Jesus. Is this what I think it is?"

Sam was over her shoulder in an instant.

"Look, Sam. Footprints, right? Heel scuff here. Toes here and here, smeared like a kick, then dragged across the glass." Sonora pointed, not touching, not quite.

Sam pointed at a spot to the right of the steering wheel. "Point of impact. Must have been a hell of a kick."

"Big struggle, and she kicks the windshield." Sonora got out of the car, walked around to the passenger's side, opened the door. "Dent, right here in the armrest. Ah. Okay. Let's say her head's here, butted up against the door."

"If her head put that dent in the headrest, it was some kind of struggle."

"No blood anywhere I can see, so he didn't cut her up in here."

Sam looked at Sonora. "He *killed* her here though. Look at that windshield."

"The M.E. says her hyoid bone was broken, and she had patriarchal hemorrhaging in that left eye."

"Conclusion strangulation."

Sonora felt queasy. The heat was getting to her. "So let's say he's driving. She's sitting here." Sonora pointed. "He stops the car, turns sideways, leans over her, puts his hands around her neck."

Sam nodded. "Her head slips down to the armrest, she kicks like a son of a bitch and cracks the glass in the windshield."

"But he's a big guy and she's dead. Why didn't he clean up?"

"Time? No paper towels?"

"He had time to play butcher and button button with the body parts."

"Interrupted?" Sam said.

"Maybe. This is her car. He kills her in the car, then moves the body someplace where he can take his time. Meanwhile his car is clean."

"Yeah, but then why does he drop her car off at the airport and not clean it up?"

"He's not going to want to be seen with her car. And now he's got a body on his hands, he's got to get it to a safe place. Remember that guy we found with his wife in the trunk?"

Sam grinned. "Wasn't his lucky day."

"It's a pretty safe bet the car rental guys are going to clean up the car. If this had been Avis or Hertz, the car would have been processed and cleaned that day or the next. Maybe he doesn't realize Money-Wise doesn't do airports. You didn't."

Sam spit tobacco. Nodded.

"There you go, then." Sonora stuck her head back in the car. Sniffed. Hot vinyl. Baked Armorol. "I think she died here, Sam. I think he strangled her right here in the front seat."

"Makes it our jurisdiction then, for sure. She may have been dumped all the way up and down I-75, but she got killed in Cincinnati."

38

It was close to seven when Sonora got home. The sun was still high and hot and it hadn't rained at her house. She pulled her car into the tiny garage space located between boxes full of what she did not know, garbage bags, and kids' bicycles. She could not understand how she wound up with two kids and five bicycles, but she knew there had to be a good reason, because Tim had explained it to her once.

Heather was sitting on the front stoop wearing last year's swimsuit. Her chin was propped on her hand and she looked thoughtful.

Sonora got out of the car, skirting a hockey stick, and an open bag of unused grass seed from a yard project, unfinished, as usual. She could not look at the garage without getting depressed. She did not look.

She left the garage door open, and went up the front steps.

"What you doing, kidlet?"

"Hi, Mommy." Glum.

"What's wrong?"

"I was going to swim, but Clampett won't get out of the pool. Can you take me swimming, Mommy?"

Sonora considered it. Public pools. Band-Aids floating in the water. Children screaming. The humidity and the heat and trying to fit into last year's swimsuit. Attractive.

"Did you forget, it's your night with Baba. And I have a date."

Heather lifted her head. "Is it that guy who took me to the park?"

"Yes."

"Will he bring his dog?"

"Heather, I never try to predict what a man will do on the first date."

Sonora went in the front door, thinking clothes, hair, makeup. Someone had left a squeeze bottle of Aunt Jemima's genuine imitation maple syrup in the foyer, and the find had been discovered by an orderly line of fat black ants, their bodies sleek and shiny like patent leather.

She was going to have to readjust her thinking. House, then clothes, hair, and makeup. Should have arranged to meet him somewhere else.

39

Sonora realized, as they walked in the front door, that she had given Smallwood the wrong signal when she'd told him the kids were at their grandmother's and the coast was clear.

Calm, that was the word she remembered using.

She could not very well explain that she did not always feel like dealing with the capricious manners of children who had never liked a man on a first date, and had even gone so far as to get rid of one in particular by asking him if he was their new daddy.

Single men had a habit of not believing you when you said you were not looking for a father for your children. And it was insulting to explain that you did not wish your children to become attached to someone who might very likely be a temporary presence.

Nope. Smallwood had assumed she wanted sex.

Clampett was as friendly as ever, which meant that Sonora had to drag him by the collar into the backyard so that Smallwood could regain his balance.

"How do you take your coffee?" Sonora asked.

"In a beer can."

Subtle, she thought, opening the refrigerator. "You're not getting any of that Bud Light around here, Smallwood."

"What you got?"

"Corona."

"In a pinch."

She shoved a bottle in his general direction. "You want to bite the cap off, or do I look for the opener?"

He smiled the smile of a man who was almost ready to make his move.

What to do? she thought. She ran the list of body parts and possibilities, deciding in advance what would and would not be allowed. She thought of Keaton. She did not want to think of Keaton. She went back over the mental seduction list, checked off a few more boxes.

That should keep her mind off things.

They sat side by side on the couch with the lamp on low. Outside, heat lightning arced against a black sky, and the wind began to blow.

"Mind if I get rid of the light?" Smallwood asked.

You could make fun of men for their lack of subtlety, but really, what *were* they supposed to do? She couldn't say she hadn't been warned.

It had been different with Keaton. She had been sure with him.

Sonora turned the lamp off.

Smallwood scooted closer. Put his arm around the back of the couch. Touched her temple with his fingertip.

"Thanks for having dinner with me," he said.

"Thanks for the dinner."

He ran the finger up and down her temple with a firm pressure that felt good. Then he leaned close and kissed her.

He tasted like beer and he kissed like a man who would not be hurried. He kissed well. But he didn't kiss like Keaton.

Sonora leaned close and Smallwood slid a hand into the back of her blouse.

Too fast, she decided, but did not do anything about

it. She closed her eyes, still feeling the wine buzz, liking the way his hands felt on her back.

His fingers were firm on her skin. Pressing. Slipping beneath the thin strip of bra line. She wasn't quite sure when it unfastened, because he pulled her close, into his lap, so that she was facing him.

His right hand went round her neck, fingers stroking her behind the ear. "Such a pretty neck," he said, softly, in her ear.

And when he said it like that, so softly, she believed that maybe she did have a pretty neck.

She was an equal opportunity lover. She began unbuttoning his shirt, which he seemed to take as encouragement. Fool.

But then he moved his hands to the front of her blouse and lifted it over her head, pulling her into his now bare chest.

Sonora put her head on his shoulder. Definitely not on the list. He kissed the side of her neck, grazing the skin ever so lightly with his teeth. He dipped his head low and took her into his mouth, hands moving up under her skirt, tracing the insides of her thighs.

More things, not on the list.

He had the top of her pantyhose in his fingers, and he was pulling them down, slowly, over her legs.

The next moments were awkward, but familiar, the kind of moments that made women snort when men spoke of betrayals in terms like "our clothes just sort of came off." Twisted pantyhose, and socks and shoes, and shock that, yes, a condom was more a necessity than an option. Men were such innocents, Sonora thought. They seemed not to have the faintest idea about babies and AIDS.

And somehow she wound up bare, in his lap, which

any man might take as a yes. But when she looked at his face, she saw Keaton's face. She closed her eyes and pretended. Smallwood sat up and she wrapped her legs around his waist. He pulled her in close until he was touching her, and he would have been bewildered and appalled if he had known she was still making up her mind whether or not to do it.

She rubbed herself on him, gently up and down, and he made a noise that let her know she had his undivided attention.

He felt good. God, he felt good.

She lowered herself ever so slowly until he took her shoulders and pushed.

They both sighed.

He wrapped his arms tightly around her back, pulling her in close and hard, and something about the position made him hit her in just the exact right place.

She thought she might not get rid of this couch after all.

He kissed her while he made love to her and she liked that very much. She came quickly and hard, Smallwood right behind her, gentlemanly, as always.

40

Sonora woke up suddenly, feeling like she couldn't breathe. Her left foot and arm were numb. She was still on the couch, and Smallwood had her encircled in a tight grip. She knew she was breathing, but did not feel she was getting enough oxygen. She felt hot.

It was a feeling she remembered from years ago, sliding down that long icy slope toward divorce, only Zack had died before they'd gotten to the courtroom.

Panic attack. Smallwood. Not a good sign. What on earth had possessed her to wind up on the couch like this?

Sex, she guessed. That old thing.

It was heavy dark out, probably around two or three. She had taken her watch off, so she wasn't sure.

She missed Keaton. She missed how familiar he was, and comfortable, and right.

She wanted a long hot bubble bath and her very own bed, all to herself. Mainly she wanted to be able to breathe. The first thing she needed to do was get out of this death grip.

She moved Smallwood's arm slowly, and when that didn't work, shoved and got up. He stirred. She went into the bathroom. Decided it was best not to turn on the light and look. She brushed her teeth, splashed water on her face. It helped a little but not a lot.

She looked into the mirror, saw the outline of her

face in the dark. That's what you get when you bring a man home and move too fast. Trapped.

Now what?

She headed back toward the kitchen, saw Smallwood standing in the hallway. He smiled sleepily and pulled her into a hug. She hugged back politely, but she wanted him to leave. He muttered something, headed into the bathroom, and she went into the kitchen thinking sex was one level and intimacy was another, and maybe things worked better when you were ready for both at the same time.

The light over the sink had gone out. She opened the refrigerator, reached for one of the emergency cans of Coke she had hidden in the vegetable crisper. She put one on the counter for Smallwood. Rubbed her forehead. Wondered how long he planned to stay. Wondered why it was up to him.

Maybe Sam's Southernness was wearing off on her and she was getting too polite.

She did not particularly want to think about Sam right now. He violated the three rules of successful singlehood—don't sleep with married men, your co-workers, or your friends. She wondered who she was supposed to sleep with.

If Smallwood said anything to anyone about what had happened between them, she would deny the hell out of it. Then she would kill him.

She noticed a shadow in the doorway and looked up.

He had not bothered to put on any clothes.

She held up the Coke. "This or beer?"

She handed him the Coke before he answered. No more beer, she wanted him to drive. He took the Coke, but didn't open it.

"I'm not an insecure man, so there's no way I'm asking how it was."

Sonora wished he would not make her laugh. It made her like him too much. "Oh baby, oh baby, I want you. Feel better now?"

"It'll do." He scratched his stomach absently.

She wondered if she knew him well enough for him to be scratching his stomach in her kitchen. Ridiculous. She'd just slept with the man.

"You have a nice comfortable bed somewhere, or are we stuck on the couch?"

She wondered why he expected to stay all night. And why she was difficult enough to object. Somewhere, someone must have written rules about this, and she wished she had a copy. *First encounters entitle both parties to fifteen minutes in the host's bathroom, and twenty minutes of postcoital small talk is considered polite. Anything else is pushing it.*

She knew she was being a pig. In the movies, they always woke up together in the morning, unless the man snuck out and left the woman a note. It had always seemed callous on the man's part, but she began to see the point.

If he was expecting omelets and fresh-squeezed orange juice, he was going to be disappointed. There was nothing in the house but Lucky Charms.

She would never have had this problem if this had been Sam. She pictured him suddenly, reading *Green Eggs and Ham* to Julia Winchell's babies.

Focus, she told herself. Think fast.

Sonora frowned at Smallwood. "Sorry if the phone woke you up."

"The phone?"

"Yeah, that's what got *me* up, but I was hoping you'd sleep through it."

"Something up?"

Sonora sighed. "Heather, again."

"Your little girl? She okay?"

"Oh, she's fine, she's just missing Mommy. She does this. Says she wants to spend the night, then I get these"—she glanced at the clock on the stove—"these three A.M. phone calls and she's homesick for Mommy." She made a silent apology to Heather, who generally tramped off to overnights without a backward glance for anyone except Clampett.

"You need to go pick her up?"

Sonora ran her hands through her hair. "I don't know. Usually I just go over and get her, but maybe it's time she outgrew this kind of thing."

Smallwood put the Coke back on the counter. "Don't do it on my account. Maybe you better go on and get her."

"But what are you going to do? Did you get a hotel room?"

"Nah, I was just going to drive on back."

The hell you were, she thought. She had felt guilty about throwing him out. Now she felt better.

She followed him into the living room, watched him put on his clothes. He smiled at her while he pulled his pants up, gave her a quick kiss and fastened up his jeans. Now that he was leaving she was a little bit sorry to see him go. He was very cute.

"It's a long drive," Sonora said. Not that she gave a shit.

"Hell, I do it all the time. I've had a good sleep, I'm fine."

"Well," she said. "If you're sure."

Sonora took a long hot bubble bath (pineapple and mango), then curled up into a tiny ball beneath her favorite blue quilt. It felt so good to have the bed to herself that she let Clampett up to share it.

But she could not sleep. When she closed her eyes, she saw Keaton, and wondered if she would ever feel that way about anyone again.

Clampett scratched frantically. He looked at Sonora and gave a mournful whimper.

Flea bath, she thought, visions of flea bombs and daily vacuuming dancing in her head. Bad idea, letting him up on the bed.

She patted his head, rubbed a silky ear. "Let me bring Caplan down, okay, Clampett? Then I'll take care of you."

She spent the rest of the night curled up with autopsy reports. Cop glamour.

41

Sonora arranged to meet Sam, early, at Baba's. Heather had forgotten her stuffed penguin and Sonora had promised to drop it by. And they could catch the sixty-four exit about five minutes from her mother-in-law's street.

No one was awake at Baba's, so Sonora left the penguin on the kitchen table, locked the front door on her way out. Sam was waiting for her in the circle driveway, leaning up against their official Taurus, arms folded. He looked like he'd just stepped out of the shower, fresh shaved, cheeks still pink. It was already getting hot out. His sleeves were rolled up. White cotton shirt, khaki pants.

"No tie?" Sonora asked.

"It's in the car. You tied yours wrong."

"Please. No criticism before coffee."

"Ooou, it's cranky this morning. When did you get to bed last night?"

Sonora gave him a second look. She had not mentioned dinner with Smallwood. "I was up all night with autopsy reports. Julia and Micah. Tell me why the district attorney didn't indict, when Micah died."

"They don't usually go after the grieving husband unless they've got a pretty sure thing. And his family has money, I think."

"I've gotten death penalty convictions on less stuff

than they had him on. I mean, Sam, she had skin frags under her nails. And he said she scratched his back during sex? Her body is found by the creek, and she's supposed to have drowned there, but there's no creek water in her lungs? That makes sense?"

"It may not make sense, but it doesn't convict Caplan."

"He's got no alibi during the time of the killing. He had scratches, which he said were from hiking. I saw the shots they took of his arms and those scratches looked fresh."

"Sonora. His wife was seven months pregnant with his child. She was held under water in a creek on a rainy night. You going to convince a jury a man's going to pull something that vicious, you better have it sewed up tight. He's not just killing the wife, he's killing the baby. And don't forget that little overnight case she had in the backseat of the car."

"Yeah, Collie, his other wife, she brought that up. Like at seven months pregnant, Micah is having a thing."

Sam put on his turn indicator. Pulled into the parking lot of a McDonald's, went for the drive-up window. "You hungry?"

Sam ordered an Egg McMuffin and coffee. He looked at Sonora. "What'll it be?"

"Three hash browns, and a large coffee with cream."

Sam made her wait till they were on the interstate and down one hash brown before he swallowed a large bite of Egg McMuffin and cleared his throat to talk.

"The overnight case made it look bad, Sonora."

"She was seven months pregnant. At the end of the day with her feet swollen double you think she's off to meet a lover? You think Caplan didn't pack the damn thing himself and stick it in the backseat?"

"Yeah, actually, I do. And I also think we're going to catch six kinds of hell going after him. And I think he'll be hard as hell to convict. You haven't been into the office this morning, but I have."

"What do you mean?"

"On your desk, and mine. A thousand and one little messages. Inquiries from everybody who is living and breathing in the DA's office. Some of them I thought quit years ago."

"What do they want? Are they threats?"

"Threats? Get real. Of course not. Just requests for information, cooperation, copies of this, that, and the other. Pain in the ass make-work on every case you and I ever touched, and some that we didn't."

"That's good, Sam. We're getting to him."

He didn't answer.

"Sam? You want to back off?"

"Hell, no. Let's fuck up our careers and go after the bastard."

42

It was a little after 11 A.M. when they took the second London exit and headed left down a two-lane country road that led them past a tiny, whitewashed Baptist church. The highway had been a wagon train of cars from Ohio, towing boats. They'd passed two exit signs for Laurel Lake, Holly Bay Marina.

"Drop the other shoe," Sam said to Sonora.

"No, no, that last rest stop should hold me for a while."

"Maybe twenty minutes. I mean the sign. I'm waiting for your nasty remark."

"The Dog Patch Trading Center? I figured they had one in every Kentucky town."

Sam put his right turn indicator on, moved the Taurus out of the intersection. It was a narrow road, a lot of twists and turns, nobody doing less than fifty. Sam was in his element. He had a smile on his face. The closest he ever got to looking angelic.

A car towing a houseboat passed slowly, crowding them close to the edge of the road.

"Why is it all these people with boats come down from Ohio," Sonora said. "We got lakes in Ohio. We got rivers in Ohio."

"We got laws in Ohio."

They passed farmland. A tractor parked at the crest of a hill.

"I don't get that," Sonora said.

"Boating laws in Kentucky are about as common as unicorns and what they have they don't enforce. You can come down here, drink till you can't stand up, and drive like a maniac through the water."

"You kidding?"

"Absolutely not. Hell of a lot of fun."

"What about the tractor?"

He looked at her. "What tractor?"

"The one we passed. Why did they leave it at the top of the hill? Seems like one push, and—"

"We're here, Sonora." Sam pulled the car up, parallel to the yard. There was no curb between the lawn and the street. Sonora opened her door and got out.

The house was a freshly whitewashed wood frame nestled on a large corner lot. A white picket fence surrounded the backyard, and on every tenth picket rested a wooden bluebird, sporting a lush red beak.

Sonora wondered how they had nailed the bluebirds up there. As she got closer, she saw that each bird wore a little tiny vest that she thought might be called a weskit, and each had a different facial expression, more human than birdlike.

There were flowers everywhere, herded neatly into beds that were bordered by landscape timbers. There was a birdbath in the front yard and a bird feeder by the driveway.

The metal storm door had dents in the middle and wasn't hanging true, but the front door looked like it had been painted a deep crimson just last week. A heart-shaped door knocker, made of wood, said WEL-COME.

The man who came to the door had a big smile, and a large hearing aid clipped behind his right ear. His brow was wrinkled, in spite of the smile, and Sonora decided he was worried.

People tended to look worried when the police came to their door.

"I'm Detective Blair, this is my partner, Detective Delarosa." Sonora showed her ID. "I talked to Mrs. Ainsley a few days ago about coming down?"

The man nodded and opened the door, offered his hand. "I'm Grey Ainsley. Come on inside."

The house was cool, windows thickly covered, but all the lights were on and it was cheery. The carpet was thick and new, covered with a multitude of bright area rugs. Grey Ainsley led them to a couch and invited them to sit.

"I'll go and get Dorrie—it's supposed to be Dorothy, but nobody gets away with calling her Dorothy or Dot."

"I *hear* you Grey, I'm coming in. This isn't Buckingham Palace. I don't have to be announced."

Grey exchanged looks with Sam, who grinned, and Sonora saw a quick kindling of the mysterious thing called male rapport. Too bad she could not send them out to play.

Dorrie Ainsley had a small girl candy voice, midregister and soft. She was short, and she walked slowly, leaning on a cane and taking Grey's elbow gratefully.

"Let me put you in your chair," Grey said, settling her into a white brocade chaise lounge.

Sonora looked around the room for pictures. A large shot of Collie hung on the wall next to one of Mia and Micah sitting on a pink ruffled bed with a huge stuffed alligator. Sonora made a count. Four of the granddaughter, two with Micah, and one of Collie. None of the son-in-law. Interesting.

"Excuse me for stretching out like this." Dorrie

winced as she settled back on the chaise. "I have terrible knees—degenerative arthritis."

"She can barely walk. She needs to get those joints replaced."

"I think I'd like to give them a little more time for research. I want them to get it right."

"They do a wonderful job with hips," Grey said.

"Hips aren't knees."

Sonora noticed lines of pain on the woman's face. Likely she'd given the matter plenty of thought.

Sam was looking around the room.

"Enough knickknacks in here to start a store," Grey said. "Dorrie makes them. She paints."

"Did you do the bluebirds on the fence?" Sonora asked.

It was the right thing to say.

Dorrie's smile got big and Grey leaned forward. "Did you notice their faces at all?"

"Oh, honey, she couldn't see something like that from the street."

"But I did," Sonora said. "They had people faces."

Grey laughed and slapped his knee. "Painted one for everybody in the family. Kids, grandkids."

"Do you have one for Mia?" Sam asked.

Grey was nodding. "Mia, Micah, and Collie. We've just about adopted that Collie."

It was a conversation stopper. Grey fiddled with his hearing aid. Dorrie leaned forward.

"Let me get you something. A cup of coffee or some lemonade?"

"No thanks," Sonora said. Sam shook his head.

"We're investigating the homicide of a woman named Julia Winchell," Sonora said.

The Ainsleys were politely attentive, guarded.

"According to phone records from her hotel room up in Cincinnati, she called your house a day or two before she disappeared. We're pretty sure she was down here." Sonora did not explain about the credit card receipts. Either Julia Winchell was here, or someone used her card.

Grey was shaking his head. "Name's just not familiar. I don't think we know her."

Sonora took a picture out of the maroon vinyl briefcase that her children had saved up and bought for her birthday two years ago. She passed the picture across the coffee table, around the potpourri.

"It's Micah's friend." Dorrie had a stricken look. Her voice, soft at the best of times, went so quiet that Sonora barely heard her.

"She was here?" Sam asked.

Dorrie nodded. Grey's hand went to hers, and she squeezed it. He moved his chair closer to hers.

"You say she's dead?"

Sonora kept her voice as kind as possible. "What did she say when she called? Why was she here?"

"She called and said she went to school with Micah. To college."

"UC?" Sam asked.

"No, Micah went to Duke." Grey's voice was gruff, but his chin went up. Proud daddy.

Sonora exchanged looks with Sam. Julia Winchell was not an old college buddy of Micah's. Julia Winchell went to UC.

"She did teach at UC," Dorrie said. "On a research grant. Micah was—"

"She was smart as a whip," Grey said. "One of those Asian whiz kids. I found Micah in an orphanage when I was in Korea. She was part Japanese, part Korean, and part American. The kind of ancestry that pisses everybody off. Three years old and about this high." His voice cracked. He held his hand low to the ground.

"I can't have children of my own. I think that's why Collie and I bonded so well right off."

Grey squeezed Dorrie's knee. "Except now Collie's expecting this miracle baby."

Dorrie nodded, smiling gently, and Sonora wondered why women like Collie and Dorrie had trouble carrying children when they were both clearly top-of-the-line mom material.

"I'm sorry. You're here to talk about this other little girl, not Micah." Dorrie handed the picture back and Sonora leaned forward to get it.

"I think there's a connection, Mrs. Ainsley. Talking about one is going to lead to the other. What did she say when she called?"

Dorrie thought for a minute. "She asked if she could stop by and see me. She said she and Micah were best friends in school. I didn't . . . I didn't want to be unfriendly. But when Micah died, there was a lot of notoriety and we got bad phone calls."

"Whole world's going bad," Grey said.

Sonora thought of the bluebirds on the fence.

"I told her she could come, but then when she got here, I just felt funny. It didn't seem to me like she knew my daughter. And I got worried, and I guess I panicked. What I did, I called Mia's father, I called Gage and asked if he knew her, or if Micah had ever mentioned her. She said her name was Jenny Williams."

Sonora looked at Sam. Jenny Williams sounded plenty made up.

"Did he know her?" Sam asked.

Dorrie nodded. "Well, he did—I mean, not right at

first. But we talked about it and he remembered her after a minute or two. I gave him her number at the hotel in case he wanted to check her out. He said it was safe to have her in. That Micah had mentioned her, now that he'd come to think about it. Grey was here and he took her out to see the bluebirds, you know, on the fence. That's when I called Gage. And when I described her and . . . you know, she was really very striking. The kind of girl you remember. And she had that tattoo. The little dragon over her ankle. It was so odd because she seemed like the last kind of girl to get a tattoo. But as soon as I reminded Gage about the tattoo, he remembered her."

Sonora exchanged looks with Sam.

"So he was definite about that? That he knew her?"

"Oh yes. He said that she and Micah were real close, and for me to roll out the red carpet. And I did. She ended up staying to lunch."

Sam leaned back on the couch, stretched his arm out across the back. "What do you think, Mrs. Ainsley? She really know your daughter?"

"Nothing she said about Micah rang true. She talked about how hard Micah worked and how she loved to study, and to tell the truth, Micah never did follow that Asian stereotype. She had American habits, didn't she, Grey? Liked to be out having fun, doing stuff with her friends. She was just so smart, she hardly had to crack a book."

Even at Duke, Sonora thought. Very smart.

"And she said she and Micah used to go out for pizza all the time. Only, Detective, my daughter was allergic to tomatoes and she stayed away from pizza, because the sauce made her break out all around her mouth."

Grey put a hand on the back of the chaise lounge. "We didn't know who she was, but she didn't really know our girl."

"She did ask a lot of questions, though," Dorrie said. Grey's mouth went hard and he set his jaw.

"What kind of questions?" Sonora asked.

Grey leaned forward. "See, she said she hadn't known about it when Micah died. So she was wanting to know what happened, and if they ever caught the guy who did it."

"How well do you get along with your son-in-law?" Sonora asked.

Dorrie looked at Grey. Then they looked away from each other.

"We get along fine," Grey said. Woodenly.

Sonora looked at both of them—neither would meet her eyes. "He controls the grandchild, that it?"

Sam rolled his eyes and Dorrie made a noise of protest. But Grey nodded.

"You got the size of it. And believe you me, he works it, every chance he gets."

"Oh, Grey, don't." Dorrie put a hand in the crook of his elbow.

He patted the hand absently, but did not take his eyes off Sonora. She recognized a man sorely in need of venting.

So did Sam. "Mr. Ainsley, would you take me around back to get a look at those bluebirds?" He grinned, friendly, at Dorrie, who tried to smile back. "I didn't get much of a look when we came in. If you don't mind, I'd like a chance to see them up close."

"Glad to. Let me show you around." Grey stood up, headed toward what was logically the kitchen. Sonora heard the hum of a refrigerator shifting gears.

She studied Dorrie Ainsley. The back door banged shut, official exit of the men, and Dorrie took a deep breath.

Sonora tried to think of an easy way into son-in-law

territory. "Mrs. Ainsley, what kind of impression does Gage make on your friends?" She waved a hand. "Family?"

Dorrie's eyes lowered, then her head came up. She lifted her chin. "People always like Gage. He's full of . . . full of fun, when he's in the mood to charm."

Sonora was nodding, friendly, sympathetic. You could not just open a valve to people's minds and let the information trickle out. Sam was right when he preached patience, patience, patience. She would never tell him that, though.

"What about when he wasn't in the mood to be charming?" Sonora asked.

She looked up, caught Dorrie Ainsley's eye. Whatever she had said had been the right or the wrong thing. The woman was swallowing hard again and her eyes were filling with tears. Sonora dug her fingernails into the tender palms of her hands.

It was painful, watching the woman try not to cry.

Sonora let her voice take on the strong but soothing cadence that worked so well. A combination cop/mom voice. She wished, sometimes, that someone would talk to her like that.

Dorrie Ainsley looked down at the recorder. "He's not . . . he's never been anything but nice to all of us. He was a wonderful—" Her voice cracked and she took a breath. A shudder went like a wave through her small stooped shoulders.

Sonora waited, but Dorrie Ainsley could not finish the sentence.

Sonora hoped she could count on Sam to give her plenty of time. She turned off the recorder. There were things she needed to know.

"It's the grandchild thing, isn't it? Mia? Your daughter's

dead and he's in control now. It's up to him when and if you get to see her. And he holds that over you."

Dorrie Ainsley looked at her steadily. "I have to keep her safe."

"His own daughter? You have to keep her safe?" Sonora did not know why she was surprised, not if Caplan was the man she thought he was. It was meeting him, she guessed. He was funny. He made her laugh.

People did not lose their sense of humor when they killed.

Dorrie Ainsley had a hard look in her eyes and the tears were gone.

The woman could barely walk and she had a soft side that led her to paint human faces on bluebirds. Sonora had no doubt that she had crocheted the afghan that was draped over the back of the couch. But she had Caplan's number, and she was dealing with him.

"He's not the man you think he is," Dorrie Ainsley said.

Sonora thought perhaps he was.

43

He killed my little girl."

Sonora glanced at the recorder, decided it was too risky. "Tell me about it."

"You've read Micah's file, or whatever it is you people keep?"

Sonora did not like being called you people, but she let it pass, like she always did.

"His skin was under her fingernails. He had scratches—whatever he said they came from, liar. He lies—he's pathological, he lies like he breathes the air, I've seen him do it a hundred times. And Micah was *not* having an affair."

Dorrie Ainsley shook her head like a woman who has heard all the arguments before and does not want to hear them again. "Being born and raised in a small town doesn't make you stupid. People are people everywhere you go. I thought Micah *should* have had an affair, in her shoes I would. I would have gotten a divorce. But she was afraid of him. You think what happened there by that creek was the first time he tried it? No, ma'am. That was just when he finally got her."

"I need details," Sonora said. She flipped on the recorder.

Dorrie Ainsley either didn't notice or didn't care. "He bought her a horse. A horse they could *not* afford, believe me. I don't know where he got the money."

Sonora waited.

"You have to understand the timing on this. Micah was eight weeks pregnant with Mia, and she'd already had two miscarriages. Now you and me know that losing two is hard, but it doesn't mean you can't have any. But Micah was convinced she couldn't carry one to term. She even told him to divorce her if he wanted kids.

"Then he goes and gets her a horse when she's two months along? It's not like *he* knew a thing about horses, and Micah was *afraid* of them." Dorrie picked at a seam on the chaise. "She was afraid of a lot of things; Micah was timid. I don't know if Grey and I overprotected her—but I just think that was the way the Lord made her. And Gage was always making her do things that scared her, and she was always trying to please him.

"He was so different when they first met. He was always athletic and energetic and liked to do things, but he treated Micah like she was a little china doll. And Grey and I—we welcomed him. We liked it that he took such care with her. At first we did. And then it was too late. She was in love with him, and dependent on him, and they got married and there was nothing I could do."

"What happened with the horse?"

"Nothing. The lady at the stable watched Micah ride and gave her some lessons, then told them to get a quieter horse. Gage lost interest, and they were in a money crunch, as usual, so they sold him. And you can't tell me he didn't fool around on her the whole time they were married, but it took her forever to figure it out."

"You told her?"

Dorrie Ainsley shook her head. "Not my place. She never asked me, so I never said so."

"How'd you know?"

"At my age, Detective, you know."

This, Sonora decided, she would accept for the time being. She tapped a finger on the armrest of the couch. "Did he do anything besides buy her a horse?"

"It sounds silly, doesn't it?" Dorrie's voice had gone flat. "It's hard to make people understand about him."

"I understand," Sonora said. "But I need it all. The more you give me . . . the more I'll be able to do my job."

"And what do you consider your job?"

"To find Julia Winchell's killer. And if I solve an older homicide that's still on the books, that's my job, too. And it may take the one to convict on the other, so talk to me, and don't worry about how it sounds."

She could play devil's advocate later, with Sam. And Crick would be quick to deflate anything flimsy. "Give me something I can use in court."

"I would if I could. All I know is, Gage always was making her do things that scared her. Little stuff, mean things. Petty. It sounds stupid, but there's this section of road between here and Cincinnati. It's steep and curvy, and not too bad, it's I-75—you probably came down it. But Micah always hated that part. And I guarantee you, every time they came home he'd get sleepy around Berea and they'd stop and change over so she would have to drive that part. And she told me, she'd ask him, you know, to let her drive the first hour or two out of Cincinnati. She didn't mind the way they drive up there, which is what scares me, it was the mountains that made her afraid. You want to know what I think?"

Sonora did, and she nodded, but there was no need. Dorrie Ainsley did not get to talk frankly about her son-in-law to someone who understood, and she was on a roll.

"I think that drive was a punishment for coming home." Her voice broke and the tears came. "He was punishing her for coming home, to see her mama. And *sometimes* he didn't ask her to drive, but that was when it was his idea to come."

Sonora felt her face getting warm and her stomach knotted and she waited for the pain, but it didn't come. The ulcer really was gone.

But she knew what kind of man Gage Caplan was. She'd been married to one once.

Dorrie knuckled the tears with an impatient gesture that was almost harsh. "Much as you might think he dotes on that little girl, he was in a rage when Micah told him she was pregnant."

"You know that for a fact?"

"I *do* know it for a fact. If you could have heard her voice on the phone . . . she was so . . . crushed. She cooked him this romantic dinner, with candles in the pewter sticks her Aunt Gracie gave her when they got married, and she was so excited. But he . . . but he . . ." Her voice dropped to a whisper. "She never told me all the things he said. She was too embarrassed. All I knew was what I heard in her voice. And it was bad.

"And then him coming down here and saying 'I'm going to be a *daddy*!' And picking Micah up and twirling her around. Like he couldn't be happier. He *cried*. He took me aside and told me in private he was scared that something would happen to Micah or the baby, and I guess he had no idea Micah had called me when he acted so bad. And to look at him now you'd think he was just crazy about that child. But here's what I know. He's a good daddy and a loving husband when people are *looking*. Not that I'm saying he knocks them around, or any of that normal abuse."

What a world it was, Sonora thought, when knocking your wife and child around could be called normal abuse. But she knew what Dorrie Ainsley meant.

"But when people aren't watching, he's something else. I don't know what, but it's bad."

"You said you needed to keep your granddaughter safe."

"I've been keeping her safe since before she was born. I honestly think—and even Grey thinks I'm crazy—but I honestly think that if I didn't have Micah stay with me those last couple months, Mia would never have been born."

"Why did she stay with you?"

"We told Gage that the doctor said Micah had to be flat on her back those last weeks, but it was a lie. That was what we told him to get her down here, where I could take care of her."

"Was Micah afraid?"

"Oh yes. I'm her mother, I could tell. It's not like she'd say so, everything was under the surface and unspoken. It was a wonderful time, those two months. I'd say, Micah, if you feel well enough, you best get up and not lay in bed all day. We rented tons of movies. Watched TV. Read a million books. And she and Grey would take long walks, and go down to the lake, and I'd have their supper waiting. I fixed all their favorite stuff and we were a family again." Dorrie placed her hands in her lap. "I think of those two months as a gift."

"How did Gage take it? The two months she was here?"

"I expected him to be difficult and he wasn't. It was almost like he was relieved. I couldn't believe he was just going to let her come down here, but he was nice as you please. He was so nice it gave me bad dreams." She stared at the floor. "Doesn't make sense, does it?"

It made sense to Sonora.

"But I know he found out we lied to him after Mia

was born, because the doctor talked to Micah later, when it was just her and me, and he made a point to tell her that she could have more kids if she wanted. And that if she got pregnant again, she didn't need to stay in bed all that time unless something unforeseen came up. So he *had* to have talked to Gage about it. Gage must have told him what we said and the doctor set him straight. But Gage never said word one to us about it."

"Odd," Sonora said.

"Everything with Gage is under the surface."

Sonora thought of Caplan's desk the first time she'd seen his office. Clean pristine desk and bookshelves, drawers stuffed with such a jumble they barely closed.

"Did the police talk to you when Micah died?"

"I called *them*. I knew he did it, and so did that Detective Byer. But the DA's office never took it on. Gage was a lawyer himself, and he knew people. I mean, they investigated him. It's just, Gage is . . . he's a charmer. People like him. And then he goes to work for those people! I talked to a lawyer about getting custody of Mia, but I didn't have a chance. All I would do is cause a big mess.

"Then Gage called me, after things died down. We'd had a lot of words, I have to tell you. And he said that he knew that the trouble between us—that's how he put it—was just my grief taking over. And he hoped I would *settle down*. That's what he said, settle down. Because he said Mia loved me and was asking for me and it would be better for her if we got along." She swallowed hard. "You don't know how hard it was for me to back down. But I did. Because it was the best thing for Mia. So I apologized and I ate crow, *then* he tells me he thinks there should be a cooling off period." She took a breath. "He didn't let me see my granddaughter for a year. She was only three years old, then, same age as Micah when Grey brought her home to me. And if you don't think that was a happy day. If I could go back to that day, I'd take my little girl and just hide."

Dorrie Ainsley looked Sonora straight in the eye and if she'd expected to see sorrow and grief, she was mistaken. Sonora knew stone-cold hatred when she saw it.

"If it wasn't for Collie I don't know what would have happened. But thanks to her I see a lot of Mia and I love Collie like she was mine. I can't imagine why a high-rolling son of a bitch like Gage married her. She's too good for him. But it was a godsend for Mia, and for me and Grey."

But Sonora knew exactly why Gage had married her. Vulnerable, unattractive—but intelligent, playful, fun. Strength of purpose just when you expected her to fold. A quality woman with a clown face.

This was one he could break, and control, and play with for a while.

44

In the best of all possible worlds, which this was not, the men would not have come back in until Sonora was ready to be interrupted. They did not head back into the living room, for which she was grateful, but settled in the kitchen. Sonora heard the refrigerator door open and close. The clink of ice in a glass.

"Can I get you something?" Dorrie Ainsley slid forward on the chaise lounge, but Sonora shook her head. "This little Jenny girl that came to see me. You say her name is Julia? Who was she, then? Was she one of Gage's girlfriends?"

"No ma'am. She wasn't one of Gage's girlfriends."

The refrigerator door slammed again, and Grey came in, followed by Sam, holding two glasses of lemonade.

"How about that?" Grey handed a glass to Sonora, and one to Dorrie. "You girls are doing an awful lot of talking. Probably need something to—" He looked at Sonora, face darkening to a dusky red. "Not supposed to call you girls, am I?"

Sonora smiled. "Ten points toward being politically incorrect."

He gave Dorrie a second look, then turned to Sonora. "She's been crying, so I guess you're all filled in on the Gage and Micah situation." He sat down on the edge of Dorrie's chaise lounge. "We got no choice but to get along with the boy. No matter what we think happened. It isn't an easy thing."

"No," Sam said.

"But it's been a whole lot better since he married Collie."

Not for Collie, Sonora thought.

Grey was nodding. "Over a hundred and ten percent. She makes it easy on us. She was scared to death to meet us, bless her heart. She and Gage come down to use the cabin, and no telling what he told her, but—"

"What cabin?" Sonora asked.

"We have a cabin down on Laurel Lake. It's got a little dock, and we have a boat we take down there, to fish and swim. It's real pretty out there. It was one of Micah's favorite places. I think Gage and Collie get down there more than he and Micah did—Collie likes to bring Mia down. I pretty much give them free rein of the place. Dorrie and I just don't get out there, and I get to see my granddaughter when Gage and Collie bring her down."

"They're supposed to come in the next couple of days," Dorrie said. "They're going to leave Mia with us and take the boat out, though dragging Collie out in this heat with her so pregnant seems the height of stupidity. But maybe that's just me. I don't like the heat."

Sonora considered the cabin, thinking that if Caplan killed Julia Winchell in the rental car, like she thought, he'd have to have somewhere private to butcher the body.

"What time did Julia Winchell leave? That day she came down?"

Dorrie looked at Grey. "A little before one, wasn't it?"

"Yeah. She had a drive back, and she was anxious to hit the road."

"And how far is it from here to Clinton?" Sam asked.

"No more than an hour, hour and a half."

"You stay on I-75 to get there?" Sonora asked.

"Up until you get to the exit," Dorrie said.

Sonora exchanged looks with Sam. He stood up.

"You folks mind if we take a look at that cabin?"

"Hell, no," Grey said. "Take you out in the boat, too, if you want to go."

45

The cabin was a good sixty feet from the lake, one of those vacation home packages, with a roof that slanted in a V and a wood deck wrapped all the way around. Sonora heard the waspy buzz of a boat engine, somewhere close on the water. There were other houses, close by and in sight, scattered at random in the trees, all with boat docks and trails to the lake.

Would Caplan have brought Julia Winchell here? Lots of people around, in the summer, lots of people to see.

But at night, with the body wrapped in plastic, he could have lugged her in under the trees. People were camping, fishing—who was to say he wasn't lugging a sleeping bag or something for the boat?

Grey led them up onto the porch, engine running on the blue Chrysler LeBaron in an attempt to keep the interior cool for Dorrie, who had insisted on coming along. He seemed shy suddenly, shoulders stiff, wiping his feet on the deck for no particular reason.

He unlocked the front door and pushed it open, but did not go inside. "I best let you do your job. I'll go keep Dorrie company in the car. Holler if you need something."

Sonora smiled at him, relieved. It was inhibiting to search a house under the homeowner's worried eye, and she was grateful Ainsley had the grace to go back to the car.

Sam nodded thanks and Sonora led the way.

It took a minute for their eyes to adjust, even with the lights switched on. All the windows had blinds and they were down and shut tight, like eyes that would not see. Sonora sniffed. Some odor here, familiar, but she could not place it.

"What's that smell?"

"I don't notice anything," Sam said.

Sonora headed to the kitchen, sniffing again. Just a trace. She could not place it. A sort of clean chemical odor, and she knew it was common as eggs. What was it?

The cabin was immaculate. Living room carpet newly vacuumed, tread marks showing. None of the furniture was new, everything had the secondhand air of things that were pre-owned and serviceable. There were prints on the wall of farms in winter—the kind of thing that provided color for under twenty dollars.

Sonora checked the kitchen sink. Dry as a bone and gleaming. She opened the cabinet underneath. It was the usual lair, dark and scummy. A green cleaning bucket, an open canister of Comet—yellow top, so it had a lemon scent. Sonora sniffed it, frowned. Not the smell she'd noticed—too lemony. A sprinkle of the blue/yellow powder had spilled onto the bottom of the cabinet. Sonora opened the door wide. The cleaning supplies had been crammed in so tightly that a plastic squirt bottle of Windex had fallen sideways on top of the Endust and the Four Paws Pet Stain Remover. The can of Raid (Kills Bugs Dead) was laid sideways across a black box of ant traps.

But on the right-hand side was an empty spot, a blue dusting of Comet trailing across the circle of empty space. Sonora picked a yellow tab of cardboard off the pile of blue dust.

It had come from a box of garbage bags, Dairy Co-op House Brand, the large lawn and leaf size.

Julia Winchell's head, hands, and feet had been tied in brown plastic bags, lawn and leaf size. Sonora wondered if they could match the roll.

"Find anything?" Sam said, sticking his head in the door.

Sonora rocked backward on her heels and lost her balance.

"Sorry, girl, didn't mean to scare you."

"I meant to do that. No, really, my knees were tired." She looked up. "Got your little penlight?"

"Yeah."

"Shine it in here."

"Sonora, if it's something horrible will you just tell me first?"

"You never did get over the time they sent you into that dark room when you were a uniform and you screamed."

"Damn right I screamed. Place was dark as an oven, and when I turn on the light there's a body hanging from the ceiling fan? What would you do?"

"No body parts, Sam, come on, shine it in."

He squatted down beside her, groaned when his knees cracked.

"Getting too old for this, Sam."

"All ex-football players have bad knees. Even the young ones."

"So you must have had yours for years."

The light made bright circles in the dark recesses of the cabinet.

"Did you know that when you say 'must've' it sounds like 'mustard'?"

"You know, Sam, you are the only person who tells me things like that. Thanks for being a friend."

Sam squinted, looking inside the cabinet. "Is this doing anything for you? Because it's not doing anything for me."

"Okay, see that?"

"See what?"

He was close enough to kiss and he had that little smile that Sonora didn't see very often, and the tone of voice he'd used to say "see what" was without a doubt flirty.

Her voice, worldly wise and jaded, came back to haunt her, and she had a mental image of herself, preaching to young Sanders, about how she had taken the cure and was henceforth no longer interested in married men.

She wondered if there was some universal force that got set in motion to make people eat crow when they made noble pronouncements.

"There, Sam. In the scum, by the Comet."

"I . . . Sonora, I think it's a clue."

"Pull me the hell up off of this floor and I'll explain it to you." She held up her hands.

Sam stood up, bent over her. He still had that smile. "What will you give me, if I do?"

"Anything you want."

"Yeah, I heard that about you."

She shoved him out of her way. Wondered if he knew he'd just missed being kissed by an expert. "Okay, here's the deal. See, under the sink, the clear spot? Something's missing."

"For one thing, there aren't any sponges."

"What?"

"No sponges, no cleaning rags. See, look in that bucket. Plastic gloves and a toilet brush. No sponges. Where are they? Because somebody's gone over this place, and they had to use something."

"Used the sponges to clean up something nasty, like blood and guts and bits of bone?"

"Eye of newt." Sam lowered his voice. "So that's the big clue, Sonora? Empty spot under the sink?"

"The big clue is a tab from a box of garbage bags that were bought in Cincinnati."

"Lawn and Leaf? Brown? Like we found her in?"

Sonora nodded.

"Millions of them out there."

"We need to find the box. Match the one we found to the roll."

"Yeah, plus we need to find a murder weapon and walk on water. All in a day's work."

"Remind me to stick a gold star on your forehead."

Sam looked at the carpet. "Okay, you think Caplan was up to no good, right here in the in-laws' cabin. Let's run with it. Where's the vacuum cleaner? Might be interesting to burrow into the bag."

"Being a cop means never having to say you're normal. Let's try the closet."

"First one finds it buys lunch."

Sonora headed toward the stairs that led to a loft. There was a closet in the pocket of space beneath. She put her hand on the knob, then looked at Sam over her shoulder.

"Wait a minute. *First* one finds it buys lunch?"

He grinned.

She opened the door and looked inside. "Extra blankets, a humongous jar of banana peppers."

"Banana peppers? You liar." He was there, looking over her shoulder. "Banana peppers. One of those things you buy at Sam's Club when you start getting carried away."

"But no vacuum cleaner."

They checked upstairs. Found a loft bedroom that had a pine dresser with coloring books and crayons, and a little girl's swimsuit hanging in a genuine cedar closet. A comfy red quilt was spread across a double bed, but no vacuum cleaner.

Sonora peered out through the bedroom window. The lake looked green and clean, shocks of sunlight bouncing off sedate ripples. It was a good deal cleaner than the Clinch River, where they'd found Julia Winchell's remains.

Sonora wondered where the rest of her was. Were there arms and legs, discarded by the side of the road, awaiting discovery? Had they been carried away by animals?

Where was the torso?

"What you looking at?" Sam said.

"Boathouse, or toolshed. Some kind of thing."

He looked over her shoulder through the blinds.

The toolshed was up the slope from the muddy edge of the water, about a hundred yards from a wood picnic table that bordered the tree line on the left side of the property. It was the kind of inexpensive storage shed you could buy at Sears and put together in an afternoon, the kind where you stored your lawn mower and grill.

Sam squinted. "Can't tell from here, but looks like a combination lock on that door. I'm sure Grey will let us take a look. Think there might be a vacuum cleaner in there?"

"God knows. Make sure Grey doesn't follow us down there."

"I wasn't planning to. Don't backseat cop, Sonora."

46

A fly buzzed Sonora's head as she picked her way down the muddy path that led to the storage shed. She listened for the telltale hum of a swarm, but heard nothing out of the ordinary. A breeze blew in off the river.

No body parts, she decided, trying not to feel disappointed.

Sam was muttering. "Eight, twenty-six, four. Eight, twenty-six, four. Eight—"

"Why don't you write it on the palm of your hand."

"Hush."

The door on the shed was bowed in so that Sonora could see the particleboard flooring—beige with an overlay of grime. Red rust flaked on the door hinges. Sam worked the combination lock, fingers thick and graceless. The lock clicked open. He glanced at Sonora over his shoulder.

"Drumroll right about now."

"Ta da, Sam."

The door stuck when he shoved it, but he put his shoulder into it and it slid out of the way, a metallic squeal heralding progress.

It was dark inside. Sonora smelled oil, dust, with lake water and mud overtones. No odor of sweat putridity, no swarm of flies or maggots, tattletales of gore. Sam had the large black Maglite, cop issue, and he held it high over his shoulder, as they'd been taught to do years ago.

There was a sawhorse on the right, dirty and faded beach towels hanging over one end, an old six horsepower boat engine mounted on the other side with a vise clamp. The engine looked dry and rusty, crud fouling the propeller. A dark spot on the floor beneath had dried raisin-black years ago.

"Oil," Sam said, catching Sonora's look.

A bottle of Clorox sat to one side of the sawhorse, snug to the right-hand side by the wall. A stack of inner tubes was piled in the left-hand corner, some of them partially inflated. Cecil the Sea Horse, a pair of pink water wings, an orange ring, a purple life vest that had seen better days, and a Mae West that looked like it had been run over with a truck. A red tube-shaped bicycle pump was hung on the left wall, along with a rack of tools. Back in the left corner, behind the vests and water toys, was a red upright Eureka.

Sonora pointed.

Sam grimaced. "If he did bring her here, that bag will be a gold mine. All it takes is some hair. Carpet fiber from the car. Blood traces."

Sonora went in careful, on the lookout for spiders. "You can't vacuum up bloodstains, Sam."

She pulled rubber gloves on, studied the Eureka. POWERLINE was written down one side in black; 9.5 AMPS.

"Canisters work better than uprights when it comes to dust mites," Sam said.

"When it comes to dust mites, I'll call you."

"They're all around you, Sonora."

"Vacuum cleaners?"

"Dust mites."

It was hot and close in the shed. Sweat ran down Sonora's back. She smelled hot metal. She was tired and annoyed. She was never at her best in the heat.

She popped the hard-shell front of the Eureka. "*Yes.*"

Sam squatted next to her. "I don't know about you, girl, but I never thought I'd be this happy over the contents of a vacuum cleaner bag."

"Face facts, Sam, it's a glamorous job."

Sam shone the light along the floor. "Look what else."

"Toolbox!" It was black plastic, from Sears. Sonora bent down and flipped the latch. "What you want to bet there's a hacksaw in there?"

"If there is, I'll start believing in the Fairy Godmother of Evidence."

Sonora used a gloved finger to poke through socket wrenches, pliers, a hammer. She lifted the top tray and looked into the bottom of the box. She tilted her head to where she could see Sam.

"Bring the light over, and get ready to clap for Tinkerbell."

"Why?"

"Hacksaw. Right here, in the bottom of the box."

47

They took the toolbox outside to the picnic table to get a better look. Sonora squinted, tripping on the path. The sun was high and bright and it took a long minute for her eyes to adjust after the darkness of the storage shed. The picnic table was well shaded. It felt good to stand in the shade and feel the breeze coming up off the water.

Sam laid the top tray to one side. Picked up the hacksaw with a gloved right hand. His left was bare.

"Why are you wearing one glove?" Sonora asked.

"Don't need but one."

A boat went by on the lake—the boat looked as if it had been painted with blue glitter and it looked new. The man driving wore a red life vest and white swim trunks. He waved at Sonora. Even as far away as she was from the water's edge, Sonora could see he was very tan.

Her girlfriends were always complaining that they did not know where the men were. Maybe they were all at the lake.

Sam held up the hacksaw. "This thing looks new, it's so clean."

"Paint's cracked all along the handle. Sam, it's not new."

"Most of these tools are a sorry mess. Look at the claw end of the hammer."

Sonora looked. Dried mud and a tangle of grass were caught between the two metal prongs. She thought about what Caplan might have cleaned the hacksaw with, remembered the Clorox bottle in the tool shed, the smell in the cabin kitchen.

"Okay, Sonora, you got that shit-or-go-blind-look, so what's in your head?"

"Clorox."

"Say again?"

"There was a bottle of Clorox under the hobby horse in the shed."

"Hobby horse? What hobby horse?"

"On the left-hand side."

Sam walked back to the shed, looked inside. "*Saw*horse, Sonora."

"Did you see the Clorox?"

"Yeah. Think he used it to clean the saw?"

"That's the smell I noticed when we first went inside the cabin. I smelled it in the living room and in the kitchen. And that place under the sink that's cleared out? I bet that's where it used to be."

"Bleach. To clean up."

"Look at the rest of his stuff." Sonora pointed to the toolbox. "Everything an oily, dirty mess."

"Just one notable exception."

"That vacuum cleaner bag pans out, Sam, we could make half a casebook on that alone." Sonora sat on the edge of the table, looked out at the lake. The water was blue-green and lazy. "He strangles her in the car, and brings her here, where he gets his private time, undisturbed."

"Think we can nail the guy with stuff from a box of garbage bags, a clean hacksaw, and one vacuum cleaner bag?"

Sonora gave Sam a lopsided smile. "Caplan could probably pull it off."

48

There was a kid sitting on the hood of Grey and Dorrie Ainsley's blue Chrysler. He looked to be about seventeen, but he had the wide-eyed stare of a child. He was eating mandarin oranges out of a can with his fingers. A yellow striped sweat bee darted in and around the lip of the open can.

It landed on his index finger and he did not notice it till he brought it close to his mouth. He screamed, threw down the can, and scooted off the car, bare legs squeaking across the metal.

He began to cry.

"*Bees.*" He rubbed the back of his legs, which were red from where they'd been sweat-stuck to the hood of the car.

Grey put a hand on the boy's shoulder. "Bee's gone, Vernon. It's okay now."

Sam had set the toolbox down, ready to go to the rescue. He picked it up again. They had put the hacksaw back inside, and latched it securely.

Grey lowered his voice. "This is Vernon Masterson. His family has that mobile home we saw on the way up, the double-wide. Vernon, these are the police officers I was telling you about."

"Hello, Vernon." Sam extended a hand.

"Go on and shake," Grey told the boy.

Vernon stuck out his left hand.

"Other one. 'Member how I told you."

"Other one." Vernon put the left hand behind his back and extended the right. "Shake?"

He and Sam shook hands. Vernon looked at Sonora. "Shake?"

"Absolutely."

His hand was sticky with mandarin orange juice. Tears had left tracks in the sweat-reddened cheeks. His white Hanes tee was oversized and his cut-off shorts went to his knees; he wore red flip-flops and there was a dirty Band-Aid on his left big toe.

"You catch bad guys. Grey told me."

Grey was picking up the mandarin orange can. Vernon held his hand out.

"No, Vernon, I better throw this away. It's dirty."

"Mama says I can have as many of the mandarin oranges as I want because of no fat." He kept his hand out.

"Yeah, but these have been on the ground, Vernon, so they're dirty."

"Dirty."

"That's right. You wouldn't want them."

"No, I wouldn't want them."

Sonora thought of her own two children, healthy and bright.

Vernon's hair was cropped close in a crew cut, and the stubble was blond. He had a heavy case of acne. His eyes were brown and soft-looking, like a deer's. He smiled at Sonora. That was what was charming about him, she thought. A teenager who smiled.

"You catch criminals, too?" he asked.

"Only the ones that don't run too fast."

He grinned and thumped his nose. "I run really fast. Celly says so." One of his front teeth was crooked. "And Mr. Gage puts criminals in jail."

Grey secured the lid on a metal garbage can, fitting it snugly over the lip. "Gage and Vernon are big buddies."

Vernon held his hands wide. "Big buddies. We go fish and do trains. He's not putting me in no jail because I'm good. If I'm not good, he would have to turn me in because of the job. *Even* friends."

"You like to fish?" Sam asked.

Vernon grinned hugely. "I like to get them and then throw them back. I like to see the splash."

"Well, there you are, Vernon, pestering people again." A girl came out of the trees, barefooted, smiling.

"Hey, Celly," Vernon said.

"Hey yourself."

He went to her like a dog to its master, and gave her a great big hug which she returned with absentminded enthusiasm. What could be seen of her legs was brown and slim, and an ankle bracelet glinted over her left foot. Sonora wondered if Julia Winchell had worn an ankle bracelet to set off the tattoo.

This girl wore a sleeveless jean jumper that hung calf length and looked lightweight and comfortable. Sonora had seen them for sale at The Limited. Her arms were tan and muscular, and she had a scoop-necked baby tee, in a soft powder pink, underneath the jumper. A gold, heart-shaped locket hung around her neck.

Her hair looked freshly washed and shiny—a professionally highlighted light brown. Her toenails were painted a shell-shimmery pink that coordinated with the baby tee. When she got close, Sonora could smell that unisex perfume that they gave out in samples in all the major department stores.

She looked at them all, smiling in an absent, friendly way, then she looked behind them and frowned.

"Gage around?" she asked.

The voice was high and girlish and Sonora revised her estimation of the age. Fifteen or sixteen. She could pass for twenty. She and the boy were no more than a year apart.

Brother and sister, Sonora decided, studying the kids' faces.

Sweat was beginning to work its way through the girl's makeup. She looked hopefully at the cabin.

Sonora, watching Celly, realized she had this sort of thing to look forward to in a few years with Heather.

"Gage isn't here," Grey said.

"Oh. Well. I mainly came over to make sure Vernon wasn't pestering nobody." Celly turned to leave, but Sam stopped her by putting out a hand to shake.

"Detective Delarosa. Cincinnati Police Department."

Her eyes got large and interested, and as she shook Sam's hand, her air of disappointment dimmed.

"Celly Masterson."

Sam clapped a hand on Vernon's shoulder.

"This is your brother?"

"Yes sir."

Sonora caught Sam's look at being relegated with one well-placed "sir" to the legion of the old, and she grinned and tried to catch his eye.

He ignored her. "You know Mr. Caplan?"

Celly nodded, unable to contain the enthusiasm, and the warm look which immediately gave her away.

"When's the last time you saw him?"

She moved closer to Vernon, arms tight by her side. "Is something wrong?"

Sam smiled at her. "Why would you think that?"

"I don't know."

Grey was watching her. Dorrie rolled the car window down, turned off the engine.

Everyone seemed to sigh. Sonora realized how annoying the engine noises had been, now that they were gone. A large bird flew overhead.

"Osprey!" Vernon jumped and pointed.

Everyone looked except Sonora. The tension that had suddenly sprung up began to ease. Dorrie waved at the girl.

"How's your mama, Celly?"

"She's fine. Working herself to death."

"Heard from your dad?"

"Nope."

Only in the South, Sonora thought, would it seem perfectly natural to interrupt a police investigation with neighborly chitchat.

But Dorrie was setting the girl at ease and establishing adult control, so she kept her mouth shut and waited.

Grey folded his arms and leaned back against the car. "You were up, weren't you, last time Gage and Collie brought Mia down to swim?"

"The cookout? Yeah. When Gage put that barbecue sauce he made up on all the burgers."

"They was good," Vernon said. Then he frowned. "Mama said for me not to bother you folks."

"You're a buddy, not a bother," Grey said.

Sonora looked at Celly. "You see him since? I think he was down one night, a couple of weeks ago." She watched the girl, thinking she might lie.

"If he was here, I didn't see him." Frowning. Puzzled.

The girl had acquired a wary look.

"You see him, Vernon?" Sam asked, looking at the boy.

Vernon shook his head. "*No* sir. But if he come up

after dark, I wouldn't of, 'cause I go to bed every night at nine o'clock. Nine o'clock is later in the winter. In the summer it's a kid bedtime, 'cause outside it's still light. But I need to go on to bed because of my medicine routine." He looked at Sam with apology. "I may be seventeen, but I am still a kid."

Sam clicked off his recorder.

Celly sighed and tugged Vernon's T-shirt. "We better get on home. Nice seeing you all." She glanced at Dorrie. "How is Mrs. Caplan doing? She had that baby yet?"

"Baby hasn't dropped yet, Celly, so I say we got another six to eight weeks."

"Tell her I said hey."

Celly turned away but not before Sonora saw the wistful look that passed across her face. She knew exactly what the girl was thinking—that to be Mrs. Gage Caplan, and pregnant with his child, would be close to heaven on earth.

Not an analogy that came readily to Sonora's mind.

The boy and girl headed off, Vernon plucking at Celly's dress and talking nonstop, she not paying any attention. Sonora wondered if her feet hurt, going barefooted like that.

Grey waited till they were out of earshot, then inclined his head toward the toolbox. "Find something?"

Sam grimaced. "Hate to leave you without your toolbox, but—"

"That's not mine, it's Gage's. I don't give a hoot in hell what you do with it."

"You identify it for certain as belonging to him?" Sonora had the recorder going, but they'd used it enough with the Ainsleys that it had become nothing more than background.

"Hell, you think I keep my own tools crapped up like that?"

Dorrie leaned out the window. "Grey, simmer down." She glanced at Sam. "He keeps his tools neat and put away. His mother always told me he never even broke his crayons when he was little. He's as picky as they come." She leaned out the window, pushed his hip playfully. "Probably do you good to break a crayon once in a while."

"I don't think it's *picky* for a man to keep his tools in order." His shoulders were stiff. "A man who can't keep his tools in order is a sorry kind of a fella, if you don't mind me saying."

Another strike against the son-in-law from hell, Sonora thought.

"His initials are right here." Grey headed toward the picnic table, pointing. "Spent a fortune on the box, and next to nothing on what's inside. And everything inside a tangled-up dirty mess. I hate lending him tools, because he never cleans anything up. "

Except for the hacksaw, bleached clean, likely with that bottle of Clorox, Sonora thought. She'd take that along, too.

Sonora had been aware of the crunch of gravel beneath tires, and she was just turning to take a look when she heard Grey's intake of breath, saw Dorrie go white and clutch his arm.

Sam said "son of a bitch" under his breath.

On some subconscious level, she must have known what to expect, because when she turned and saw the red Cherokee Jeep Laredo with Gage Caplan behind the wheel, she did not feel surprised.

49

Gage nosed the Jeep right behind Grey and Dorrie's Chrysler, blocking them in. He shut the engine off, got out of the car.

He had a big grin, dark sunglasses.

His suit coat had been draped over the headrest on the passenger's seat up front. His tie was loose, the cuffs on the navy pinstriped shirt rolled back.

"Hello, Mama. Grey." He walked to the Chrysler, a man in no hurry, leaned down and brushed Dorrie Ainsley's left cheek with his lips.

Grey stumbled forward to shake his hand.

The Ainsleys looked older, all of a sudden. Beside them, Caplan seemed to reek of strength and robust health.

"Detective Blair . . . and you must be Delarosa. I don't believe we've had the pleasure."

Sonora looked at Sam. He had a faint smile on his face.

"Yeah, I'm Delarosa. You're Caplan, that right?"

They shook hands, like boxers anticipating a grudge match, neither one of them in a hurry.

"Detective Blair, I have to say I'm surprised to find you here."

"Why do I doubt that, Mr. Caplan?"

"I don't know, Detective, why *do* you doubt it?"

She wondered how he'd known. The Ainsleys could

have called, but one look at Dorrie's white face put that one to rest.

Molliter? Was he Caplan's conduit into the investigation?

Somebody was.

Caplan had a smug smile. "I just came by to see my in-laws."

"Just happened to be in the area, a four-hour drive from home?"

Caplan shook his head. "If you'd swallow that one, you wouldn't be much of a cop, now would you, Blair? I'm here to make plans with Dorrie and Grey for a surprise baby shower for my wife. I'm bringing her down in a couple of days, and I thought it would be fun to surprise her." He smiled at Dorrie. "Isn't that right, Mama?"

Dorrie swallowed. Looked at Sonora, then back to Caplan. "That's fine with me."

"Don't whisper, Mama. People can't hear you when you whisper. Grey will have to turn up his hearing aid."

Grey folded his arms. "I can hear her fine. If you can't, Gage, that's your problem."

Caplan gave him a lazy look, no more than a flick of the eyes. "Detective Blair, I see you've collected a few goodies. If I'm not mistaken, that's my toolbox your partner is holding."

Sonora saw Sam's hand move, saw that he'd clicked the tape recorder on.

"Sam, set the toolbox back down on the picnic table there. Let's let Mr. Caplan make absolutely sure that these are his tools." Sonora smiled at Caplan. Waved a hand toward the picnic table.

Caplan returned the smile. Patient, waiting. Sonora watched him. Was he making mistakes? Was she making mistakes?

He knew the hacksaw was clean. And he knew Grey and Dorrie would have already identified the toolbox. He had nothing to lose here.

Why was he there? she wondered. It told them immediately that he had an "in" to their investigation. Why show his hand? What did it buy him?

Caplan went to the picnic table, opened the box of tools. "Yes sir, Detective Delarosa, this belongs to me."

Sam pointed to the hacksaw. "This yours, too?"

"Yes sir, it is." Caplan smiled slowly. "What were you planning to do with my tools, if I may ask? And . . . is that a vacuum cleaner bag?" He looked over his shoulder at Dorrie. "Late on the spring cleaning this year?"

Sonora cocked her head to one side. "Now don't tell me, Caplan, the vacuum cleaner bag belongs to you, too?"

Caplan looked at his in-laws. "Folks, both of these detectives are out of their jurisdiction. Did they show you any kind of a search warrant? Any paperwork at all?"

Grey was still.

"Folks?" Caplan's voice had acquired an edge.

Dorrie Ainsley said no, very softly.

Caplan shook his head at Sonora. "Detective, you must know better than this. You're miles out of jurisdiction, two whole states away. You're collecting evidence from a private residence without a proper search warrant. Even a man's trash has protection under the law. You can't come in and carry these off without taking a big risk that everything you've got here will get thrown right out of court." He looked over his shoulder at Dorrie and Grey. "This is the kind of sloppy police work that makes my job so difficult."

"We've got permission," Sonora said. She looked at Dorrie. Back me up, she thought.

Caplan shook his head slowly. "I don't think so. Not for a minute."

Sonora watched Dorrie Ainsley. Saw the struggle.

"They already have my permission, Gage."

Grey sighed softly, looked his son-in-law eye to eye. "We felt sure you would want us to cooperate with the police. You're kind of on the same side, aren't you, Gage?"

Caplan gave him a gentle smile. "I'm sure the both of you are doing what you feel you have to do, and whatever happens, happens." He put his hands in his pockets. "In a way, you know, I admire you, both of you. I always have."

Caplan's shoulders sagged, just a little. But Sonora looked into his eyes, and knew that inside, Caplan was smiling.

50

Sonora did not know what had woken her up. In her mind she could hear Dorrie Ainsley, telling her that Collie and Gage would be taking the boat out. She wondered if Collie was a good swimmer. If she wore a life vest out on the lake.

How well did a woman swim when she was seven months pregnant?

Sonora turned onto her side. Decided she could not think until she went to the bathroom, so she did that, then got back in bed, stopping to get her blue quilt out of the closet.

She propped up her pillows, made the bed up, except for the spread, and curled up in the quilt to keep off the chill of the air conditioner.

It often happened this way, a moment of complete mental clarity just as she was waking up, where she was able to look at things practically, unemotionally, objectively. Able to tell if she was denying a problem, or making one out of nothing.

This felt like a problem.

Collie Caplan lived with Gage Caplan every single day. She was alive and well. She had not asked for protection.

And maybe, after what had happened down at the cabin with the Ainsleys, the lake trip would be called off.

There was nothing Sonora could do but close her eyes and go back to sleep, so she could be rested and brilliant enough to catch Caplan before he did it again.

The doorbell rang, and Clampett leaped up with a combination bark and howl that brought the hair up along the back of Sonora's neck. She reached for the pair of sweats she'd left in a wad on the floor by her bed, glanced at the clock: 5:40 A.M.

What the hell.

It was still dark out. Clampett stayed by her leg, barking, his ruff standing in a ridge on his back. Sonora looked out the side window by the front door.

A sheriff's car was parked in front of the house, headlights blazing into the darkness. A pudgy blonde with a ponytail and a uniform that likely caused pain when she bent over waited patiently at the door.

Sonora unlocked the dead bolt. She did not like the woman and she did not like her smirk. "What is this?"

"Are you Sonora Blair?"

"What's going on here?"

"You're Blair."

Some instinct warned her. "No, you've got the wrong house."

"The hell I do." The woman tossed an envelope on the porch. "You've been served."

Clampett growled. Sonora seriously considered letting him out in the yard to play.

51

Sonora met Sam in the parking lot of the Hilton Hotel. He was standing by the Taurus, looking at his watch. "I see you got my message."

Sonora locked up the Blazer. "To meet you here? Good guess, Detective. Where the hell you been all day."

"In court."

"Court? For what?"

"The Deaver hit."

"You didn't have anything to do with that case."

"No kidding? I still got subpoenaed at six o'clock this morning, said I had to be in court at eight."

"They came to my place first."

"I wondered."

"Bitchy blonde with hips?"

"That's the one."

"I didn't have to appear until one. Crick got it quashed."

"*Somebody's* got prosecutoritis."

"Let him play, Sam. That much sweeter when we jump his ass." She followed him across the parking lot. "So why are we here, baby, you get us a room?"

He smiled in a way that let her know the thought had crossed his mind. "Thought we might have a talk with Caplan's Aunt Georgie. Get some background on the bastard, I believe were Crick's exact words. Look for a sweet spot."

"Anything to get out of the heat."

"Got *yours* quashed, did you?" Sam waved her forward, through the automatic door into the lobby of the Hilton. A bellboy looked at them, inquiring.

"Where's Suite A, the Alabama Room?" Sam asked.

Sonora shivered. It was ice cold in the lobby.

The bellboy gave a knowing look. "You're here for the Babylon Models Internacionale?" He eyed Sam's suit and haircut. Looked Sonora up and down.

"I don't think so," Sam said.

"They're the ones who booked the Alabama Room," the bellboy said.

Sonora shrugged. "I guess that's who we want then."

She headed in the direction the bellboy pointed— around a fountain and huge potted plants and a gift shop that sold toothpaste for over three dollars per tiny tube.

"Not you," Sonora said, leading the way.

The doors to the Alabama Room were propped open. A blonde in a black power suit stood next to a table, arguing with a man in a brown corduroy jacket. His hair was cut a la *GQ*, and he had the careful beard stubble Don Johnson made popular in the old *Miami Vice* television series.

"I did the last one," the man said. "Why won't you take this one?"

The woman shook her head. Her lips were pressed tight. "Not in my contract."

"But why? You shy or something?"

She shook her head, glanced at the clipboard.

The man caught sight of Sonora, flashed a smile as reassuring as a shark fin in the water. "Are you here for the seminar?"

She glanced into the Alabama Room. A coffee urn was set up on a table at one end of the room. Metal folding chairs were placed in front of a dais that was bracketed by a table and chairs on either side. A video was playing on a television at the front of the room—forgettable music with a driving beat and some kind of fashion show where thin girls were gliding down the runway with plastic fruit on their heads.

"We're looking for Georgie Fontaine," Sam said.

"Go on in and sit down," the man said. "She'll be along after the talk."

"What talk?" Sam's voice was rougher than usual.

Probably suspicious of men who wore corduroy in the dead of summer. Sonora peered into the Alabama Room, where an aura of nervous hope and expectation was as thick as the smell of coffee in the corner. Most of the metal chairs were full, girls of all ages with their moms beside them. There were a few lone males, most of them in their teens or early twenties.

Everyone was dressed up. Little girls had their hair piled on their heads, teenage girls had curled and moussed enough for a Vidal Sassoon convention. They all studied each other out of the corners of their eyes, like contestants in a Miss America competition.

Sonora looked at Sam, saw he'd have no chance at Miss Congeniality if he kept that scowl on his face.

"What is this, anyway?" she said.

Corduroy jacket didn't like her question. "Aren't you here for the seminar?" he asked. "If you'll fill out this form—"

Sonora ignored the pencil and clipboard he tried to hand her and flipped her ID. "Police Specialist Blair, Cincinnati Police. We're here to see Georgie Fontaine, and would appreciate it if you'd track her down."

Corduroy jacket had gone very wary, but the blonde was paying attention. She pointed off to the right.

"Headed that way for a smoke."

"Thanks," Sonora said.

Sam followed, head swiveling to give the blonde a second look. A dark hallway veered off to the left. Sonora smelled cigarette smoke, saw a sign that said REST ROOMS. She looked into the dark corridor, saw a woman leaning up against the wall, inhaling from a cigarette as if it was the sustenance of her life.

"Georgie Fontaine?"

"Who wants to know?" The voice held the deep husk of a veteran smoker, the self-confident amusement of a jaded woman of the world, and a hint of curiosity. "You guys aren't the cops I talked to, are you?"

Sam walked over to the wall the woman had propped a very nice shoe against, and showed her his ID. "Detective Delarosa," he waved a hand at Sonora, "and Detective Blair."

"Hell, you are the cops. Sorry. I had to get away from the youngsters, they've been bitching at each other all day. Should have retired when I had the chance."

"Could we go somewhere and talk?" Sonora asked.

"Let's get some coffee in that little sports bar by the gift shop." She glanced at Sonora. "Duncan should be giving his spiel by now. He talks slow, they won't need me for a while. Unless he's got the girl doing it." She peered around the corner, as if reluctant to show herself.

"It's not in her contract," Sam said.

The crowd in the sports bar was thin. The air was filled with stale cigarette smoke. All of the tables were sticky with beer rings and crumbs, and wadded napkins constituted most of the table decorations. No doubt the night before had been a big success.

A bartender moved slowly on legs like jelly, wiping glasses dry. He did not seem happy to see them.

Georgie Fontaine took the cleanest table in the far left corner of the room, away from a noisy group of men wearing the kelly green pants and knit shirts that proclaimed golfers. There were four of them, two were smoking. They drank beer and Beefeater martinis and watched the tournament on television. Sonora's head began to ache.

She took the seat at the table facing the television, because she knew that if Sam could see it he would watch it, no matter what was on. A smattering of applause broke out from the large screen as a man with a potbelly made a difficult shot, and the announcer spoke with the kind of muted enthusiasm used by disc jockeys at classical radio stations.

Sonora put her elbows on the table, felt water soaking through the sleeve of her blouse.

Sam had his recorder out, and Georgie Fontaine was reeling off her name, address, and serial number. Age sixty-two.

"Not possible," Sam said.

"What isn't possible, sweetie?"

"I couldn't have heard that right. You're forty-two."

"This is what sixty-two looks like in the nineties." But she smiled at him tolerantly, as she would at a son.

"Just for the record," Sonora said. "Gage Caplan is your nephew."

Fontaine lit up another cigarette, took a quick puff. "Only one I got. Rest are nieces, I have three of those. Easier to buy for at Christmas."

"Are you and Gage close?" Sonora said.

Fontaine's eyes narrowed.

Could be from the smoke, Sonora thought. But she wondered.

"Never see him."

"Why is that?" Sam asked.

She waved a hand. "I work long hours. He works long hours. He's done very well. I'm proud of him." She did sound proud. Surprised, too.

"You see much of your nieces?"

Fontaine rolled her eyes. "All the time." It sounded like a complaint but she smiled fondly. "Baby-sit their kids when I have some time, which isn't all that often."

She took another drag on the cigarette, glanced over at the bartender. He avoided looking at their table.

"See much of Mia?" Sam asked.

Fontaine thought about it. "I saw her once at some Christmas thing. It was right after her mother died, and Gage was kind of at loose ends. Poor baby, I never saw a kid look so tiny and lost. She cried a lot, asking for grandmama. The other one, Gage's mom, is dead. I remember wondering why he didn't have her down with Micah's folks for Christmas—I think they live in the hills or something. Tennessee or Virginia."

"Kentucky," Sonora said.

"Whatever."

Sam grimaced but did not say a word. Sonora wondered how often Mia had asked for her grandmother, wondered if she'd learned not to ask.

"You said Gage's mother is dead?" Sam asked.

Fontaine nodded. "Very tragic. Gage was just a little guy when it happened, six, I think, if that old. I think he was in kindergarten. Kimmie was maybe seven months pregnant. She'd miscarried once and was trying like crazy to have another child."

"She was your sister?"

Fontaine shook her head, waved away a cloud of smoke. "No, my sister has all the girls. My brother married Kimmie when Gage was four or five. Her first husband just ran off and left them. They were living in the projects and really going it hard. Alex was very comfortable, financially, my parents had money and, you know, they gave us a very nice life. Got us started when we left college, then left us alone. We both went into business—me into modeling, then running this modeling school. Alex went into law. Specializing in bankruptcy. Consider the last decade or two. He sure hit the right specialty. And loves it. Believe it or not, people need a white knight when they're going bankrupt. Creditors get mean if you don't yank their leash, and if people don't know the law they aren't protected. I know he does a lot of work out of pocket. Which he can do, thanks to good old mom and dad."

She spoke of her brother with a great deal of fondness, Sonora thought. She spent a lot of time with her nieces. And yet had almost no contact with Gage. Interesting. Was it because he was not really family, the blood issue, or was it something else?

"What happened to your sister-in-law? How did she die?"

Fontaine's face settled into the worn grooves of old grief. She stubbed her cigarette out in a gold foil ashtray that was full of other butts, some lipstick-stained, at least two shades of red.

When Fontaine spoke, her voice was matter of fact. "She drowned in the bathtub."

52

Sam looked over at the bartender, who nodded and headed over. "How could she die in a bathtub? She epileptic? Pass out?"

Fontaine shook her head. The bartender stood next to Sam, a question in his eyes.

"Coffee," Sam said, pointing at himself and Sonora. He looked at Fontaine.

"Bring me a whisky sour." She blew a smoke ring, looked at the waiter. "And wipe the table, if you would, please." Fontaine moved a dirty glass to one side, and the bartender gave her a mournful look, as if he knew he should never have come over.

"Alex and Kimmie had this big ole house. Brand new, out in Indian Hills, land all around. It was a long drive for him to the office, but Kimmie had her heart set on living there. Gage went from the projects to this enormous house. And Kimmie was pregnant when they were married, and they lost the baby, tore them both all up to hell. I know it was hard on Gage. They had this nursery they put together—Kimmie never had anything, so she outfits her nursery with everything she ever wanted when her first was coming along."

Sonora nodded. "How did Gage feel about all of this?"

The bartender came back with a plastic tub. He put all the glasses in the tub, tossed the ashtray in on top, and wiped the table with a drippy rag, leaving a swath of wet beads for everyone to dodge.

"Drinks be right up," he said.

Sonora reached into her purse for a bottle of Advil.

Fontaine was thinking. "That's kind of hard to say. He didn't seem to not like Alex, but he didn't seem to like him either. Like Alex was part of the furniture. I know he was kind of clingy with Kimmie, I remember he used to watch her all the time. If she was in the room, Gage was always in touching distance. He was a smart kid. Ahead for his age. Coming out of a bad school, but still sharp.

"I know he kept asking why Kimmie didn't have all that baby stuff when he was born, and she kept trying to explain it was because of Alex. He never did seem to get it. He and Kimmie had this thing where he was the old baby, and this was the new baby. But instead of making him feel better, it seemed to make it worse. He was really . . . bothered. Kimmie and Alex talked about it, but they were so distracted, so in love and excited about the new baby. I know I was worried about Gage getting short shrift there, and I think Mom said something to Alex. But Kim was like a little girl in a fairy tale and I don't think her feet were touching ground. She and Alex were so obsessed with each other it was nauseating. We were all just kind of tolerating them till the 'honeymoon' cooled off. And then she lost the baby. And it was like their whole world went dark.

"They locked the nursery door and wouldn't let anyone go in there, and Alex took Kimmie off for a cruise and left Gage with my mother."

The drinks came. Fontaine sighed softly when she saw the whisky sour. The waiter left plastic cartons of cream and Sam took a drink of steaming black coffee and

stacked the creamers into a short and stocky white tower.
Sonora opened one, poured it into her coffee.

Fontaine snapped her fingers. "I almost forgot. I
brought pictures." She rummaged in her purse, a large,
shapeless leather purse that looked to have endless capac-
ity and was worn down and soft with age.

She took out an envelope with a breath mint stuck to
one side, opened the flap, removed a stack of prints. She
laid the pictures out in a row like a hand of solitaire and
she snapped them as she laid them down, just like you
might with playing cards. Sonora thought of Butch
Winchell, lining up pictures of Julia and her two baby
girls.

Fontaine pointed a fingernail coated with deep red
polish. "This one's cute."

Gage, age three, sat cross-legged in a dingy living
room. There was a television on behind him, and the kind
of couch people put out by the side of the road (or,
Sonora thought, in her living room). Gage's hair was long,
curly, and his face was round and full, cheeks chubby like
a Gerber baby. Even then he looked like a little line-
backer, thick sturdy legs, a solid build. He had a hand
crammed deep into a box of Cracker Jack's and there was
a piece of caramel corn on the front of his shirt. He was
smiling and happy and seemed not to have a care in the
world.

The row of pictures told the story. Gage and Kimmie,
together against the world. The team. Money very tight.
Gage's clothes all with the worn look of hand-me-downs.
Christmas trees with a few toys, some give-away coloring
books, the tiny boxes of crayons they gave away in restaurants. Sonora thought of Kimmie, hoarding those boxes so
her little boy would have more things to unwrap.

There were pictures of the new house—Kimmie

twirling in empty rooms, none of Gage here. Where had he been that day?

And pictures of the nursery. Pretty as a wedding cake, white and lacy and coordinated with hardwood cherry baby furniture—canopy crib, bassinet, a little reading nook with a bentwood rocker and a shelf full of brightly colored books.

"You say his mom drowned in the bathtub? Anything funny about it?" Sam asked.

Fontaine shook her head. "It was tragic, but it was an accident. They had one of those antiquey type tubs—large and deep with feet on it. Alex had it put in special for Kimmie. She'd been having a difficult time with the pregnancy. She had fainting spells. They think she ran the water really hot, and all the blood rushed to the surface of her skin, and she just . . . passed out. And drowned."

Sonora picked up one of the pictures, held it up. Not a very good shot. Someone had been trying to get the nursery from the hallway. The room was light, sun streaming in, but not centered, and half the shot was of dark hallway. Standing in the shadows, next to the bright sunny nursery, was little Gage Caplan.

A year had made quite a difference. The happy, care-free child was gone, if he'd ever really existed. Gage was looking at the camera and posing with a smile so earnest it was painful to see, knowing that the man or woman wielding the camera had probably not even been aware he was there.

Sonora flipped the picture over. Someone had written NURSERY in block letters on the back. Not NURSERY AND GAGE. Just NURSERY.

53

Sam pushed the swing door into the bullpen and let Sonora go ahead. "What about Caplan's current wife?"

"What about her?" Sonora said.

"I don't feel good about her situation. Pregnant. Living with a wife killer."

"Me either."

"Maybe we should talk to her. Drop a hint."

"Oh yeah. Meanwhile, Caplan will tear our heads off. Besides, I already did."

Sam stopped at the edge of the desk cluster. "I've seen ant hives look lazy compared to this."

Sanders was putting on her jacket.

"Lose another clown?" Sonora asked.

"We've got the killer."

Sam whistled. *Way* to go. What happened?"

"Caught the sucker red-handed." Gruber's voice, as he came in through the swing doors between the crime scene unit and homicide. His tie was loose, and there were circles under his eyes, but his step was light and he had that eager attitude cops get when they circle in for the kill. Sonora envied him. She wanted a warrant for the arrest of Gage Caplan and the same kind of feeling in her stomach.

"Thanks, Gruber, I was scared I might have to finish a sentence." Sanders tilted her head and peeped at him.

He grabbed his chest. "Direct hit, young Sanders."

"But what happened?" Sonora asked.

"One-armed Bobo in a dunking booth. We were out surveiling Indian Hills, and this guy hits? Only Bobo's waiting for him now. Got a handgun in his pocket—don't even take it out. Nails him through the jacket pocket as soon as he catches sight of the deer rifle. Good thing he got him with the first shot. Kick knocks him off the platform and into the water, and now his gun's with the fishes."

"Kill him?"

"No such luck. Winged, right arm, but to hear this guy squall you'd think he got repeatedly gutshot with an AK-47."

"What's he like?" Sam said.

Sanders narrowed her eyes. "Nebbishy. Skinny guy in cowboy boots and a concave chest."

Gruber was nodding. "Yeah, I noticed that first thing. Concave chest."

"Oh, shut up," Sanders said.

"Uniform is cuffing him, know what he's doing? Crying. Saying don't hurt me don't hurt me, get me a doctor. *Son* of a bitch. What a tough guy." He looked at Sanders. "Hospital's going to release him into our custody, we're going over to get him right now, if Sanders here's got her lipstick on straight."

"I borrowed yours," she said, eyes shiny.

Gruber glanced back at Sam and Sonora. "How's your thing coming along? 'Cause if you got time on your hands, you can, like, dust Interview One for us."

Sonora looked at Sam. "Is it my imagination, or is this man insensitive?"

Sam showed him a middle finger. "Dust this, babe. We got work. Where's Crick?"

"In his office celebrating, I'm sure." Gruber followed Sanders out the door.

Crick's door opened just as they got there. He did not look like he was celebrating. His gaze rested on Sonora and her knees went weak. The man did not look happy.

"There you are," he said. Mildly over the volcano. "Just the two I want. In my office."

He didn't have to add now. Sam exchanged looks with Sonora and they went inside. Sonora sat down without being asked because standing up was hard when Crick had that look on his face. Crick did not keep them waiting. He sat on the edge of his desk—too close and too big.

When he spoke, it was in a very steady tone. "I've had a call from the district attorney's office, and I want to get a few facts straight."

Sonora wondered how much trouble Caplan was going to cause. She'd just been to London, Kentucky to see his in-laws and commandeered his toolbox. For every action there is an equal and opposite reaction—that she had learned in grade school.

"Sonora. How often have you interviewed the counselor alone?" Crick watched her steadily. The cat-at-the-mouse-hole look.

The question did not sound good. Sonora frowned. "He was supposed to meet me at his house a few days ago, but didn't show. I talked to his wife—"

"You talked to his wife?"

"Yeah and—"

"Why?"

"Why *what*?"

Clearly, in his eyes, she could see he did not like her tone of voice. But she did not like being interrupted and cross-examined rudely when she was busting her ass on a case.

"Why did you go to his home and talk to his pregnant wife?"

"Why not?"

Crick looked at her. "Then what?"

"After I talked to his wife? He asked me to drive her to his office, and then he said he'd talk to me there."

"He asked you to come then? During his big victory celebration?"

Sonora leaned back in her chair. Wary. "Yeah. He did."

Crick looked at Sam. "What about you? Where were you?"

"I was running follow-up on this guy Barber, and the people who saw Julia Winchell at the conference."

"How come you two split up?"

Sam shrugged. "Just worked out that way."

"You're excused, Delarosa."

Sam looked at Sonora. He made no move to leave.

Crick did a double-take. "I said you're excused. Detective Blair and I have some private business to discuss."

Sam kept looking at her. Sonora nodded her head and he got up, squeezed her shoulder with his left hand, glanced back at Crick, and headed out.

"Close the door behind you," Crick said.

Sam shut the door firmly. Sonora put her hands in her lap.

Crick sighed. Rubbed a hand across his face. "District Attorney Caplan has had a talk with the lieutenant."

"I'm sure he has."

Crick raised an eyebrow. "Oh you are, are you? And why is that?"

"Because he's a killer. And he's a DA. And I'm going

to nail his ass, and he knows it. I'm just surprised it didn't happen sooner."

Crick leaned back, folded his arms. "That's not the nature of the complaint."

"What is the nature of the complaint? Sir?"

"Caplan says you've made unwelcome advances toward him, hounded his wife and family, including his mother- and father-in-law, and shown up in his office at times orchestrated to embarrass him."

"*What?*"

"Sit down, Blair. Caplan knows about what went on with the Selma Yorke thing last year. About your relationship with a family member of one of the victims. What he said, basically, was that you were at it again."

Sonora dug her fingernails into the palm of her hand. "Conceited, arrogant, son of a bitch."

"Is that all you've got to say?"

"You *know* what he's doing. You know Sam and I are getting floods of make-work requests from the DA's office, you know we've been subpoenaed to appear in court on cases we had nothing to do with. And. *How* did Caplan know I was at his in-laws'? We got a leak, sir, otherwise how could he have known?"

Crick laughed so hard it was a howl. "Got a leak to the prosecutor's office? No shit, I wonder who it could be. I can think of only fifty possibilities. And for that matter, how do you know his in-laws didn't call him?"

"I don't believe that, sir."

"What matters here is what I believe."

"Did you expect Caplan to take this sitting down?" Sonora clenched her jaw.

"I know Caplan is riding high since he nailed Drury. I know he gets along with almost every cop who's worked with him in court. I know he's got a lot of friends and a lot of influence."

"How about the cops that investigated the murder of his first wife? Did they get along with him, too?"

Crick didn't answer.

Sonora got up and walked out.

54

Sonora stopped by her desk long enough to kick the chair, then headed for the women's bathroom. The door was on a "slow hinge" and refused to slam. She ran water in the sink and splashed some on her face, aware, suddenly, that something was hanging from the mirror.

A jockstrap.

She had called this one wrong. She wondered what had made her think she could gross out male cops.

She snatched the jockstrap off the mirror, pulled the elastic back like a slingshot, and jettisoned it.

The bathroom door opened and Sam stuck his head in. "Girl, you in there?"

"Yeah?"

"Correct me if I'm wrong, but that was a male undergarment, wasn't it?"

"So?"

He came in carrying a chair, two Cokes, a package of peanut butter crackers. He jammed the chair up against the door, flipped the latch, and sat down.

"Privacy." He sighed, handed her a Coke and the package of crackers. "If your temper tantrum is over, why don't you tell me what's going on?"

"Crick just said that Caplan has put in a complaint about me coming on to him during questioning."

Sam did not look surprised. The office grapevine was in good working order, no duh. "You got your tapes, don't you?"

"All he has to say is I turned them off."

"He ain't got nothing. You're a good cop. Let your record stand."

Sonora looked at him. "Idiot. That's the problem."

"Oh hell. That Keaton Daniels thing."

He said Keaton's name like it was a disease.

"You never did like that guy," Sonora said.

"It's not that so much as it was a bad career move on your part."

"Tell me something I don't know."

He smiled at her. "Bitchy under pressure. One of the things I like about you, Sonora. You're not noble. In the South, women make martyrdom an art form."

"You have that Southerner's way of insulting me politely."

"Ingrained. But back to my point. It's a man's problem. See, what you want to do is emote and carry on and have long drawn out discussions on stuff like 'how could he' and 'what did I do to bring this on?' If you got a man's problem, use a man's solution."

Sonora unclenched her jaw. She wanted to say something about the emote and carry on remark, but wouldn't that mean she was emoting and carrying on?

"Just what is a man's solution? Shoot it? Flush it down the john?"

Sam shook his head at her. "Ignore it."

"Ignore it?"

"Yep. Then the ball's in their court. Then they got to put up or shut up, and you don't sit there and spin, which is what they want. Don't do that, girl. Just go on with your regular shit."

Sonora thought for a minute. "You know, Sam, I'm beginning to understand why men always get the upper hand."

55

Crick looked at Sonora, arms folded. He stood outside his office. "Sudden call of nature?" he asked her.

Sonora felt Sam at her back. "Yes sir."

"That's the only explanation I could come up with. I wouldn't want anybody who works for me thinking they can get up and leave because I say something they don't like."

"No sir."

Crick sat back down behind his desk. Started talking before they settled. "Not a damn thing in that vacuum cleaner bag, boys and girls."

Sonora sat down slowly, stared at Sam.

"I see by the way your mouths are hanging open, you expected otherwise." Crick snorted. "Did you really think he would use a cabin that belongs to his mother- and father-in-law? When he knows damn well they hate him?"

"That would make it all the better, as far as he's concerned," Sonora said.

"Nice theory, Blair, but it didn't pan out and he made an ass out of both of you. What we got now, boys and girls? We got the counselor, just nailed Jim Drury, and got a lot of good press and pats on the back. His first wife was murdered, heinously, but he's rebuilt his life. New wife, new baby, daughter he adores. He's made himself available to talk to you time and time again. You've been to see his wife, you've been to see his in-laws, you've talked to his step-aunt for crissakes. You make accusations and took physical evidence from a cabin where you suspect he dismembered a woman he says he never met. And guess what? It's clean. No blood, no hair, no nothing. Now the big vacuum cleaner coup is his trump card, not ours.

"The man's only crime is he owns a hacksaw. Guess how many men do? All you have is a tattooed dead woman who says she saw him kill somebody, and she can't testify, can she?" Crick placed his fingertips together. "So who in this office is ready to jump up and talk to a grand jury?" Crick put hand to his ear. "I'm listening, but I don't hear any volunteers."

"What about the rental car?" Sam said.

Crick nodded. "Okay, you're getting warmer, but you're a long way from hot. *Somebody* killed her, but you don't have Caplan's head in the noose. Mr. Caplan has declined to give us hair and blood samples, but we can get them, on down the road. The rental car could be a major screwup on his part. He's too smart to screw up so we figure he was short on time and took a calculated risk. Good. He can't have all the breaks, and we'll get something. We got soil samples, for one, which for reasons we cannot figure are similar to the residue on the shoes found at the scene of one of the Bobo killings."

Sonora leaned back. "Say what?"

Crick shrugged. "Don't ask, I can't for the life of me figure out the connection. But we will. Or rather, you will. And Caplan, through channels you understand, has made a very good observation. Which is that he's a long shot compared to Julia Winchell's husband and lover. Man has a point."

"Sir." Sonora did not like the pleading note in her

voice. She cleared her throat. "This hacksaw of Caplan's. It had been scoured clean with Clorox, even though all the other tools had accumulations of dirt and oil and rust. Why is it clean? Everything fits in for Caplan."

"Give me your theory, A to Z."

Sam shifted in his chair. "We think he killed her here, in Cincinnati, strangled her in the rental. Then put her in his car and carted her down to the cabin—okay, not the cabin, but somewhere. He cut her up with the hacksaw, put his little packages together, and cleaned up like a DA who prosecutes murders knows to clean up.

"Look at the geography—it fits him. The leg was found right outside of London on I-75 right before you get to Corbin. Another hour or two down the road is the Clinch River which flows through Clinton, Tennessee. He could have thrown that bag with the head, hands, and feet over from the interstate."

"Why go south? Why go out of his way?"

"Which would you do?" Sonora asked. "Throw body parts on a trail leading to your house, or on a trail leading to the husband of the woman you've just killed? Assuming you don't want to get caught?"

"Where's the rest of her? Arms, another leg, torso?"

"They may still be out there. Maybe they were carried off by animals."

"Maybe he kept some of her," Sonora said.

"Then he's got a lair," Crick said. "But it's not the cabin. Which leaves the rest of the world."

Sonora chewed a thumbnail.

Crick leaned back in his chair and closed his eyes. Sighed heavily and opened his eyes. "I made a phone call. Detective Owen Baylor. Know him?"

"His name was in the file. He handled the investigation into Micah's death," Sonora said.

"Yeah, he's retired now," said Crick. "Either of you talk to him?"

Sonora and Sam shook their heads.

"Yeah, I know, and he's miffed a little. Plenty enough to talk to you guys about Caplan, if you'd come around, that's how he put it. He thinks Caplan did her, Micah, thought so at the time. It went before a grand jury, but they didn't indict."

"Why not?" Sonora asked.

"Bad presentation?" Sam said.

"So Baylor says, and he was there. On the other hand, he thinks Caplan did it." Crick scratched his chin. "Caplan wasn't in the DA's office then. Baylor thinks that the prosecutor didn't think Caplan did it. Didn't feel like he could prove it anyway, and didn't want to go after the grieving husband unless he could really nail it down. He and Caplan seemed to hit it off. That didn't sit too well with Baylor, still doesn't. Anyway, they got to know each other. Caplan kept harping on about catching the killer who murdered his wife, and eventually applied to work as a DA. To put his grief to rest. He gets hired on, and surprise surprise, he does a helluva job."

"Experience will out," Sam said.

Crick narrowed his eyes. "The two of you. Both in agreement. You think Caplan did Winchell, you think he did his first wife?"

Sam nodded.

"Absolutely," Sonora said.

"Work from the other end awhile. The one depends on the other. So you get out there to the university, where Julia Winchell saw whatever it was she saw. And you walk it through. And you make it work, or you leave the guy alone and focus on somebody else. We clear?"

"Yes sir."

Crick stood up and his voice deepened. "Good. 'Cause I don't like assholes in the prosecutor's office playing games with my people. Rest assured there will be no more subpoenas. You better be right, and you better bring him in. I'm counting on you two to see I get the last laugh on this."

Sonora took a deep breath and scrambled out of Crick's office behind Sam. He leaned close and muttered in her ear, "It's not that I don't trust Crick, but if I see a sheriff's car in the front of the house, I'm not going to the door."

56

Sam leaned against the wall and Sonora sat in a metal folding chair. The man behind the desk was relaxed, not in any hurry. He had a mustache that was going gray, and wore the blue uniform shirt of campus security.

The office was tiny, desks and cabinets scarred and old, like the ones in the bullpen. Sonora wondered why it was a given that anyone who had anything to do with law enforcement got crappy office furniture.

She'd seen janitors with better accommodations.

The drawers in the filing cabinet had not been closed in years—much too full. Boxes of papers and forms and computer printouts were stacked chest-high in every corner, and the folders on top of the file cabinet were an exercise in balance.

A round metal trash can had been turned upside down so the security guard, P. Fletcher Hall, could use it as a footstool. Sonora wondered where they threw trash. Although it was possible, looking around the tiny office, that they kept it.

"That clock keep good time?" Sam asked.

"Yeah," Hall said, attention on the cabinet he was searching.

Sam grinned at Sonora. The clock was missing a minute hand.

The guard nodded his head. "Yep. Here it is. Thought he'd have it. Lieutenant don't throw nothing away." He read it first, while they waited, which irritated Sonora, then handed it across to Sam, which annoyed her again.

He seemed amused, mouth set smugly. "The girl was clearly a nutcase, unless it was one of those sorority things. She causing trouble?"

Sonora looked up. "That what the guy said in the report? Nutcase?"

Sam leaned over and showed her the acorn that had been drawn in the top right-hand corner of the form.

The call had been logged at 10:48 P.M. According to the security guard, Marsh, he'd been standing on the top of the concrete bridge that led from the fifth floor of the Braunstein Building, taking advantage from the let-up in rain for a smoke break, when a young woman who was later identified as Julia Hardin of Clinton, Tennessee, and a student at UC, had come tearing out of the fourth floor exit in a condition described as hysterical.

Marsh had watched her, alarmed. She was clearly in a panic, screaming for help. He had been about to call out when she spotted him. It was dark, but the embers of his cigarette were glowing, and there was light spillage from building security lights. She had run in circles for a moment, trying to find the outside staircase that led to the bridge, and was out of breath by the time she made it up.

Sonora knew who not to call in an emergency.

Marsh had clearly been suspicious of drug-induced hysteria. He had spent some time describing her physical appearance, including bloodshot eyes, and respiratory distress with a cough and a runny nose.

She had been crying and nearly incoherent. She had told him that a pregnant woman was being murdered in the women's bathroom on the third floor.

She had specified the third floor, which, in addition

to her appearance, had put him on guard. The third floor was a parking structure.

He led her back into the building and took the elevator to the third floor. When the elevator opened onto the parking structure, she had become hysterical, and in order to placate her, they had searched all of the women's bathrooms, working from the top down.

Nothing out of the ordinary was found.

She had settled on the fourth floor as where the alleged murder occurred, convinced by the presence of the Resource Room/Multimedia Lab and the mannequins in the fashion design classroom. But there had been nothing to see in the bathroom. No blood. A little water on the floor, but that could easily have been caused by a toilet overflowing.

He had questioned her carefully on drug use, but other than saying she had taken Contac for a sinus headache, she swore she was clean.

He had suggested taking her to a hospital emergency room, and at that point she had given up, except for insisting on an escort back to her dorm.

Sonora shook her head. No wonder Julia Winchell had never forgotten.

"Marsh still work here?" she asked.

"Dead two years ago, over Thanksgiving. Pancreatic cancer."

"We take this, or get a copy?" Sam asked.

"I guess I better make you a copy," Hall said. "Believe it or not, I let that out of here, lieutenant will know somehow it's gone."

Sonora took a last look at the office before she walked out, grateful that there were one or two places left in the bureaucracy that had not been computerized for efficiency. They'd never have found it otherwise.

57

Sam's pager went off while they were in the student center, looking for a place to pick up a sandwich. He headed to the bank of phones near the stairwell.

It was quiet inside, dark and cool. The lunch hour was long over and the fast food outlets were dark, locked behind metal grills. Midsummer, hot as hell in the late afternoon, very little activity.

Sam was making notes. Sonora sat on a bench and crossed her legs. Her jeans were getting looser. Had the weight-loss fairy finally come?

Sam hung the phone up, and sat down beside her on the bench, flipping open his notebook. "That was the maintenance supervisor, returning our call. Here's what we got. Braunstein Building stays open and unlocked twenty-four hours a day, people in and out at all hours. Classrooms, offices, and labs for biology, chemistry, fashion design, genetics, and biochemistry."

Sonora tapped the bench. "Sam, it's all falling into place."

"Just because the building's unlocked twenty-four hours a day doesn't prove he did it. If you think I'm going back into Crick's office with anything less than solid, you think again."

"All I'm saying is it shows opportunity. So far, so good."

"May as well forget lunch, everything's closed down.

Let's have at it." He flipped his notebook shut, stuck it in his pocket. "They got maps at the information counter."

The campus could not have been called crowded. The occasional students wore loose shorts, sandals, backpacks hanging off their shoulders. A few suits here and there—administrative types. No one else dressed like that in the heat. A background cacophony of jackhammers and beeping machinery kept a film of grit in the air. Construction workers in yellow hard hats were grimy with heat and sunburn.

Sam studied his map, stopped in front of the ground floor entrance to the Braunstein Building. A truck pulled up. Sonora saw Sam's mouth move. She waited till the truck, brakes squeaking, lumbered away.

"What'd you say?"

"I said she probably came in right here."

Sonora pointed. "Concrete bridge, right up there. Probably where she saw the security guard." Sonora tried to imagine the place at night, in the rain. "You really think she saw him in the dark?"

Sam scratched his chin, stepped off the curb, looked around. "Yeah, probably. There'd be lights on. She might even have noticed him as she went in. I'll buy it. Come on, let's find us some air-conditioning."

The double glass doors led into a foyer, dark tile, staircase to the left, and a drink machine glowing DIET PEPSI in the right-hand corner. Sam opened the metal doors on the right, like he knew what he was doing.

"I think we should go left," Sonora said.

"Are you serious? Go right, come on."

The metal doors slammed behind them, making an echo, like prison. The walls were beige, concrete block. Ugly mustard-yellow doors led into the FRESHMAN RESOURCE ROOM & MICROCOMPUTER LAB.

"See that?"

Sonora looked inside. Bookshelves, tables, plastic chairs. Study carrels, and to the left a computer lab. The room smelled old.

"It's where she left her purse," Sonora said. "I've got the weirdest feeling. Like she's right here beside us."

"It's the heat, girl. Fried your brain. Do us both a favor and don't mention things like that to Crick."

A girl in a study carrel looked up. Sonora and Sam ignored her. Police business. They left the lab and moved back into the hallway.

A door squeaked loudly and boomed shut, making what Sonora knew her son would call reverb. Their footsteps were loud. Sonora's Reeboks squeaked. The hall had a yellowed look, linoleum buffed over a heavy wax buildup. Big round clocks stuck out from the wall, like in elementary schools and hospital rooms. The minute hands jerked with the pulse of every second. The lighting, fluorescent and harsh, spilled squares of reflected light on the overwaxed floor.

Sam stopped at the floor directory, studied it for a minute, went left down the corridor. Voices echoed, Sonora could not place where. She imagined Julia Winchell, coming into the building from the dark, rain-swept campus. She would be drenched, her feet wet, sandals squeaking like Sonora's tennis shoes. She would pass the glowing drink machine, the metal doors would clang behind her, and she would stand, worried, in front of the resource room.

Her purse would be sitting on a desk, right where she had left it. She would take a minute and look inside—checking for the fifty dollars and the earrings from her sister. And they'd be there. She'd be relieved and happy. She would think that her ordeal was over.

"Here," Sam said. "Four-thirty-two. Micah Caplan's office. Her old office."

It belonged to somebody named Harry now. There was a cartoon on the door—an alligator, with the caption, "Trust me, I'm the boss." The paper was dirty and curling at the edges. Sonora wondered if it had been there eight years ago. She wondered if Micah had put it up.

She took two more steps, then stopped. "Sam, what floor are we on? I thought we were on the fourth floor."

"We are."

"Then how come that little black door has a three on it?"

He walked back toward her. Looked at the opposite wall. "You mean this?"

"How many other little black doors do you see?"

"It's a dumbwaiter."

"No kidding. It's still got a three over top, why is that?"

"You're worse than my kid, I don't know *everything*."

"Yeah, but wouldn't you think, if you saw a three over a door, that you were on the third floor? This is where she got confused. This is why Julia Winchell thought she was on the third floor."

"Don't go overboard, Sonora, it's not going to buy us a warrant."

"It's indicative, Sam."

"That I'll give you."

"Right before Julia heads into the ladies room and descends into hell, she sees this little black door with a three over it. Which explains why later, when she went for the security guard, she told him she was on the third floor."

"Which buys Caplan time to make off with the body. Another thing we're going to have to figure out." He headed back down the hallway. "Women's rest room, Sonora. The scene of the alleged crime."

Sonora stood outside the door. She was aware of a metallic background hum, as if they were close to a physical plant. Display cases lined the right-hand side of the wall, with printouts and faculty lists mounted under glass.

She wondered how it had sounded, the noises coming from the bathroom that night eight years ago. It was an odd, echoey building. People far away sounded close. You could hear voices and doors closing, and still not see a soul.

What had it been like for Julia Winchell, alone, or nearly alone. Hearing the splash, the choking noises. Having the courage to open the door.

"Sonora?"

"Yeah, go ahead."

He pointed to the blocky black outline of a stick figure in a skirt, denoting female. "I think, seeing how this is the ladies room, maybe you better go in first by yourself, make sure there isn't anybody else there."

Sonora leaned sideways against the bathroom door and pushed. Behind her, someone came out of a doorway. She caught the dark silhouette out of the corner of her eye, before whoever it was turned a corner and was gone. The bathroom door creaked, and she went in.

"Loud door. Why didn't Caplan hear her?"

"Think what he's doing, Sonora. Micah's making a lot of noise. He's involved. Crying, if Julia Winchell didn't make that up."

"You think he didn't know a thing till he looked up, then voila, there's Julia? Watching and witnessing?"

"Celebrate the moments of your life."

The first thing Sonora saw walking into the bathroom

was the opposite wall. Julia Winchell must have found that disconcerting. Yellow tile wall, mustard-brown linoleum. Then you veered right, and there were the sinks and soap dispensers on the right-hand side, a row of mirrors, opposite a line of individual stalls.

A towel dispenser and inset trash can were on the far wall. All stall doors were open, all cubicles empty. Sonora opened the door and looked at Sam.

"The coast is clear, come on in and adjust your panty hose."

"I could probably get arrested for this," Sam muttered.

"I promise to swear I don't know you."

They stood side by side, staring into the cubicles, as if there was something to see.

"I wonder which one it was," Sam said.

"Which what?"

"Stall."

"That one," Sonora said, pointing to the one second from the left.

"Why that one?"

She shrugged.

Sam turned and faced the mirrors. "She saw it there first."

"The reflection? Probably. Saw something, and turned and looked."

The bathroom door opened. A girl in plaid shorts and chunky shoes came in, arms bare and sunburned. She stopped suddenly, looked up at Sam.

"It's opposite day, right?"

Sam and Sonora scooted out.

Sam took a deep breath once they were in the hallway. "What is opposite day, anyway?"

"Pay attention, Sam. We got Julia Winchell running

screaming out of the bathroom. She goes . . . this away, maybe?" Sonora headed to the right. The corridor ended in T. Green swing doors, one propped open, which led into a large lab-type classroom. Clustered next to the door were three dress forms and two mannequins, hanging on a wall by the door.

Sam stopped. "Look at that."

"Didn't she say something—what was it? She thought she saw people, but it turned out to be mannequins?"

"Everything's clocking."

"God, Sam, can you imagine? She sees Caplan in the bathroom, drowning Micah, she runs screaming for help, thinks she sees people, comes full tilt in here and gets . . . this. No people. She must have had nightmares for years."

"Let's go back to the bad guy," Sam said. "What's Caplan do with the body?"

"He knows the cavalry's coming and he's got to move fast."

"There's a lot of doors, up and down the hallway. He could have gone in any one of them."

"At night, Sam? Lot of them will be locked."

"The mannequin room isn't locked."

"Think he brought her in here?"

Sam wandered in, and Sonora followed. He pointed. "Right there. Big black trash barrels. Could have put her in one of those, temporarily. Mail cart right there, could have slid her right on in." He stepped into the hallway. "Dumbwaiter is right down the hall. Could have loaded her onto that."

"Suppose someone was at the other end?"

"He's moving fast, now, Sonora, taking risks. How about these lockers." He stepped out into the hallway. "Think he could have fit her in one of those?"

The lockers were painted army green. A few had combination locks on them, most didn't. "Full length. Looks possible."

Sam opened the locker that was second from the end. "Get in. She was littler than you are."

"Hey. She was pregnant."

"Except for that."

Sonora ducked and scooted in. "Easy fit, actually."

"There must be fifty ways to store this body."

"So he stashes the body, then waits till Julia and the security guy leave. Maybe waited a couple hours till everything is dead quiet. She was a little bitty thing. He could have rolled her out in the mail cart. I wonder if he planned to leave her here in the building, his original plan, before he got discovered, or if he'd planned that business at the creek all along."

"We'll never know," Sam said.

"Unless he tells us." Sonora chewed a thumbnail. "If that guy, Marsh, had made a better search, they'd have found her that night."

"Sonora, look at it from his point of view. Co-ed comes running out and says there's a murder going on in the women's bathroom on the third floor, which just so happens to be a parking lot."

"People get confused."

"He looked in every bathroom. There was still nothing there."

"Let's take a look at that parking garage."

They headed down the hallway, found the elevator. Sam ushered Sonora in, pushed the button for three. Sonora leaned against the wall, thinking about Julia Winchell, pressed against this very wall, trying to catch her breath, trying to get back in time.

The elevator door opened into a dark cavern of

asphalt and noise. The brash sound of a car horn floated in with the smell of oil and gasoline fumes. Sam walked out into the parking lot, looked around, then came back.

"So he doesn't have to haul her body out the front door. He can come down the elevator and put her right into the car. Mighty damn convenient."

"Hey, Sam."

"Yeah."

"There's one other place he could have hid her."

"What?"

"He could have hung her up, with the rest of the mannequins."

"You're a sick puppy, Sonora."

"So is he."

58

Sonora was on the phone with Heather when she heard Sam tell her that Gruber wanted them. She put her hand over the mouthpiece. "Just one second, okay, Sam?

"Yes, I promise to read the whole magazine article, but I'm telling you, Heather, it's a come-on. We can't get rich raising chinchillas and the smell is—" Sonora paused. "Heather, listen. You don't worry about the Visa bill. Mom takes care of that. We are not going to raise chinchillas." Sonora hung up the phone. "You seen Gruber?"

"Last I saw he was headed into the women's bathroom."

"Must still be opposite day. Let's see what he knows about those soil samples on the Bobo killer's shoe."

Sonora and Sam found him washing his hands. He grinned at Sonora as they came through the door.

"You girls ought to clean up once in a while." Gruber checked his hair in the mirror. "I got something for you two, don't know if it's of any use. But I know forensics came up with creosote on the carpet in the Winchell rental car. Same as they found in Bobo's tennie."

Gruber turned the faucet on, slicked down a piece of hair that was lying funny. He reached for the paper towels. Sam handed him one before he got to the dispenser. "You know, Delarosa, you ever get tired of police work, you have a promising career as a bathroom attendant in your future."

Sam held out a hand.

Gruber looked at Sonora. "He expect a tip?"

Sonora nodded. "I always tip him."

"Here's your tip, kiddos. Bobo killer is one of those model railroad hobby guys. You know, the ones set up those little tracks in their basement and build little houses and stuff to go around it. He goes train watching on his lunch hour."

Sam frowned. "What's that?"

Gruber wadded the paper towel, threw it into the trash. "It means he watches trains, Einstein. Goes to railroad tracks and switch yards and basically just hangs around like a dork."

"A train groupie," Sam said.

"Whatever. But that's where the creosote came from. Railroad tracks." Gruber headed for the door, looked back over his shoulder at Sonora and Sam. "Nice bathroom you got here, ladies. Needs reading material."

Sonora waved him off. "Everything you'd need, Gruber, is scrawled on the walls."

Sonora's phone was ringing as she and Sam headed for the bullpen. She tripped over Molliter getting to it.

"I took a message for you while you were out," Molliter said. "And I washed your coffee mug for you." He put the dripping mug on top of her stack of bills."

"You took a message for me? You don't have work, or were you afraid my answering machine wouldn't get it?"

Molliter took a breath. "Look, the woman sounded upset."

"What woman?"

"Don't jump down my throat. Dorothy Ainsley. I told her you'd get back to her."

Sonora grabbed the phone. "My seven year old lies better than you do, Molliter. Get the hell away from my desk."

Molliter headed for the file cabinet, hands full of papers. "I don't know why I try to get along with you, Sonora."

"Hey, Molliter," Sam said. "She was kidding."

"Homicide, Blair." Sonora heard noise on the other end, something like a copy machine in the background, phones ringing. "Hello?"

"Is this Detective Blair?"

A woman, and she sounded familiar. Sonora frowned, trying to place the voice. "Yeah, this is Blair. How can I help you?"

"This is Bea Wallace. I'm Gage Caplan's—"

"Chief of staff, yes."

"I was going to say secretary."

"What can I do for you, Mrs. Wallace?"

"Mr. Caplan has dictated a chronology of his actions on July the eighteenth. He asked me to fax them to you."

"I see. And you need the—"

"Yes," Wallace interrupted. "I got your message about the fax machine being broken."

Sonora stayed quiet, thinking. The fax machine was fine. She hadn't left a message. And Caplan knew everything that went on in the bullpen. "Mrs. Wallace, I really need that chronology right away. I'm sure you understand that in an ongoing murder investigation—"

"Detective, Mr. Caplan has instructed me to . . . I believe the word he used was *facilitate*. My job is to help you out. Whether or not I want to personally doesn't enter into it." Her voice was tight, just on the hairy edge of rude.

Smart lady, Sonora thought. Wondered what she had

to say. Thought a minute, trying to provide a safe venue for her to say it.

"Any chance you could drop by the office and pick it up?" Bea Wallace asked.

Surely not, Sonora thought, with Gage Caplan breathing down their necks. "Ma'am, my boss has just instructed me not to harass your boss and the last thing I want to do is show up in your office." Sonora looked over her shoulder. Saw Molliter was listening. He'd worked with Caplan several times last year, hadn't he? "Why don't you meet me out front in the lobby? I should be there in half an hour. That all right? Caplan unchain you from your desk long enough to run downstairs and hand me a piece of paper?"

"Detective, I don't like your tone of voice."

"Like it or not, Mrs. Wallace, you be there. I'll try not to get held up."

She hung up, saw Sam staring at her.

"My God, you're in a bad mood."

"Come on, Sam, we got places to go." Sonora looked over her shoulder. "Hey, Molliter. Anything you want to ask me? Like where I'm going? What I'm doing? Will copies of all forensic reports I get make it easier for you?"

He looked at her. "You're crazy."

"And you're shit."

Sam grabbed her arm. "Come on, girl, you're already in enough trouble for one day."

59

Bea Wallace was standing outside the building when they got there. She held a piece of paper that fluttered in the hot breeze. She looked very solitary, standing close to a fountain, watching the street.

"Park already," Sonora said.

"Nowhere *to* park," Sam said. "You get out and I'll circle around and come back and pick you up."

Sonora opened the car door part way.

"Wait for the . . . *shit*, Sonora, look before you jump out."

"Sorry."

"Go. Now, before the light changes."

"Thanks, Sam."

Bea Wallace was looking at her watch as Sonora approached. Her pink striped shirt was coming loose from the waistband of her navy skirt, and her shirt had been buttoned wrong, giving the front a lopsided, unfinished look. Bea Wallace had put on lipstick recently, and was in the process of chewing it off. She stood with her weight shifted to one side.

"Got here as quick as I could," Sonora said. The wind blew a fine mist of water from the fountain across her face. Felt like heaven.

Bea Wallace gave her a tight smile. "This is for show, in case the counselor is looking out his office window. I wanted to do this in full view. If he can see me, he won't think twice about this."

Sonora reached for her recorder, but Wallace shook her head.

"Pull that out and I walk. I value my job. I'm here to do somebody a favor."

Sonora kept the recorder in the purse. "Who?"

"Collie. She's a nice little girl, and I don't want anything happening to this one."

"You said 'this one,' Mrs. Wallace."

"I'm well aware what I said."

"What happened to the last one?"

Wallace looked at her. She had dark brown eyes, bloodshot, outlined in black eye pencil. She did not look like she had been sleeping well. Which, Sonora thought, could mean she had something on her mind, or that Caplan worked her hard. Possibly both.

"I'm not going to dance with you, Detective. I'm short on time and you look to be short on patience. I don't *know* a thing, but I have worries. The first Mrs. Caplan had one or two near misses before she was murdered. All of them when she was pregnant. And now this thing with Collie and the canoe."

Sonora moved closer. "What thing with the canoe?"

"You didn't hear about this? He set it up right under your nose, that day in the office when everybody was celebrating the big victory. Going down to the lake where Micah's mama and dad have a cabin. Mr. Caplan goes there all the time. Collie—she's not much for the water or the heat, and still, they're out canoeing in the middle of the afternoon. And the canoe goes over, and nobody's wearing a vest. I talked to Collie myself this morning. Sometimes that girl tells you things without knowing it. And what she told me I don't like."

"Canoes go over all the time," Sonora said. Was this what Dorrie Ainsley had called about? Had she seen the canoe go over?

"This one went over because Gage was conducting a 'safety drill.'"

Sonora raised an eyebrow. "With a pregnant woman in the boat?"

"Yeah, and right in the middle of the lake. I don't know how much you know about that area, but that water is miles deep in some places. People dive there. Collie goes under *there*, never see her again."

"She swim?" Sonora asked.

"Enough that she got to the shore. With no help from our hero. She's really shook up and I don't like the way this sounds. I wonder if you ought to talk to her."

"Did you?"

Bea Wallace looked at her. "Tell you the truth, I barely know the woman. But she . . . something about her makes you want to look out for her. She's sure not looking out for herself. She's got a baby to protect. Maybe you can get her to see sense."

"I don't think she's going to see any kind of sense that doesn't take Mia into account."

Bea Wallace's lips went tight. "That's how he keeps her in place. One trick in a bagful." She handed Sonora the sheet of paper that constituted Gage Caplan's paper-thin alibi. She turned and began walking away.

"Mrs. Wallace?"

"Yes?"

"That fax machine isn't likely to get fixed anytime soon. You need to send me anything else, don't hesitate to call. You can get me at home, I'm in the book."

Wallace gave her a steady look. "Tell Collie to get the hell out, Detective. At least till after the baby is born."

60

Collie met them at the door in a frayed pink corduroy bathrobe. It hung loose, buttoned every other one. A long belt hung from the loop on the left and trailed behind her like a tail. She stared at them through the storm door, running a hand through short straight hair, dingy brown streaked into highlights by the sun. Her hair would be almost pretty next time she got around to washing it.

"Afternoon, Mrs. Caplan. May we come in for a minute, and talk?"

At first Sonora thought she was going to turn them away. But Sam was so low key and appealing, ducking his head shyly and giving her a little smile, as if it would hurt his feelings to be turned away. He always knew when to be nice and when to be tough.

"This really isn't the best time," Collie said. But she opened the door. She was barefooted. Her toenails had been painted hot pink. Sonora wondered who had painted them. She could not picture Collie bending that far over this late in her pregnancy. Mia, most likely.

Sonora tried to imagine a way for this thing with Caplan to play out so that Mia did not get hurt. She could not think of one.

"Mia's sleeping over with a buddy," Collie said, as if following Sonora's thoughts. She led them down a staircase off the kitchen into a dark den in the basement.

It looked like the house refuge for messy people.

Sonora had the feeling that Collie and Mia spent a lot of time here. A television was going without sound. One of those shock talk shows, where teenagers were shouting at their parents, whose faces were a despairing mix of hurt, bewilderment, and outrage. Sonora was glad the sound was off.

The downstairs couch was an old beige sectional, forming a cozy horseshoe that was littered with paperback books, Barbie dolls, Bryer horses, and an economy size pack of M&Ms, plain, not peanut.

"Sit down," Collie said. "Can I get you something?" She handed Sam the open bag of M&Ms with an air of distraction.

Clearly the woman had not slept. She stared at Sonora, chewed the end of a fingernail. Sonora wondered if Caplan had passed his sexual harassment complaints on to his wife. She was glad Sam was with her.

Collie put her head in her hands.

Sam leaned forward and touched her lightly on the shoulder. "Are you all right, Mrs. Caplan? Should we come back at another time?"

"No, I'm okay. Just a headache and an upset stomach. I can't even drive around the block without feeling bad. Pregnancy and this heat, I guess."

Her eyes had dark hollows beneath, and her lips were dark red.

"I understand fishing is a hobby of yours," Sam said.

She looked at him dully. "Umm. Yes."

"Does Mr. Caplan like to fish?"

"No. Not with me, anyway. Gage doesn't really have any hobbies. Except reading biographies."

"Doesn't build those ships in the bottle, do woodwork, or build model railroads?" Sonora asked.

Collie looked at them. "Just biographies and ball games on television."

"You go fishing with your dad a lot?" Sam asked.

Collie sat sideways, looked at him. "Yeah, I guess so. Who told you that?"

"Gage."

"Oh. Yeah, I do. Why are you asking me these questions?"

"When was the last time you got a chance to go up there? Your dad live close?"

"Bowling Green. Mia and me went up in July. Couple weeks ago."

"That would be the eighteenth? On a Tuesday?"

She waved her hands. "Could have been, I don't exactly keep the date lodged in my brain. Tuesday sounds right."

"Catch anything?" Sam asked.

"Mia did pretty good."

"I'm surprised you got that far away from home, with a baby coming so soon," Sonora said.

Collie tilted her head to one side. "My dad called, and he sounded kind of . . . I don't know. Like he really needed me to come up. And I'm glad we went, Mia and me had a great time. My family really made a fuss over me. My sister came and we had a . . . it was fun."

"I spoke with your father, Collie. He said Gage called and asked if you could come up because you were tired and needed to get away. He even canceled his plans for that weekend."

She clutched one of the buttons at the top of her robe. "Gage called him?" She sounded out of breath.

"We also understand you had an incident out in the canoe this weekend." Sonora kept her voice low, matter-of-fact.

Collie took hold of the loose belt and wrapped it round and round her hand. "Gage tell you about it?"

"What exactly happened?" Sam said.

"I just . . . it was my fault, I'm so clumsy. Even when I'm not pregnant, I'm a klutz. I just, I zigged when I should have zagged, I guess. Fell right out. If it wasn't for Gage, I probably would have gone straight to the bottom."

"He a good swimmer?" Sonora asked.

Collie nodded.

"Bet he jumped right in after you and pulled you to shore," Sam said kindly.

Collie was still nodding, but slower, and Sonora saw it in her eyes. Uncertainty. Hurt. She wondered how much Collie would shield him.

"He jumped in after you?" Sonora said. A question.

"He kind of had no choice, the canoe went right over. It was all my fault," she said softly.

Sonora wanted to shake her.

"And he towed you to shore," Sam said.

"It all happened so fast, I just . . . we both made it to the shore, so I guess it turned out fine. Except there he is on one side and me on the other, so I had to wait forever for . . ." She trailed off.

Sonora tilted her head. "So if he's on one side and you're on the other, he ditched you and left you there on your own in the water."

Collie looked at her feet, put one bare foot over the other. "My ankles are swollen."

"I'm sorry to hear that," Sonora said. "He's a good swimmer, your husband. You said so yourself, and other people have told me the same thing. How is it he left you out in the middle of the lake, when you're seven months pregnant, and don't swim all that well? I have a hard time with that, Collie."

Collie leaned forward as if her stomach hurt. "Not

everybody can be brave when there's a crisis. It's nice if they are, but people are people. You can't make them be heroes. Do you know how embarrassed Gage was for leaving me out there like that? He cried! Don't you dare tell anybody I told you this, but he *cried*."

Sonora was remembering Julia Winchell's voice, on tape. That the man she saw kill Micah was crying as he held her head down in the toilet. "When did he start crying?"

"Right before . . . I guess he saw what was coming up and panicked. I know I looked up and he was starting to cry—eyes all red and full of tears, and I remember thinking, well, what in the world? Then the next thing I know, I'm in the water, going under and down. And I was treading, my arms and all, and finally I get my head up. And I'm calling him, and looking for him, and I'm scared to death he's drowned. And the boat is way out of reach, and it's going farther out. And I still don't see him. But then I see that little red Coleman cooler, and thank God. I grabbed a hold of that and kicked with my feet, but I made it. Took me forever, but I made it. Then I crawled up through the rocks and sand, I'd lost my flip-flops. And I sat down, I was so tired. And I look across the water, and there he is, Gage, safe and sound. Just looking at me."

Sam sat forward on the couch. "Why weren't you wearing a life vest? If you don't swim well, you should have been wearing one."

"I know, and I almost always do. But . . . we left them in that toolshed by Dorrie and Grey's cabin, and decided not to go back."

"Who decided not to go back?"

"I don't remember."

"Yes, you do," Sonora said.

Collie licked her lips. "What are you trying to say?"

"Let me see if the afternoon didn't go more like this. Didn't your husband tip that canoe on purpose? Didn't he make sure you didn't wear a life vest? Didn't he go off and leave you in the water on purpose, hoping you'd drown?"

"Of course not!"

"Really? You were there, Collie."

"I am seven months pregnant with this man's child!"

"Micah was seven months pregnant when she died," Sonora said.

Collie stood up. "This is a miracle baby. We wanted this child forever!"

"We, Collie, or you? How did he react the first time you told him you were pregnant?"

Collie's mouth opened, then closed. "He . . ." She sank slowly to the couch. "He yelled at me and screamed at me and broke the picture frame with me and my mom and my dad and my sister. He said any baby of mine would be a . . . an ugly baby. Oh God. I never saw him so mad in all my life." She put her head in her hands. Shut her eyes tightly. "I know he loves me. He's just difficult sometimes. He's got a high pressure job, and his childhood. Just not the best. It's not surprising that he acts like he does."

"What he does doesn't surprise me near as much as you, the way you take it, Collie." Sonora stared at her.

Collie blinked. "Are you in God's good truth trying to sit there and tell me my husband is trying to kill me? You think I'm just so desperate to be married to Gage, or to anybody, that I'll put up with anything? Is that what you think?"

Sonora kept her mouth shut. It was what she thought.

"Because I'm overweight and have a goofy face and a big nose. I have to take what I can get."

Sam looked at her. "I don't believe it."

"Not that you *have* to," Sonora said. "Just that you think you do. Protect that baby of yours, Collie. Make a formal complaint. Let us open an investigation."

"I have two babies to protect. Mia's mine, too. And unless the laws have changed just recently, the only rights I have toward Mia are the ones Gage lets me have. You going to tell me what to do now?"

Sonora put her business card on the table, jotted her home phone on the back. "Call if we can help."

"Nobody can help me, Detective."

Sam stood up. "Take care, Mrs. Caplan. And good luck."

61

Sonora always thought of mad scientists and old Frankenstein movies whenever she went into the crime scene side of the bullpen. There was always so much going on—vats of liquid, glass cases with who knows what suspended in the middle. The room did not look modern or pristine—in fact, it reminded her of high school labs, with that same air of aged equipment and people all around mixing chemicals and running experiments that she did not understand.

Terry had a smudge on her cheek. Not unusual for Terry. Her long, straight hair was coming out of the braid, falling across the high broad cheekbones. She was rail thin, wearing white overalls and a lab coat, and she pushed her cat glasses back on her nose and smiled at Sonora.

"You want me to start?"

"Crick wants to do this in his office. He and Sam are there now, waiting for us."

"Oh." Terry looked around the lab, as if she were a fish forced to leave her tank. "I guess."

She followed Sonora through the swing doors into the bullpen.

"Hey, Molliter," Sonora said.

He stood at the coffee machine. Turned his back.

Crick had a fresh pot of coffee and plenty of extra cups.

Terry helped herself to coffee. Added cream and sugar. She raised both eyebrows and leaned against a file cabinet. "Let me know when you want me to start."

Crick waved a hand. "Start now."

She nodded her head up and down, up and down. "You guys have been keeping me busy. Any particular thing you want me to start with?"

"Free hand," Crick said.

She cleared her throat. Went to the end of the room, as if she were prepared to lecture in a hall. Sonora and Sam turned their chairs around so they could face her, and Crick sat down behind his desk.

"Let's start at the beginning, which was eight years ago, with the homicide of Micah Caplan. I've studied the file on that, done a little futzing around, and I can tell you definitively that the water in her lungs did not come from the creek where her body was found. Two months before she was killed there was a sizable agrichemical theft in that area. Very well organized crime ring going after the dealers—you can get a couple hundred dollars per gallon container—and somebody was ripping them big time. The upshot is that thanks to a well-placed informant, the police were pretty much able to give chase. In an attempt, unsuccessful I might add, to destroy the evidence, one hundred pounds of simazine and twice that of Treflan were dumped into that creek.

"No traces of either chemical were found in Micah Caplan's lungs, but traces were found in her hair and on her clothes."

"So her killer dunked her in the creek, but she was drowned somewhere else," Sam said.

Terry chewed her lip and nodded. "I'd say so. The water in her lungs had traces of surfactants, phosphorus, calcium carbonate, hypochlorite bleach, various detergents.

Elements consistent with the kind of chemicals used to clean bathrooms."

"Toilet water," Crick said.

"Right."

"Good. Go on."

She took a sip of coffee and winced. Hot. "Cosmetics. There were traces of lipstick and foundation and saliva on the armrest of the rental car. The cosmetics are a match for what you brought me out of the vic's hotel room."

"Rum Raisin Bronzer," Sonora muttered.

Terry nodded. "I studied the soil samples from the rental car—very similar to what we found on the Bobo killer's shoe. I studied the density gradients, mineralogical profiles. Pollens." She looked at them expectantly.

"Ooooo," Sonora said.

"Ahhhh," Sam added.

"Thank you. I came up with oil, pea gravel, creosote present in both samples. But sample one, from Bobo, has pollens indigenous to Cincinnati. Sample two, from the rental, is from farther south. Pollens you'd find in Kentucky and particularly Tennessee, where they have a lot of dogwood and azalea. These pollens are also present inside that plastic bag that held Julia Winchell's head, hands, etc. They're in her hair, under fingernails and toenails."

Sonora looked at Sam.

"It gets better," Terry said. "Silica, clay . . . let's call it river mud. Consistent with the Clinch River and Laurel Lake area. Found in the soil sample from the rental car, and in that plastic bag of remains."

"So he used her car. To kill her, then cart her around in later. Dropping off his little packages."

"The packages were well wrapped then," Terry said. "And he didn't do the butcher work in the car. But he may well have used it for delivery."

Sam waved a hand. "And there's nothing, not a damn thing in the vacuum cleaner bag that would make you think Julia Winchell was ever in that cabin?"

Terry shook her head. "Forget the cabin. You need to start looking for railroad tracks."

"Railroad tracks?"

"The creosote was in one of the bottommost layers in that soil sample. Whoever it is went through the mud, and went across railroad tracks." She looked at Sonora. "Wish list. Bring me the box of garbage bags he used. Bring me the box and I'll match the one that had Julia Winchell's remains to the next one on the roll. Then the prosecutor will love you."

"In this case," Sonora said. "Maybe not."

Terry pushed her glasses back on her nose. "This guy killed his first wife when she was pregnant, that right?"

Sam nodded.

"And you guys think he's going for wife number two, and she's pregnant? Is it the pregnancy thing?"

Sonora shrugged. "Who knows?"

"Why doesn't he just get a vasectomy?"

"Be easier," Sonora said.

Sam looked at Crick. "Only women could think of a vasectomy as an easy solution."

Crick folded his arms. "And for this guy, probably not as much fun."

62

Gruber was coming in the door as Sonora and Sam were going out. "Look, kiddos, your phones were ringing back and forth, one then the other, so I figured it was somebody had both your numbers and going crazy. You know a lady named Dorrie Ainsley?"

Sonora moved faster than Sam, and got to the phone first. The receiver that was off the hook was on Sam's desk. She picked it up.

"Mrs. Ainsley?"

"Is this Detective Blair?" The voice was tight, throbbing.

"Right here, Mrs. Ainsley. I'm sorry, I should have gotten back to you right away, I had—"

"Detective Blair, I just got a call from Mia. She . . . this makes no sense, Detective, but she says she's at a park by the water. Downtown by the river. She says there's a flying pig? And barges?"

"I know where she means," Sonora said.

"Collie took her down there. She left her at the playground and said she'd be back in about twenty minutes. That was over an hour ago. Mia said Collie hasn't come back. She said that they went to the park in a cab, and that Collie made her pack a bag and that Collie had a bag. Mia tried to call her dad, but she can't track him down. Grey's on his way, but—"

"We'll pick her up."

"Something else I better tell you. When Collie and Gage were down here, they—"

"Is this about the canoe?"

"Yes. You know about that?"

"Yes, Mrs. Ainsley. But I appreciate you letting me know."

"That's what I was calling about earlier. There's something else. Two nights ago I had a phone call from Gage. He was very upset. Or he acted like he was. He cried."

Sonora frowned. Bad things happened when this man cried.

"He said that he found out Collie was having an affair. He was afraid she was going to leave him."

"Do you think this is plausible, Mrs. Ainsley?"

"He said she had one of those on-line lovers. You know, on the Internet."

"Is Collie a hacker?"

"I don't know. I know she has a computer she fiddles with. Gage said he got into her E-mail, and that she and this man, this Elvis, is what he calls himself, he and Collie have been carrying on for months. He wanted to know if Collie had confided in me about this guy, and what he should do. Whether he should mention it, or hope it played itself out."

"What did you tell him?"

"I told him he was crazy."

"What did he say?"

"He said he hoped I was right."

Sonora pulled the bottom drawer open in Sam's desk. "You still got that extra pair of cuffs?"

"Yeah, so?"

"Where'd Molliter go?"

"You know damn well where he went, I heard you say 'fuck' under your breath when he went over to talk to Terry."

"Can't hide anything from you, can I, Sam?"

"What are you up to?"

"Trust me, you don't want to know. Where's Crick?"

"Out to lunch."

"Just as well."

63

What's he want me for?" Molliter asked.

Sonora scratched the back of her head, playing it irritable. "How the hell would I know? I got stuff to do, and I'm late. He asked me to come get you, I came and got you. Maybe they figured out where the smell was coming from."

Sonora opened the door to the men's room. The light was off, and the smell was a presence. She had counted on Molliter cringing and being distracted, just long enough.

"Get the light, will you, Molliter?"

"I'm looking for the switch."

"Somewhere over there, I think." Sonora guided his hand into the open cuff on the pair that she'd hooked to the drain pipe. The key to good police technique was the advance work.

She had Molliter's cuff snapped while he was still groping for the switch. She took his gun out of the shoulder holster, just to be safe.

"What the hell are you doing, Blair?"

"You been a cop all these years and you don't recognize handcuffs, Molliter?" She flipped on the light. Molliter looked pale and perplexed. And angry. She took a step backward. "I'll put your gun in your center desk drawer, Molliter. For safekeeping."

"Man. It *stinks* in here."

"Yeah. And all you guys are using the women's bath-room, so I don't guess anybody is going to find you."

"Are you crazy?"

Sonora shrugged. "I think you're the one, Molliter. Somebody's calling the DA's office and keeping them up to date on this Winchell thing. And now the second Mrs. Gage Caplan is missing, and I don't want Gage getting the play-by-play over the phone. So to be on the safe side, you're going to spend a while in here."

"I'll just call for help."

"I anticipated that." Sonora took a roll of strapping tape out of her blazer pocket. She covered his mouth quickly, speed was the key here, keep him off balance. "I'm sorry, Molliter. You don't look all that comfortable, and with any luck at all, you're going to be here a while. Now, I could be wrong, and if I am I'll owe you a great big apology that you'll never accept, so likely I won't bother.

"I think after a while you'll just get used to the smell."

He made a noise in the back of his throat. Sonora did not like the look in his eyes. She was glad he was cuffed.

64

Mia was on the swing set in the third play area they searched. Sonora took a deep breath when she saw her, and Sam squeezed her shoulder.

The little girl had a stoic look, legs pumping, no eye contact or interest in anything going on around her. She swung with precision, up, down, joyless.

It was muggy out and hot. The air was clouded with gnats and the hum of bumblebees. Some of the other children studied Mia. She did not acknowledge their presence.

From the playground, you could not see the river. Sonora wondered where Mia had found a pay phone. She had evidently ranged far and wide.

A small green backpack and a battered blue Samsonite suitcase sat next to the metal frame of the swing set. Mia glanced over periodically, as if to be sure they were still there.

"Mia?" Sonora stood with her back to the sun.

Mia squinted.

"How you doing?" Sam said.

"Fine, thank you." She stopped the swing by dragging the toe of her hiking boots through the sand.

"Remember me?" Sonora said. "I'm the police detective that came and talked to Collie."

Mia nodded.

"This is Sam. He works with me."

"Did I do something wrong?"

"No, honey," Sam said. "We came to make sure you're okay."

"How did you find me?"

"Your grandmother sent us."

"You know my grandmother?" Wonder in her eyes. And suspicion.

"Yes. Her name is Dorrie Ainsley, and she lives in London, Kentucky, and she paints bluebirds with faces on them. I've seen them. One of the faces is yours."

"And one is Mommy, and Daddy, and Collie." Mia looked at Sonora. "Did she tell you that Collie didn't come back?"

"That's why we're here. We're going to find her. After we take you home." Sam crooked a finger and she came running.

Sam carried the blue bag and Mia took the backpack. "Mia, there's a lot going on we're not sure we understand."

She nodded. She stayed quiet and watched everybody they passed. Looking for Collie.

"You sure you have no idea where Collie went?"

"She went to meet the friend."

Sonora opened the back door of the Taurus, helped the little girl find her seat belt. She was wearing a pair of red cotton shorts today. Shorts and a sleeveless white denim shirt. Her hair was held back with a plastic white hairband. She looked hot.

"Why don't you tell me everything that happened since you got up this morning. Could you do that?" Sonora asked.

Mia nodded. "First thing, I got up. Then I ate some cereal. Lucky Charms."

"That's what my little girl likes."

"You have a little girl?" Mia asked.

"Yeah. Detective Delarosa has one, too."

"They must have been having a sale on little girls that year," Sam said. He started the car. Pulled out of the lot where they were illegally parked.

Mia gave them a faint smile. "Collie was in the shower. She came out and checked the messages. There was one from the car place."

"What car place? Do you know the name of it?"

"No. But it's the car place where Collie likes to go. I think they must have called while Collie was in the shower and I was still in bed. So Collie called them up and talked a minute, and then she started crying."

"Why did she cry?" Sonora asked.

Mia shrugged.

"Did the phone ring in between? Did somebody else call?"

"I don't know. I don't think so. I didn't hear it if it did."

Sonora caught Sam's look. "Maybe it was a big estimate."

"Yeah, right. Okay, Mia, she cries. Then what?"

"I took her some Kleenexes and a Coke and a cookie."

Sam looked over his shoulder and smiled at her. "Want to come and live at my house?"

"Then Collie blew her nose but she wouldn't eat the cookie so I did, because my Lucky Charms were getting soggy."

Sonora nodded.

"Then she just stopped crying. She said, that's that then. Weird, I guess. Then she hugged me and said she loved me, and that it was time to face the facts. Then she told me we were going to go be with a friend for a while.

"I asked her why. She said it was grown-up business, and that I should do what she told me, and she would try to work everything out. And then she hugged me again and said she would always keep me safe."

Sonora looked across at Sam. "We need to go to the house."

"It's where I'm headed. Mia, did she tell you anything about this friend?"

Mia thought for a minute. "Just that he was very nice, and very understanding. That he really cared. That he was easy-going and didn't lose his temper, and that he liked little girls."

Sam looked at Sonora. "How could she figure all that out on-line?"

"Probably told her so himself."

65

Sonora half expected Gage Caplan to be in the doorway waiting for them, but the house was empty and unlocked.

Mia ran in ahead of them. Sonora and Sam followed. Mia went straight to the basement calling Collie's name. She was back up in a minute. Did a room-to-room search, looking.

The answering machine was in the bedroom. More white. Bedspreads, white carpet, heavy mahogany furniture, with peach accents on the wall. Expensive and bland.

The closet door was open, a dress on the floor like a blasphemy in the otherwise immaculate room. Sonora pressed the message button on the answering machine.

"Mr. and Mrs. Caplan, this is Wilfred Boggs, calling from Boggs Auto. Please call me at the following number, about your 1996 Nissan Pathfinder, regarding repairs." Sonora wrote the number down on the scratch pad by the phone. Saw that someone else had written the same number down earlier.

"Should we call them?" Sonora asked.

Sam shrugged. "No stone unturned. Something made her cry. Want me to do it?"

"Yeah, I'm going to see if I can track down that computer."

She found Mia sitting cross-legged on the top bunk of her bed. Sonora stood in the doorway.

"May I come in?"

Mia's arms were folded and she was staring into the jumble of sheets, bedspread, and blankets.

"Yes." Voice barely audible.

"Nice room."

Mia nodded. Words were too much effort. Sonora looked around the room with a smile, thinking that whoever had put this one together was an opposite to whoever decorated the rest of the house.

The bed was fire engine red metal, and there was a desk and dresser, simple blunt cut wood, maple. A big bear rug sat in the center of the room and it was evident that the bear head was groomed from time to time. Ribbons adorned the dead fur ears, and someone had colored his teeth with crayons, and stuck the head of a Barbie doll in his mouth. There were posters all over the wall—Patrick Swayze with a horse, a mama cat curled up with her kittens, and a hippopotamus with its mouth open wide.

The bookshelf was a jumble of Fear Street, Sweet Valley Twins, and some ancient Nancy Drew books. Sonora went to the shelf and picked up a yellow hardback copy of *The Secret of the Old Clock*. She opened the flap, saw Collie's name written inside in purple cartridge pen.

"Collie gave me those," Mia said. "She liked to read my Sweet Valley Twins and Fear Street books, but made me promise not to tell, so people wouldn't tease her about reading kid books. She'd get Daddy to buy them for me, then we'd sit in the den and eat sandwiches and read. Daddy fusses at us when we do that because he says we don't have enough light. So we try to do it when he isn't home."

Mia swung her legs over the bed, turned so that her belly was against the mattress, and jumped down.

Sonora assumed the ladder was only for the faint-hearted.

"Do you think Collie will come back?" Mia asked.

Sonora hedged. "I don't think Collie will leave you. Remember, she had you pack a bag. She took you along."

"Just because she has another baby, doesn't mean she doesn't want me. She already told me that. I'm not going to have sibling stuff. I want a sister."

"What does Collie want?"

"A baby. A boy or girl will do."

"Where's her computer, Mia?"

"In the den. But it's got a password. Collie told it to me so I can put on the dinosaur CD and do the kid thing for America Online. The password is Mia. She named it after me. The computer is downstairs in the den."

"Here's what I think. I think you should get something to drink, and eat if you're hungry. Then you should curl up in front of the TV and zone out for a while, try not to worry. And while you do that, I'm going to try and figure out where Collie went."

"How come Daddy's not at work?"

"Maybe he had an appointment."

"I have Nintendo in my room. Can I stay in here?"

Sonora nodded. Headed downstairs for the den.

The computer was tucked into a corner, away from the little horseshoe of couch, TV, books, and toys. It sat on a small oak pressboard computer table—streamlined, and no frills—right by a rowing machine and a Nordic-Track that were both layered with dust.

The computer was not dusty. Sonora sat down in a black rolling chair, which was much like the one she had at work, without the armrests.

She was not good with computers. She only knew the system she used at work, and the old Apple 2E that she and the kids had had for years. She wished her son was with her.

She turned on the desk lamp that curved over the work area, and smiled.

A multicolored apple was inset at the bottom of the monitor. Collie had a Macintosh, a Performa 637CD.

Computers for normals. There was hope.

Sonora studied the keyboard. Probably the key in the top right-hand corner with an arrow on it. Nothing else looked likely, and this one would be the obvious choice. Sonora pushed the button.

Heard the splay of music that meant she'd hit pay dirt, closed her eyes and smiled.

"Sonora?"

Sam's footsteps on the staircase. He was walking lightly.

"Down here, Sam."

"Is Mia with you?"

"She's in her room playing Nintendo."

"Good. I know why Collie bolted."

Sonora swiveled in her chair, watched him come down the stairs. "Over here," she said. She pulled a beanbag chair close to the computer. Sam looked at it, sat, and sank almost to the floor.

"Comfy." He stuck his legs out and wiggled sideways. "Talked to Mr. Boggs. Sounds like a good mechanic, by the way. Anyway, Collie dropped the car off yesterday because it was vibrating like crazy, some kind of problem with the U-joint. Boggs said he'd talked to Gage about it a few weeks ago, but that Caplan said money was tight and he was busy with the Drury prosecution, and was going to wait a while on the repair.

"Evidently Collie got fed up waiting and took the car in herself yesterday. Boggs called to tell her that he couldn't get to the U-joint till he got authorization to fix the exhaust."

Sonora narrowed her eyes. "What kind of problem with the exhaust?"

"Well, it seems that Mr. Boggs and his employees had the Nissan running in the garage, and it ran them out. Filled the place with carbon monoxide. They had to air the place out before they could go back to work. When they did, Boggs took a look and found a big hole way up in the exhaust system. He said it struck him as odd. They don't usually break through there, and that you could look the whole system over and not find it unless you were really looking. The upshot is that carbon monoxide has been pouring into the cab of the car, and he thinks it's been going on for a while."

"I'll be damned." Sonora twisted from side to side in the chair.

"That's why she bolted. Because if Caplan did make that hole in the exhaust, she passes out behind the wheel, drives the car into a light pole, or head-on across the highway. Remember what she said when we talked to her? She couldn't drive around the block without feeling bad? Put it down to heat and being pregnant?"

Sonora nodded. "The only thing holding her back was Mia. And if he rigs the Nissan, then Mia likely gets killed or hurt along with Collie and the baby. So now Collie cuts her losses, because now she's got nothing to lose. Why didn't she come to us?"

"Mia, Sonora. She comes to us, she gives up the kid. She's a stepmother, she's got no legal claim. What'd you come up with?"

"I got the computer turned on."

"Veeeery good." He leaned forward, came up on his

knees, and pushed a square button on the monitor. "Now you've got a screen, too."

"My hero." The password barrier came up and Sonora typed in MIA. "I got the password, too," Sonora said.

"Your two to my one."

Sonora pulled the EDIT screen down and hit FINDER, then searched for America Online. The file came up immediately, again demanding a password. Sonora tried MIA again, and it worked.

"This is too easy," Sam said.

"It's a Mac, Sam. It's supposed to be easy. Tell the truth. Your Pentium is back in the box because it's such a pain in the ass."

"The kid uses it."

YOU HAVE MAIL! the computer told them.

Sonora hit the picture of the mailbox. The screen changed. Showed a communication called ELVIS TO COLLIE. She clicked it and pulled it up on screen.

> Collie, I got your note, and I think you are *absolutely* right.
>
> It's not safe for you, or the baby, or Mia. Of course I want you to bring her! We've talked around this before, and if I didn't make myself clear, I will now. *I WANT TO PRO-TECT YOU AND THE BABY AND MIA.* I don't want anything to happen to you. Please just do me one favor.
>
> When you come to the meeting place, come by yourself, just for a minute.
>
> Please understand. I want our first real life meeting to be private. You've never seen me. I am somewhat attractive, but not great. I

want you to see me and look at me and not feel pressured. I want you to be able to say, look sorry, I'm calling this off. And I don't want to do that with Mia watching.

And remember whatever happens be- tween us, we are friends. There is no pressure on you to be anything but a friend. I will give you safe haven, while you need it.

Be careful, and hurry.

Sonora shook her head. "Too good to be true. He's telling her exactly what she needs to hear. I never met a man who did that, and it wasn't some kind of con."

"Look at the screen. Now we've read the mail, it's got a little red check. So evidently Collie didn't get this."

"She must have. Why else did she leave Mia on the swing set, and tell her she'd be right back?"

Sam pushed a button that said KEEP AS NEW. The check mark disappeared. YOU HAVE MAIL! the computer told him.

"That was easy," Sam said.

Sonora looked at him. "But stupid. Why would she do that? So someone could find it?"

"Let's go back into the folder and see if she kept any correspondence."

"Surely she wouldn't."

"Why do people do anything, Sonora? Because they're people."

"This isn't hanging right, Sam. She wouldn't want Gage to find it."

He ignored her and took over the keyboard.

And hit pay dirt.

A saved file, full of correspondence with her on-line lover. Elvis.

They had started talking on-line three months ago. Just friendly chatting. Two people who needed a friend. Collie was trusting and confiding, and ripe. She opened up to Elvis immediately, commented often on how he always seemed to know when she'd had a bad day, or was upset. Elvis hinted that perhaps he'd found a soulmate.

"Soulmate," Sonora decided, was a term that had gotten women in almost as much trouble as "just this once." She had seen women, and men, endure years of agony, because they were afraid their sweetie was a soulmate, and irreplaceable. Sonora had not believed in soulmates for years. Her soul was on its own.

"At least we know why she calls him Elvis," Sam said.

Sonora looked up. "Why?"

"Didn't you read this one?" Sam scrolled back. "See? He gives her this sound thing to put on her program that says *Elvis has left the building* instead of beeping. Haven't you ever heard that one? We had it on our computer a while, but it starts to drive you crazy."

Sonora looked over Sam's shoulder.

Elvis,

Mia and I got such a kick out of the Elvis thing you gave me for the computer. Believe it or not, Gage hated it. I had to take it right back off because it gave him a headache. I think he's just tense from this Drury thing. I bet when it's all over he'll think it's funny.

Sonora checked the date, saw the correspondence was early in the relationship.

"Sam, Caplan has that Elvis thing on the PowerBook

in his office. How come he tells her to take it off her computer?"

"How come she keeps a file of mail that Caplan can get to with no problem at all?"

"And how come the mail said it hadn't been read, when we know it had?"

"To get the attention of whoever brought the program up."

"Somebody looking for Collie. Like a homicide detective investigating her death or disappearance. Like a homicide investigator who has already talked to Dorrie Ainsley and been told that Caplan suspected her of having an online affair."

"What are you saying, Sonora?"

"Try this theory, Sam. Caplan's first wife is murdered. Suspicious enough. The second one gets killed, he's going to be suspect number one. Unless another good possibility comes up. Like some on-line lover who turns out to be a nutcase."

"Caplan's the on-line lover," Sam said flatly. "Whole thing has been a setup from day one."

"He's in a perfect position. He knows she needs a friend. He knows when she's upset. He knows exactly what makes her tick, so he can be the on-line lover of her dreams. He knows that when Gage the husband comes home grumpy and difficult, Gage the on-line lover can leave a little E-mail note to brighten her day.

"Look at the messages. All ego-boosts. You make me laugh. There's no one in the world like you. You're a quick wit, lady. Tell me what you use for bait when you're fishing. But not a lot about old Elvis himself, is there?"

Sam rubbed his chin. "There's no message about where they met. I looked. Can't find the actual setup."

"That's no mistake," Sonora said.

"So where is she?"

"She may not even be alive."

Sam frowned. "Look for the railroad tracks, that's what Terry said."

A loud thumping made them both sit up.

"Someone at the door?" Sonora asked.

Sam put a hand on his gun. "Let's go see."

66

The door to Mia's room burst open as they made it to the top of the stairs.

"Collie?" Her face was bright, eyes big, and she ran down the hallway toward the front door.

"Hang on," Sonora said.

Sam moved into the living room.

"Let's have Sam go to the door and you and me wait right here."

Mia stopped in the hall. Her face was tight and thin, and she cocked her head listening. She took a breath.

"That's Granddaddy."

"You sure?"

She nodded, straining forward.

"Go," Sonora said.

As if she could have held her back.

"Where's my little granddaughter?" Grey's voice sounded cheerful, bombastic. Sonora rounded the corner in time to see the face did not match the voice, until Mia ran into the room. He swooped her up into his arms, and the lines of fatigue and worry eased back. He hugged her tight.

"*Granddaddy.*" She was crying.

"Wassa matter, chicklet? Granddaddy fix it, whatever it is."

She lifted her head up off his shoulder. "We can't find Collie. She left and didn't come back, and she's not like that. Something's really wrong, you've got to believe me."

"Well, heck, yeah, something's wrong. We know Collie wouldn't go off and leave you, chicklet. Unless she got lost trying to get back."

Mia looked up. "You think she's lost?"

"Honey, I've got no earthly idea, and believe me, I'm worried. But it's not like we're going to sit around on our butts, little girl. We've got a plan. We've got two police detectives going to find her—these people are trained professionals and they know just what to do. And you and me are going down to Gramma's to wait. Because when Collie comes looking for you, that's the first place she'll check. Isn't it?"

Mia nodded.

"We got trouble, hon, but we're going to handle it. Now get your bag packed up, while we do some grown-up talk."

"I already got a bag." She pointed to the backpack that was still in the hallway.

"*That* little piddly thing? Honey, your gramma's down in London cooking like there's no tomorrow, you going to have to stay a while just to eat it all up. Now go get some more clothes and those scary things you like to read. Bring all your favorite stuff. Be a female and don't pack light, 'cause I got that big Chrysler and room is the one thing we do have." He set her down. "Go on, baby doll. The sooner you get packed, the sooner we can hit the road."

Mia seemed lighter, somehow, when she ran down the hall, and Sonora looked at Grey, thinking that she wouldn't mind having him for a grandfather herself.

Grey waited till she was out of earshot. Took a breath. "What you know?" he said, voice going tight and flat.

Sam gave him a half-smile, and rubbed his chin. "I think the question, Mr. Ainsley, is what do you know?"

"What do you mean?"

"I mean that your wife called us forty-five minutes ago, and here you are. It's a three-hour drive at seventy. Even that Chrysler didn't get you up here in forty-five minutes."

"You got me there. If you don't mind, I'm going to sit down on my son-in-law's damn off-limits couch." He sat, groaned. "There. Okay, here's what I know.

"Collie called Dorrie a couple days after that canoe thing. She was all worked up. You hear what happened?"

Sonora sat in the leather wing chair, and Sam sat next to her on the footstool. "We know," Sonora said.

"Scared her. Scared her a lot. Dorrie and I don't know exactly what Collie is up to, but we trust that girl, and we love her like our own. Here's what she told Dorrie. That if things got really worrisome, and if she got scared enough, she might take Mia someplace where they could be safe. And she said did she have our permission to do that? She said she wouldn't do something like that unless she really had to, but if she did, and we agreed, she promised that she'd keep us in touch so we wouldn't worry. And she said it would be very temporary and very desperate. She said we better not know any details, because we needed to stay neutral. She said Gage might well get Mia back, if only for a while, and he shouldn't suspect we were all in it together. Otherwise he'd keep Mia away from us, like he did that time before."

Sam tapped his ankle. "When did Gage call?"

"You mean when he cried on the phone and said Collie was cheating on him with some kind of computer boyfriend?"

"Yeah."

"Last night. Put me and Dorrie on edge. We talked about it, decided I would come down here, get a hotel room, and just stay close. I'd been on the road an hour when Mia called London. I called Dorrie from a rest stop, and she told me what was up. And I want to say right here and now, me and Dorrie didn't believe a word Gage said about Collie cheating on him. And what's more, if it is true, then more power to her. I know that boy, he's just trying to turn us against her."

Sonora looked at Sam. "I'm afraid it's a lot more serious than that."

67

Railroad tracks and the river." Grey looked up. "You think he's taking her down to London?"

"I don't know." Sonora looked at Sam. "Could have been the Clinch River, but he knows the Laurel Lake area. It's not the cabin, but it might be somewhere nearby. Familiar territory."

"Let's call Dorrie and—"

"Think, Mr. Ainsley. You don't want your wife walking into this."

"We'll call the sheriff."

"We'll call Smallwood," Sonora said.

Sam looked at her.

Grey looked in the hallway. Saw Mia. "Come on in, chicklet, I need to ask you a question."

She stood in front of him, hands at her sides.

"Your daddy ever take you train watching anywhere, maybe walking along the railroad tracks?"

She shifted her weight to one foot. "He likes to go for long walks in the woods, when we go to the lake, but he walks too far, and I don't like to go. He walks for a long time. Collie says it makes him feel better."

"But you don't know where he goes?"

"Only Vernon knows."

"Why does Vernon know?" Sam asked.

" 'Cause Vernon follows him everywhere, even when

he's not supposed to. Sometimes Vernon makes Daddy mad."

Sonora looked up. "Are there any railroad tracks near your cabin, Mr. Ainsley?"

He frowned. "There's some tracks and a siding a couple miles out."

Sam looked at Sonora. "Terry said to look for railroad tracks and river mud."

"We got both," Ainsley said.

Sam nodded. "Our CSU guys are coming to pick a few things up. Any chance you could stay, and let these guys in?"

"Sure. You two headed to London?"

Sam nodded.

"See you down there if we don't pass you on the road."

Sam shook his head. "You'll never catch us."

68

Sam used the blue cop light to get them out of the city. It helped a little. Sonora was on the cell phone, running up the bill.

"I said *Smallwood*. He working or what?"

Sam looked over at her. "Put your seat belt on, Sonora. You call Crick?"

"Yeah, he's taking care of it. Drive as fast as you can and not kill anybody, those are his direct orders. Use the light and the state cops will leave us alone."

"Man, I been waiting for something like this for years."

Sonora went back to the phone. "Tell him it's Sonora Blair and it's urgent, with a capital urge."

Sam glanced at her. "A capital urge?"

"There's a crisis here, quit picking. Watch that truck, no, dammit."

"You better sit back and close your eyes. They've got an hour and a half head start. He's not going to keep her around for chitchat."

"Yeah, but he had downtown traffic around three or so, and you know that's a bitch. Plus he's traveling with a pregnant woman. Unless he's already killed her, they'll be making a pit stop every twenty minutes. Particularly if she's scared."

"Yeah, but I'm still traveling with you, and you make a pit stop every twenty minutes, too."

"Not this trip. This trip I'll hold it."

"Hello? Sonora?"

"That you, Smallwood?"

"You sound like you're in a well."

"Cell phone. I need—"

"Listen, Sonora, I'm sorry I didn't call, I was going to try and get in touch with you tonight. I just got bogged down at work and—"

"Smallwood, this is not about that. Forget that."

Sam looked at her. "Forget what?"

"Shut up and drive." Sonora gritted her teeth. "Smallwood, we got a problem here, with the Caplan thing, and I'm going to need your help. Number one, we're on our way to London, and it's an emergency situation. We've got the lights flashing, but it wouldn't hurt to let the Tennessee state cops know who we are and that we're okay. We're cleared through Ohio and Kentucky. Crick's working on Tennessee, but if you can help us out any, feel free."

"Sure, Sonora, but I'm right here. You in that big of a hurry, why not send either me or one of the locals?"

"Funny you should ask. I can't go into details, but Collie Caplan's disappeared and we think she's with Gage Caplan."

"Doesn't she live with him?"

"Either come up to speed, or just trust me on this, okay? We think they're headed for London, and that he's got some kind of little hidey-hole down around near the cabin that his in-laws have on the lake. Someplace near railroad tracks."

"What's their last name? The in-laws?"

"Dorrie and Grey Ainsley." She gave him the address. Glanced at Sam. "There's a kid that lives near there, his name is Vernon something or other—"

"Vernon Masterson," Sam said.

"Vernon Masterson. He may know where the place is. He tags along after Gage quite a lot."

"Sonora, I hate to be negative, but you really think Caplan's going to let a kid find his hidey-hole?"

"Well, gee, Smallwood, this happens to be all I've got. Plus you clearly don't have much to do with children. Kids are sneaky, Smallwood. They find things out whether you like it or not."

Sam looked at her. "Forget what?"

69

It was 9:15 and heavy dusk when Sam and Sonora pulled into the gravel drive that led to the Ainsleys' vacation cabin on the lake. Smallwood's squad car was there, as was a dark green minivan that Sonora didn't recognize.

It was cool, here by the lake. Sonora got out of the Taurus, heard boat engines on the water, and crickets in the grass. Someone had left an orange inner tube on the picnic table. The shed door was open.

The front door swung open as Sam and Sonora made it up on the deck. Dorrie Ainsley stood under the porch light, moths circling.

"There you are. Come on in."

"Dibs on the bathroom," Sonora told Sam.

"Don't say hello or nothing," Smallwood quipped.

"She'll be back, in a minute," Sam said. "She just set a record, for her."

Sonora heard the front door open while she was in the bathroom, voices and people moving around. She dried her hands on a towel and hurried out.

Vernon Masterson sat on the couch wearing shorts and a T-shirt. His hair was rumpled and he looked as if he'd been asleep. He blinked at all the people in the room, and sat stiffly beside a woman who patted his leg, and told him everything would be all right.

His mother, Sonora decided.

She looked tired and worried. Her hair was

brunette, L'Oréal number eleven, if Sonora guessed correctly. She wore stockings and a skirt and sensible shoes. She looked as if she had not had time to change after work.

"I'm Detective Blair," Sonora said.

"Katherine Masterson. Vernon's mom."

Sonora nodded. "Did they explain that we just want to talk to Vernon?"

The woman nodded. "I hope you understand, but he'll do better if I'm here."

Sonora did understand. Mrs. Masterson had no idea who had done what to whom, and she was there to look out for Vernon. In her place, Sonora would have done the same.

"Am I in trouble, Mama?" Vernon asked.

"Just tell the truth," Mrs. Masterson said.

Sam sat down on the edge of the coffee table across from him. Not too close, but their eyes were on a level. Sonora folded her arms and settled back against the wall. Sam would be good with this.

"Vernon, we're here to look for Mr. and Mrs. Caplan. And we think you know where they might be."

"No sir, I went to bed at nine o'clock. That's my bedtime every night."

"I know, Vernon. And that's fine. But you and Gage are pretty good friends, aren't you?"

"Yes sir."

"And you go on walks together?"

"Oh, no sir."

"You don't go on walks together?"

"Oh no. I would not follow a friend. Not if he didn't want me to. There might be bees."

"Didn't you say you played railroad with Mr. Caplan?" Sonora asked.

Sam gave her a look over his shoulder. She decided to shut up.

"Oh no. We were going to? But he never got time. Mr. Caplan works an awful lot. And you don't want to follow him, because there might be bees."

"Vernon's been afraid of bees since he was a little boy," Mrs. Masterson said.

"Vernon," said Sam. "I'm afraid of bees, too. Scare me to death. I hate getting stung more than anything."

The boy nodded.

"I need you to tell me where the bees are, so I don't get stung."

The boy opened his mouth, then closed it. "I'm sorry, sir. I can't tell."

Mrs. Masterson looked at him. "Vernon, you tell that man what he wants to know."

Vernon's skin lost color and he shook his head. "Mama, we could all get hurt if I tell about the place."

"How would you get hurt?" Sam said. "Did Mr. Caplan threaten you?"

"No, no, he's my friend, he takes care of me. He promised, he would never let the brown-faced man come and get me. If it wasn't for Mr. Caplan, the brown-faced man could come to my house. He does bad things to women. I don't want to say with Mama in the room. But Mr. Caplan told me all about it. And he said the brown-faced man saw me, and might find out where I live, 'cause this is such a small town. But Mr. Caplan told him he better leave me alone. So long as I don't go back out there, I should be safe. So I never go back there. Plus, that's where the bees are. You won't want to go out there either."

"What kind of a place is it?" Sam asked.

Vernon shook his head.

"Will you tell me if I guess?" Sonora asked him.

His mother smiled at him. "You could do that, Vernon. If she guessed."

"It's a railroad car, isn't it, Vernon?"

Vernon looked at the floor. "You're a good guesser, ma'am."

"Thank you."

70

The train was on a siding. Judging by the growth of weeds and scrub through the tracks, it had been there for years. It was an old coal engine, black, three wood boxcars behind. Sonora squinted. Looked like a caboose at the end, but the track curved and she could not be sure—the tree line had grown up, encroaching the siding. A car was parked back behind the weeds, around the hidden side of the train. Sonora could see a hint of chrome bumper.

She tugged at Sam's sleeve. "Is that Caplan's car?"

"Hard to tell. Could be."

The tracks were rusted. The engine black. Bits of coal were scattered in around the gravel.

The crickets were loud here. Sonora heard music, faint, but close. A thick orange extension cord, the outdoor utility kind, snaked from beneath the railroad cars. It ran across the tracks, and into a utility pole and box that was fenced in with chain-link.

So he had electricity.

It was gloomy out, not totally dark, plenty of moon. Sonora hoped Caplan was listening to the music, and not the sound of their footsteps in the gravel.

Vernon pointed, hand shaking. "It's the brown-faced man."

"Where?" Sam said. "You see him?"

"No. But he lives in the other car. The one after this. He looks out the window." Tears slid down Vernon's cheeks.

"We'll take care of your mom," Smallwood said.

Sam shushed him. "Listen. You hear that?"

Sonora heard sobs. "You think it's Caplan, or Collie?"

"Can't tell."

"We better move."

Smallwood pointed. "If you go through that car there, it looks empty, and it should connect. Come in on him through the train. I'll head around through the woods, and go up the back way. But I'll wait and give you guys some time. That sound okay?"

Sam nodded at him. They all looked at Vernon.

"You be all right, Vernon?" Sonora asked.

The boy nodded. His face was flushed and beaded with sweat. "Be careful, ma'am."

"We're going to get the brown-faced man, Vernon. We're going to make sure he never comes after your family. You stay here and hide. Don't come out till we come back for you." Sonora looked at him. Would he stay put until the cavalry came?

The music got louder. "Paint It Black," classic Stones.

"We got to go," Sonora said. She drew her gun, headed for the railroad car.

It had been painted red in its heyday. The metal step was well worn and so high off the ground Sonora had to use the rail to get up. Sam's feet were noisy behind her. The music was louder here. Sonora listened, but could not hear voices or sobs.

It was dark inside, hot, the air heavy with the smell of dust and old steel. A rusty green sign lay on its side: JUNCTION CITY. The paint on the walls was coming away in curls, and lengths of lumber lay scattered all over the floor. Seats had been pulled out of their mooring, cushions shredded, tossed aside.

Sonora shone a flashlight, shielded by the top of her hand. Saw an arm beneath an overturned seat.

"*Jesus*. Sam."

He turned. Picked the arm up. "Mannequin part."

Sonora took a breath. Felt sweat running under her arms. They went down the center aisle to the back door.

"Boarded up." Sam pulled at the wood. "Recently, with good lumber. We're not getting in this way."

They backtracked, climbed out of the car. Sonora stayed close to the train, metal against her blouse. It was full dark out now. In the next car, she could see light, and through a window, a silhouette.

She moved closer. Her hand was shaking.

"The brown-faced man," Sam said, in her ear.

The man was clearly visible, targeted by light from inside the car. He stood quietly, looking out the window. His face was dark and wooden looking, as if he'd been terribly scarred. He stood very still.

"You think he's seen us?" Sonora asked.

Sam tilted his head to one side. "That sucker ain't real."

Sonora looked back. The brown-faced man did not move or shift position. He wore a hat, a white shirt, and pants and a belt. "Scarecrow?"

"Works. Look around, Sonora, you see any graffiti? Any beer cans or condoms? How come the local kids aren't out here, hanging out? Something is keeping them away."

"How are we going to do this?"

"Right through the door. We got no other choice."

The music got louder. Something about turning away from the darkness, then a driving beat. "Paint It Black" again, playing over and over, like a CD on repeat. And mixed in with the music, a man sobbing.

Sam looked at her. "Let's get the hell in there."

They moved, feet noisy on the steps, Sam in front. He kicked the train door open and Sonora went in on his heels.

She saw Caplan first, dressed for the office. He had shed the suit coat and rolled up his sleeves, but he still wore a tie, and it trailed across Collie's swollen belly as he bent over her, a firm hand on her shoulder, and looked into her face.

Collie was tied into the chair, hands behind her back. Sonora noticed her fingers, swollen and red. Her belly looked huge and she sagged against the ropes, eyes wide but unseeing, face tinged blue.

There was a plastic bag over Collie's head, pulled tight around her neck. She wasn't struggling.

Sonora stared, hoping to make the image go away. They could not be too late. They could not just have missed her by minutes. She could not be dead.

"Watch him," Sam yelled.

Caplan was on the move, headed her way. He shoved the scarecrow and the brown-faced man came crashing toward her. The boom box went sideways, and the music stopped.

Sonora was aware, on some level, that Sam was with Collie, ripping the bag off her head, his mouth over hers, and one part of her mind was going *please, please, please*.

Caplan miscalculated, expecting her to dodge the scarecrow instead of run straight at it, and him. She grabbed the front of his shirt and threw her body into his. He lost his balance, and his momentum and hers slammed him hard into the wall. His meaty bulk cushioned Sonora from the blow. He looked surprised. She was surprised, too. She pushed a hand against his chest and brought the gun up under his chin.

It was a short, but oddly timeless moment where he decided whether or not to move and she decided whether or not to shoot.

"Gage Caplan—" she had to stop a minute, catch her breath. "Gage Caplan, you are under arrest."

Sweat ran in rivers down his face, mixing with tears. His shoulders shook. Laughing? Crying? Sonora could not tell. Dark rings of misery shadowed his eyes. He looked like a man in another time and another place. Sonora smelled him. She crammed him farther back to the wall and he stayed.

"You have the right to remain silent."

He said the words with her, his lips barely moving, voice soft. The familiar litany had a weird calming effect on them both.

She took the plastic rings out of her pocket and fastened his hands together. He watched her, unflinching, as if he expected something, she did not know what.

He smiled at her, and the expression on his face was as hard to read as it was familiar. He raised his hands, tightly encased in the plastic rings, and dragged a finger across her cheek in a butterfly caress.

"I was just putting her back," Caplan said, and looked down at her indulgently, almost fondly.

She studied him, watchful. "I don't understand."

Her own voice surprised her, so soft and so gentle while her heart pounded hard in her chest. She heard Sam, blowing air into Collie Caplan's lungs. The sound of crickets outside. Footsteps, someone moving in the next car. Smallwood on his way.

"Heartbeat," Sam said.

More footsteps. Smallwood getting closer.

"Breathing," Sam said. "On her own."

Sonora took a deep hard breath.

The expression on Caplan's face was radiant. "I'm so glad. I don't mean to be like this."

"I know," Sonora said. She looked around for something he could use to wipe his tears.

71

Smallwood put his head in the door, stopped suddenly, rocking forward on his toes. "Everybody okay?"

"Under control," Sonora said. It was good to see him. Sweat streaked from his temples and slicked his hair down wet. He smiled at her and came closer, close enough for her to see that his smile was shaky and he was white under the tan.

He looked down at Collie. "How is she?"

"Breathing."

"Is her baby okay?"

"I don't know," Sam said. "You want me to ask it? Where's Vernon?"

"Puking in the grass. He followed me into the car. I didn't know he was there till it was too late. You better come next door and take a look. This one's the screamer."

Caplan chuckled softly.

72

Sonora sat rigid in her chair while the bailiff lowered the blinds in the courtroom. She had seen the tape more than once. She knew what to expect.

They did not turn out the lights, so she got to watch everybody's face, whether she wanted to or not.

Liza Hardin and Butch Winchell sat side by side in the front of the room. Winchell had worn the same suit to court every day. Every day the suit seemed to get looser, and Winchell seemed to get smaller. They took no notice of Jeff Barber, who sat in the back right-hand corner, a small dark-haired woman by his side. She patted his shoulder at regular intervals.

The sister who cooked, Sonora thought.

The guy with the video camera had been a little shaky. The camera jigged up and down as he got used to the feel of what he was doing.

He had started with an outside shot of the railroad cars. The area was drenched in harsh, artificial light, cordoned off with yellow police tape. The woods pressed in from all sides, shadowy, dark, echoing with the noise of disturbed insects. Background noises were muted—a humdrum mutter of men and women at work, the sound of footsteps on metal steps, people walking near the tracks, feet sliding in the gravel.

A moth darted in front of the lens, then veered out of range.

Sonora closed her eyes for just one minute and was back in that railroad car. She glanced across the room at Caplan, every inch the pro. The look of polite interest on his face did not waver. She thought he was sweating under the weight of the expensive suit, but it might have been wishful thinking.

The camera took them up the metal steps, three of them, Sonora counted. Started with the car where Sonora and Sam had found Collie.

Caplan had given that car the VIP treatment, though Sonora hadn't noticed until she'd seen the tape for the first time. It was clean inside, no broken windows, no trash. A lamp from home, two comfortable chairs, a CD player.

The camera zoomed in on the brown-faced man, kicked into a corner. His hat had come off, revealing the tied-off opening at the top of his head. The courtroom went silent and tense. People watched and waited.

Everyone had been warned.

Sonora saw herself, just a flash, as she walked away from the camera. She looked hot on film, cheeks flushed, hair drenched with sweat. The camera caught a look of concentration on her face that could have been mistaken for anger.

Sweat lightly coated the palms of her hands. They were getting close. The camera would pan the overturned chair, the plastic bag Sam had ripped away from Collie Caplan's face. She waited for the close-up of the ropes, hanging loose from the back of the chair, severed clean by Sam's pocketknife.

A woman sobbed, then choked it back. Sonora turned and looked, like everyone else. Liza Hardin was leaning forward in her chair, one arm wrapped around her middle as if her stomach hurt, the other entwined with Butch Winchell's elbow. They edged closer together, holding hands.

The camera moved into the next railroad car, caught a state police crime scene technician bending over the deep sink that Caplan had put in one corner. The technician looked up at the camera. He wore a jumpsuit and thick latex gloves with dark stains that were clearly blood. He stepped backward and out of the way, motioning the camera closer with the bloodstained gloves.

Caplan had no running water, just jugs of High Bridge Springs Mountain water, stacked in a corner, so the sink was never properly cleaned.

The camera lingered over a clog in the drain. Hair and bone fragments, Sonora knew, glad that Liza Hardin and Butch Winchell could only see an innocuous wad. She could not help what they might be imagining.

The camera pulled back, taking a wide view of three mannequins—two of them dressed with care and a certain expense. Wigs, shoes, makeup. One of the mannequins had short black hair and wore a skirt and a tiny pink sweater with pearl buttons that Dorrie Ainsley had positively identified as belonging to her daughter, Micah. The other had a long dark wig and wore khaki pants and a sleeveless denim shirt, thought to be the clothes Julia Winchell disappeared in. The other mannequin had not been dressed. It stood next to the others, bare and faceless.

The forensic psychologist had thought it was interesting that none of the mannequins had been made up to look pregnant.

Sonora saw a flash of movement, looked back over her shoulder. Jeff Barber was bailing out, the dark-haired girl at his heels.

She studied the jury. A woman in a black power suit

looked from the screen to Caplan. He smiled at her and she looked away. The rest of them stared straight ahead. Most sat quietly in their seats. One shredded a tissue in her lap.

The camera was on the move again, swinging left to right across a table that was covered in plastic, focusing on a brand new Craftsman hacksaw that sat in the center of the table, price tag still on the handle. The camera did a swift pan, lingering a moment, as per Sonora's own instructions, on an open box of lawn and garden garbage bags that had been placed under the table. Terry had matched the garbage bag dredged up out of the Clinch River with the roll of bags in the box.

The camera veered upward suddenly, when the operator tripped, and everyone got an unexpected view of the cobwebs in the ceiling of the railroad car. The screen went fuzzy. Gradually the image sharpened as the focus was readjusted.

Gage Caplan had treated himself to a brand-new Kenmore deep freeze.

It was white. The lid was up. Water had made drip marks down the front, and there were smudges under the lip, in the center.

The camera zoomed in for a tight shot.

There was ice, bags and bags of it, lumped around the nude torso of a woman—positively identified as Julia Winchell. One slim arm, unattached and separately wrapped in clear plastic, lay beside the swell of frozen hip on the torso's left side, as if Caplan had not been able to part with it at the last minute.

Liza Hardin wailed and Sonora bowed her head.

73

The judge had called a recess, the jury excused. The press, excluded from the courtroom, waited in a thick writhing mass on the courthouse steps. Sonora headed for the basement niche she and Sam had discovered years ago. Not pretty, but peaceful.

They were talking death penalty. They had done it before in Cincinnati. They would do it again.

She felt a hand on her shoulder, and a force propelling her away from the crowd toward a deserted hallway.

"Molliter? What the hell do you think you're doing? Let go of my arm. I've got a gun, I won't hesitate to shoot."

"You did not get a gun past the metal detector, and even if you did, I've seen you at the shooting range, Sonora, and I'm not worried right here at point blank range."

He had a tight grip and it hurt. She dug in her heels and pushed him away. "What are you going to do? Handcuff me in the men's room?"

"I've had enough bathroom conferences to last me a while, thanks just the same."

She tried not to laugh. It was hard to hate someone when they made you laugh.

"Look, just walk up this hallway with me, okay? Nobody up there, and we can be private. I want to talk to you a minute. Come on, Sonora. Please."

He hadn't squealed on her. "Okay, Molliter, we can talk. But I've got some people to see so keep it short."

He took her at her word, and she had to move to keep up with him—he was tall and lanky and he took big steps. He turned a sharp corner.

"Here, okay?"

Sonora nodded. Rested her back against the wall. He turned sideways, shoved his hands in his pockets.

"How long were you stuck in the bathroom?" she asked him.

"Been dying of curiosity, haven't you."

Sonora nodded.

Molliter rocked up and down on the balls of his feet. "*Hours*. Six, to be exact. The plumber found me." He sighed. "You have likely been wondering why I didn't go to Crick on this."

"Nah, I just figured you liked it."

"Sonora, I am trying to talk civilly to you."

"Let's get something straight. You want to go running to Crick, you be my guest. Go now. Soon as word gets around you leaked confidential information to the DA's office, and assuming Crick doesn't kick your sorry ass out, you're going to start eating lunch alone. Better get used to it."

"People talk back and forth all the time. This isn't a new thing."

"It's always new when you get caught."

His breathing picked up, quick and shallow. "You have to understand—"

"You know what, Molliter? You couldn't have picked a poorer choice of words. Anytime anybody has ever said that to me, 'you have to understand,' it means they've pulled some major shit."

"You listen to me, Sonora. I worked vice and I

worked personal crime. Years of it, day in and day out, guys plea bargaining, getting off for lack of evidence, sometimes the same guys, over and over. And then Caplan comes along. This guy is *hungry* and he likes the chase. He goes after child molesters and rapists and pimps—not the girls, Sonora, the pimps. Goes to court on a date rape, when he didn't have a prayer of getting a conviction, but he did it anyway, because he wanted to try. Do you know how rare that is? Do you know how rare it is for a man to be so committed he risks his career for the sake of doing a little good in the world?"

"He had ego, Molliter, not morals."

"So what, if that's what it takes."

"Well, Molliter, there's just a small problem with this guy's favorite form of recreation."

"I'm just trying to make you understand why I did what I did."

"Understand? Meet Collie and Mia Caplan and give me understand. See a pregnant woman tied up in a shitty railroad car, turning blue with a plastic bag over her head. Give me understand."

"I'm as sorry as I know how to be. I have prayed over this, and I'm here to try and make things right. The woman is still alive."

"No thanks to you."

"What are you going to do, Sonora?"

"Me? Not a damn thing. I had a problem, I took care of it. Crick isn't stupid. Anything further comes from him."

"He . . . we've had a sort of talk. I think I'm in the clear there."

"Good for you. God looks after assholes."

"I said I was sorry."

"You don't get it, Molliter. Some things you don't get

to do, because sometimes, sorry doesn't cut it. Forgiveness may be divine, Molliter, but it's a separate issue."

He took it. Stared at her, hands in pockets.

Sonora was never very good at silence. "So what now, Molliter, you holding your temper, counting to ten?"

"Let me put it to you this way. Am I going to be eating lunch alone? When I call for backup, is anybody coming? They going to drag their feet getting there?"

Sonora folded her arms. "I see, this is all about you. You know, Molliter, I have never been able to stand you, but you used to be a good cop."

"I have a wife and kids and I'm still a good cop."

"Fine. I'm not going to gossip about you at the coffee machine, and I'm still going to watch your back. Those the words you needed to hear?"

"Yes. Thank you very much."

She didn't say anything.

"I try very hard to be a good person."

"I've given you everything you're going to get, Molliter. There's not going to be any seal of approval."

"I'd like to try and see if we can be friends again, some time in the future."

"Look, Molliter, we never were friends. I'd like to go all warm and fuzzy with you, but the truth is, it's not going to happen."

He nodded. "Okay. I'm sorry, but I thought I was right. Maybe someday you'll forgive me and we can be friends. I'm willing to wait for that day."

"You still don't get it, and you never will."

74

Sonora figured on a high probability that Liza Hardin and Butch Winchell would be hiding out in the basement—she had shown them the spot on that first day in court. She rounded the corner, heard voices.

The basement room had been some unfortunate's office at one time or another, and there was still a metal desk, and a couple of padded chairs, a bookcase with dust-enveloped law books. A tiny grilled window at the top of the room sat at street level, emphasizing the feeling of being down in a hole.

Liza Hardin was sitting on the corner of the desk, Butch Winchell looking out the window.

"How's it going?" Sonora asked, pausing in the doorway.

They turned and looked, furtive and jumpy.

Liza had been crying. Her mascara made streaks of black down her face. Someone had brought in a box of tissues, and little white clumps were scattered across the desk. Winchell had a glazed look. The skin of his face sagged with rapid weight loss. Whatever he had lost, Liza had gained. Her face looked bloated, unhealthy, neck puffy.

They would get better, Sonora thought. This was the bad time.

"I came down to check on you. Do either of you need anything? Coffee, something to eat?"

"We don't eat," Butch said.

Sonora believed him.

Liza slid off the desk and grabbed Sonora's hand. "How do you think it's going?"

Sonora smiled at her gently. "It's going as well as it can."

"Collie . . . Mrs. Caplan. She hasn't been here the last two days. Is she okay?"

"She's fine. She only comes if she has to, she's got a baby to nurse."

Collie had delivered a seven-pound baby boy, early but healthy, several hours after Sam had brought her around. She had named him Grey, for Mia's grandfather. She and Mia were staying with Grey and Dorrie, and thinking about moving to London permanently after the trial.

"Do you think he'll get the death penalty?" Winchell asked. His voice held very little inflection. It rarely did these days, Sonora had noticed that about him.

"I have my fingers crossed, Mr. Winchell."

Liza looked at her. "You were there. You . . . saw it."

"Ms. Hardin, your sister, Julia, died in a matter of minutes. Anything that happened after that—she was long gone. Hold on to that."

They seemed riveted by her words and she looked into their faces and thought, as she had before, that no one had yet come up with the right configuration of words to handle these things.

"I have something for both of you."

She saw it in their eyes, a sort of desperate hope, as if she could give them something to make it all better, as if she could give them the only thing they wanted, which was Julia, back home again, safe and sound.

That was the problem, working homicide. Nobody came home safe and sound.

Sonora handed them both a brown envelope. "I'm giving each of you a copy of the tape Julia made a few days before she died. They'll be playing it in court some time this week. She's talking about the murder, getting her thoughts down. I wish it was something else, like her telling you the things she would have said if she'd known what was going to happen, but this is all I've got. Listen to it, keep it for later, throw it away. Whatever you need. Just don't tell anybody where you got it."

"I won't be able to play it without crying," Liza said.

Sonora nodded. "That's allowed."

Butch Winchell fingered the edge of the envelope, as if he couldn't wait. "I'll play this for the girls when they grow up."

"You do that."

Sonora shook each of their hands and headed back to the courtroom. At the least, Julia Winchell's daughters would have the gift of their mother's voice.

It was a small thing, but it was all she had.

ANOTHER SIZZLING READ FROM AWARD-WINNING AUTHOR LYNN S. HIGHTOWER

"Lynn Hightower is a major talent."
—Jonathan Kellerman

FLASHPOINT

LYNN S. HIGHTOWER
Shamus Award–Winning Author of *Satan's Lambs*

Handcuffed to the wheel of his car, he was doused with gasoline and set on fire. Then the killer walked away…high-heeled shoe prints her only calling card.

Police Specialist Sonora Blair is committed to finding this killer before she strikes again—no matter what the cost to her private life or her career. But when the murderer begins to call Sonora—taunting, mocking, trying to lure her into a twisted woman-to-woman complicity—the tension of this deadly cat-and-mouse game climbs to an unbearable pitch.

At bookstores now or order direct: